ED ROBINSON

≪ THE ≫
ADVENTURES OF
LEE ROBINSON
≫ USMC ≪

outskirtspress
DENVER, COLORADO

This is a work of fiction. The events and characters described herein are imaginary and are not intended to refer to specific places or living persons. The opinions expressed in this manuscript are solely the opinions of the author and do not represent the opinions or thoughts of the publisher. The author has represented and warranted full ownership and/or legal right to publish all the materials in this book.

The Adventures of Lee Robinson
USMC
All Rights Reserved.
Copyright © 2014 Ed Robinette
v1.0

Cover Photo © 2014 JupiterImages Corporation. All rights reserved - used with permission.

This book may not be reproduced, transmitted, or stored in whole or in part by any means, including graphic, electronic, or mechanical without the express written consent of the publisher except in the case of brief quotations embodied in critical articles and reviews.

Outskirts Press, Inc.
http://www.outskirtspress.com

ISBN: 978-1-4787-2347-9

Library of Congress Control Number: 2013922912

Outskirts Press and the "OP" logo are trademarks belonging to Outskirts Press, Inc.

PRINTED IN THE UNITED STATES OF AMERICA

DEDICATED TO MY FAMILY WHO HAS MADE ME PROUD, AND I HAVE TRIED TO BE AN EXAMPLE TO THEM AS A FATHER AND GRANDFATHER.

TO MY GOOD FRIEND NANCY HATCH WOODWARD, INSTRUCTOR AT CHATTANOOGA STATE, WHO HAS TAUGHT ME MANY CLASSES IN WRITING?

TO MY MANY FRIENDS AT THE CHATTANOOGA WRITERS GUILD, WHO HAS TAUGHT ME SO MUCH ABOUT WRITING A STORY.

TO MY MANY FRIENDS AT THE HOSPICE OF CHATTANOOGA, WHO AS A VOLUNTEER, I HAVE LOVED AS MY FAMILY.

TO MY PASTOR, DEACONS, AND CHURCH FAMILY AT WHITE OAK BAPTIST CHURCH.

AND TO MY GOOD FRIEND ANNE GAILLARD, WHO HAS SPENT LONG HOURS, CORRECTING MY GRAMMAR, AND EDITING THIS BOOK.

EDITED BY: ANNE GAILLARD

THIS STORY IS A WORK OF FICTION. NAMES, CHARACTERS, PLACES, AND INCIDENTS EITHER ARE THE PRODUCT OF THE AUTHOR'S IMAGINATION OR ARE USED FICTITIOUSLY, AND ANY RESEMBLANCE TO ACTUAL PERSONS, LIVING OR DEAD, BUSINESS ESTABLISHMENTS, EVENTS, OR LOCALITIES ARE ENTIRELY COINCIDENTAL.

IN LOVING MEMORY

MARGARET L. ROBINETTE
March 16, 1931—June 5, 2009

1 THESSALONIANS: 4-13-18

13. BUT I WOULD NOT HAVE YOU BE IGNORANT, BRETHREN, CONCERNING THEM WHICH ARE ASLEEP, THAT YE SORROW NOT, EVEN AS OTHERS WHICH HAVE NO HOPE.

14. FOR IF WE BELIEVE THAT JESUS DIED AND ROSE AGAIN, EVEN SO THEM ALSO WHICH SLEEP IN JESUS WILL GOD BRING WITH HIM.

15. FOR THIS WE SAY UNTO YOU BY THE WORD OF THE LORD, THAT WE WHICH ARE ALIVE AND REMAIN UNTO THE COMING OF THE LORD SHALL NOT PREVENT THEM WHICH ARE ASLEEP.

16. FOR THE LORD HIMSELF SHALL DESCEND FROM HEAVEN WITH A SHOUT, WITH THE VOICE OF THE ARCH-ANGEL, AND WITH THE

TRUMP OF GOD: AND THE DEAD IN CHRIST SHALL RISE FIRST:

17. THEN WE WHICH ARE ALIVE AND REMAIN SHALL BE CAUGHT UP TOGETHER WITH THEM IN THE CLOUDS TO MEET THE LORD IN THE AIR: AND SO SHALL WE EVER BE WITH THE LORD.

18. WHEREFORE COMFORT ONE ANOTHER WITH THESE WORDS.

PROLOGUE

My name is Rodney Sweeny, U.S.M.C. and as promised, I'm writing a book about the adventures of Lee Robinson, a fellow Marine, and the best friend anyone could hope for, or have. Our motto says it all. Semper Fidelis, "ALWAYS FAITHFUL."

This is his story, his love for his friends and his women. I was with him in most of his adventures, and shared the fear and the courage of such a man. The time that we weren't together, I was told of his love for his wife and family, and was told of things from friends and family, that he did not know I knew about him. The battles, even his love affairs, I told him many times, that one day I would write a book, and let the world know of such a man, and our adventures.

Today, I am 68 years old and I am writing that book. Very little will I write in the first person, because I want it to be about him, this is his life, his story, and The Adventures of Lee Robinson. Rodney Sweeny, U.S.M.C. Retired.

In 1927, the Marines landed in Shanghai, China and would stay until 1941. Their main duty was to protect the United States Emissary.

In 1937, the Japanese attacked Marco Polo Bridge in Peking China, and the war had begun.

Flat Rock, Alabama 1939

Rodney had turned 18, but he was celebrating his birthday picking cotton along with his brothers out in the field. If they had a good harvest, and they would eat well that year, if not, then it would be mostly beans and corn bread. They were poor, but so was everyone else.

After a supper of beans, corn bread, and buttermilk, he would pick up a magazine that he had read many times, and then lay on his bed dreaming about faraway places. Laying that one down, he saw a new one that his brother must have brought in from town. Inside was a story about the Marines in China. He couldn't imagine how far away that must be. He had been to Birmingham several times with his folks, and even went to Chattanooga once. But China? That was another world.

He looked at the story again. The Marines had on blue and white uniforms, and they looked so brave. At the end of the story was a picture of a Marine poster pointing his finger at him: The U.S. Marines wants you?

Rod laid his head on the pillow made from a flour sack, and dreamed. *Could I be a Marine? I'm strong for my age, and I have been in a couple fights, didn't win either one, but I didn't back down, and I wasn't scared. If they would take me, they would teach me how to fight, and I may even get to go to China. And that was all he remembered.*

"Rodney breakfast is ready; you need to feed the chickens before you go back in the cotton fields." said his mother from the kitchen.

While eating breakfast he said aloud. "I bet the Marines don't feed any chickens or pick cotton."

"What did you say son?"

"Said, that I was going to join the Marines. Yes Mom, that's what I'm going to do."

"Yes honey, maybe when you get older, but now you have some work to do here."

Rodney was leaning against the rails of the cargo ship loaded with new Marines heading for China. Most of them had never been this far from home before, and it was hard to believe that he was now a Marine, and heading for China. He was sorry he left his mother and brothers on the farm, but there came a time when a boy must break ties with his family, and become a man.

He did well in 'boot camp' and was an expert with a gun. "Excuse me, rifle, you don't refer to your rifle as a gun." 'Marines manual'

Marines were shouting and pointing, and then he saw it. "China he said to the Marine next to him. We are here, now we are China Marines."

It wasn't long before he fell in the routine of being a China Marine, and made a couple of trips into the town of Shanghai, usually with several friends.

Rod had mess duty that morning, so he didn't get to go into town until late, and all his friends were already gone. But that was okay. He had never been to town before; beside he wouldn't have to be back until Monday. He had never spent the night alone anywhere, in fact there were several things he had not done that Marines do. They had the reputation of drinking, fighting, and loving women. "I guess that's what I need to do, if I want to call myself a real Marine."

After supper he walked around town, looking at the women, but none seem to be interested, but before he knew it he was getting in the 'off limit' or the rough section of town.

He came to a bar, couldn't read the name, but thought maybe he could get a Coke inside. Going in he asked for a Coke, but the bartender put a bottle of beer on the counter. That's okay; I need to learn to drink anyway.

He was on his second beer when he looked at a table in the back of the room. And there sat a Marine from his outfit with his arms around a pretty Chinese woman and with his hand up under her blouse, and the other hand on her leg. He saw Rodney looking and winked at him. Rod winked back, and turned back to his beer.

Less than ten minutes he heard voices and cursing and then chairs and tables turned over. Looking back at the Marine, he saw three Chinese soldiers holding him down and beating him. Well he remembered the saying," Marines are brothers, and you don't let your brother get beat up, unless it was by another Marine."

So Rod grabbed his beer bottle and hit the first Chinese, knocking him off. Then he pulled the other one off, and hit him with his fist. By now his new friend was getting up and knocked the other soldier against the wall. After that it wasn't much of a fight. But then some of the other Chinese in the room were beginning to get up, so they went to the bar. The bartender wouldn't serve us, but asked us to leave.

"Why? Did they jump on me," my friend asked." Was one of them her boy friend?"

"No, but it was the Captain's wife."

"I'm Corporal Lee Robinson, Company A. Thanks for coming and helping me out." He said holding his hand out.

"Private Rodney Sweeny, from Company A. Do you get into fights like that often?"

"Hell, how did I know that she was married," looking at his skinned knuckles.

And that was the first time I met Lee, and we became friends and have been ever since. Also Rod became a Marine, that night, well almost. The other part would come later.

Table of Contents

Chapter 1	Cuba	1
Chapter 2	The Battle	9
Chapter 3	San Diego	13
Chapter 4	War	21
Chapter 5	Guadalcanal	32
Chapter 6	The Bloody Battle of Tarawa—November 20th 1943	45
Chapter 7	Battle for the Marshall Islands	54
Chapter 8	The Battle of Saipan	66
Chapter 9	Honolulu- Three Days of Rest	75
Chapter 10	Iwo Jima	87
Chapter 11	Okinawa—The Last Battle of WW II	98
Chapter 12	The Last Battle -Victory	108
Chapter 13	The Bomb is Dropped-W.W.II is Over	121
Chapter 14	Killed in Action	132
Chapter 15	Christmas of 1945	144
Chapter 16	Japan	156
Chapter 17	Home	169
Chapter 18	Mary Brown	180
Chapter 19	Korea	192
Chapter 20	Inchon Korea	204
Chapter 21	Toktong Pass	216
Chapter 22	Rescued from the Toktong Pass	228
Chapter 23	The Retreat	242
Chapter 24	Home Again	254
Chapter 25	Navy Seals	265

Chapter 26	Rockdale 277
Chapter 27	Fight in the Cabin 289
Chapter 28	Mary. 300
Chapter 29	Red Dog Tavern 310
Chapter 30	The Last Adventure 320

CHAPTER 1

Cuba

Lee was slowly awakened by something crawling across his face. Half awake he took his hands and brushed off whatever it was. Then within a minute it was on his ear. This time he slapped as hard as he could, waking up and murmured "Damn flies." His face was stunned from the slap, and then he heard a laugh. Looking he saw Lulu holding a broom straw in her hand.

She was a dark attractive Cuban girl about nineteen, with a white blouse, that showed the outline of her young breast, and tan shorts worn around a slim waist. She had been sitting under a large palm tree, trying to read while the young handsome Marine slept in the hamlet… This was not the way she had planned the day.

The American Marines were no difference then the Cuban men on the island. Once they made love to a woman, they just wanted to sleep and did not want to be bothered. Well Lulu wasn't going to let that happen today, breaking off a long straw from a broom nearby, she then approached the Marine who was sleeping in the hamlet.

"Lulu why did you wake me up, I needed that nap?" Lee said, grabbing her and taking the straw away.

She kissed him and laughed, "You said you had to get back to the base at 4 p.m. It's now 2 p.m."

"No! I have a 24 hour pass. Don't have to be back until tomorrow", Lee said grabbing her and kissing her and his hands went to her breast.

If you spend the night, we wait. It's too hot now." removing his hands.

"You didn't think so a couple hours ago," Lee said grabbing her again.

"You lied to me, you said you had to go in a couple hours, and I did not know when you would be back. "

"Well I don't have to go, so let me get about an hour of sleep, and then we will go to the beach, and then I will take you to supper tonight at Carlos in town."

"One hour." she said.

Lee just dropped off to sleep again, when Lulu threw a bucket of water on him.

"What the hell… Why did you do that for? It hasn't been thirty minutes" getting out of the hamlet and he took the bucket out of her hands.

Then he went to the water faucet and filled it up, and Lulu ran toward the beach.

Lee chased her and tackled her on the beach, throwing the water on her. Then they both roll in the sand, and were kissing each other, when a loud voice was heard.

"Sergeant Lee," someone was shouting and blowing a jeep horn. " The Captain wants to see you."

Lee looked and saw Rodney sitting in a jeep and blowing the horn.

"What is it Rod. Can't you see that I am busy? "

"Lee, the Captain wants to see you now. He said to get you back, even if I had to hog tie you to the jeep."

"That will be the day," said Lee removing his arms from around Lulu.

"What does the Captain want?" Walking over to the Jeep, and asked Rodney.

"Don't know Sarg, but I think it's real important. He has been trying to find you all morning. Something has happened. I think, the gorillas have raided a town.

"Was it Gormays? " Lee asked.

"Not sure, but I think he's involved. The Captain would know." Rod said looking over at the young beautiful Cuban girl.

"Sarg every time I see you, there's a different girl. I have been here for six months, and I haven't had a date yet. What is your secret?"

"Simple Rod, look on page 10 of the Marine Corps manual."

"Lee, I have read the manual through two times, and there's nothing on page 10 about finding a girl."

"There's not? Well it should be, they are part of a Marine's life. Don't you see those Marine movies, they all have the girls."

"Rod I need to sit down with you, and talk to you about girls, hell, they are the necessities of a Marine's life. But right now, if I got to leave, I need to tell Lulu that I 'm leaving, and she isn't going to like that."

Lee walked back to where Lulu was waiting and kissed her. "Baby, I have got to go, can I see you tomorrow?"

"Lee, you told me that you had a twenty four hour pass. I had some plans for us tonight and what about our supper?"

"I know honey, but I work for the Marines, and it seems they can't do anything without me. They want me to go and catch a bad guy for them, just keep the bed warm and I will be back."

They rode down the steep mountain trail heading to the 2nd Marine Battalion base on the beach at Antigo. The 2nd Marines were part of the 2nd Division stationed in Cuba for jungle training.

"Sarg, what should I know?"

"About what, Rod?"

"About girls Lee, you said that you were going to talk to me."

"Now? You want me to tell you now? Rod, just keep driving, and watch the road, that's a long way to the bottom."

"Tell me Sarg. How do I get a girl to spend the night with me?"

Lee looked at his young friend, who had just turned eighteen three months ago, but came to his aid in China when he was outnumbered in a fight.

"Rod, this should be in the Marine Corps manual for new Marines. First you find a girl that you like, and then after couple dates and she says she likes you. That is step 1. Then when you meet her again, you act real depressed and worried. That is step 2. She will ask you what is wrong, and put her arms around you. Step 3. You will say with a sad voice that you are shipping out, and there may be lots of fighting, and you may not come back. By now you have her crying, and kissing you. Then step 4. You will say, that my biggest regret is leaving you, and we will never know what it would have been like, if we just had one night together." " It works most of the time," said Lee.

The jeep passed the sentry at the gate and pulled in front of Captain Blake's office and stopped. Sergeant Lee Robinson got out of the jeep, while Rodney went to the enlisted men's barracks.

Lee told the clerk to tell the Captain that he was here.

"Damn time," said the Captain and asked Lee to come in.

He saluted, and asked the Captain if he wanted to see him?

"Yes! All day. Where have you been Sergeant Robinson?"

"On leave sir. I was on the mountain at Naha. "

"And who gave you leave? I sure as hell didn't." The Captain said looking at Sergeant Lee standing at attention."Let me look at that pass." Lee handed the Captain a worn, wrinkle piece of paper.

"Hell! Sergeant Robinson. This pass was for last week. What are you trying to pull? I ought to send you to Officers Candidate School that would get you out of my outfit. You would make a good second Lieutenant. And looking at the way things is we may have a war on our hands with Japan, and we need some experienced officers. Interested Lee? "

"No sir, I like just staying a Sergeant please." "Is that what you wanted to see me about Captain?"

"No Sergeant, it is not. Gormays and some of his gorillas went to Odessa village last night, raped some woman, cleaned out the bank, and carried off a thirteen year old girl. And she happens to be the Mayor's granddaughter. He has asked us to help. The local police are afraid to go up in the mountains to look for her. I checked with General Mays, and he wants us to do what we can to help find her. Good public relations with Cuba, and we need that right now. "

"How many men can I take, and how long do I have to find her? " Asked Lee

"Take as many men you will need from our company, and I will give you three days to find her. Let me know your plans and where you might be in case of a fire fight, and you may need some help. I have talked to the supply Sergeant to give you any supplies you will need."

"I will take six men, myself and Sanchez for a guide; He knows all about those mountains, all that he will want will be extra food for his family. Hell, he has eight children, a wife and her mother." Said Lee

"You get him and find the girl; he will get six months of food." Said the Captain. "Lee, don't you and your men get killed, but it is important that we can return the girl. Hell, I think Castro and his men are looking for her."

"I will keep you informed of my plans Captain, "said Lee walking out the door.

"Sergeant Robinson! How long have you been a Marine? "

Lee turned to the Captain and said. "Three years I think."

"Then you have read the Marine Corps manual?"

"Captain Sir." And about saluting an officer when you leave? "

Sergeant Lee Robinson came to attention, clicked his heels

and said, "YES Sir, Captain," giving him his best salute.

"Hell Lee, if you weren't the best Sergeant that I ever had, I wouldn't put up with you. Now go find that girl, and don't get yourself killed."

Lee left the office and went to see Corporal Rodney at the barracks. Rodney wasn't at his bunk so Lee sat down and made a list of six names, of the men he wanted. He left the list on the bunk for Rodney to find. The note said contact these men for a dangerous mission and meet me at 0600 in my office, I will give you the details then.

Sergeant Lee got into his jeep and drove down the beach to Sanchez house, coming to a stop at the front porch. Sanchez was sitting on the steps drinking a bottle of rum.

"Sanchez, if you will volunteer for a dangerous mission, I will buy you a case of rum and food for the family for six months. Interested? "

"Yes Sergeant Lee, I will do anything for that much food, and a case of rum? Who do I have to kill?"

"Nobody I hope, but it's possible we may have to. Our mission may call for it. "

"Tell your wife you will be back in a couple hours, and get in the jeep. I will tell you about it as we ride and meet my other volunteers."

When he got back to his office, the six men were waiting for him. Lee had picked the best, now if they will just go with him. He told the men it could be dangerous, and if anyone wanted to back out, that would be alright, and he told them of his plans and the mission. All the men agreed to go.

Sergeant Lee then went back to see Captain Blake and

gave him the names of the men that he had picked, and said that he and the men would leave tomorrow morning. He then went to the armory and picked up some supplies and boxes of ammunition.

At 0600 Lee was awake, and He met the men and then they went to the mess hall for breakfast, and then asked the cook to fix them some sandwiches for lunch. In a raining and foggy morning they took a truck to the bottom of the mountain.

CHAPTER 2

The Battle

Sergeant Lee and his men packed their sleeping bags and enough food for three days. Sanchez had told Lee that they would need to go to the back side of the mountain because Gormay's men could spot them in the valley three miles away.

It would be a long five mile walk going in the back way, but safer. After walking three miles they came to the base of the mountain. Now they would have to climb up and go over the top, in heavy jungle and wild animals to deal with.

Half way up the mountain they ran into a mountain lion and Lee told the men to hold their ground and see if he would pass them by. They could not afford to shoot and give their position away. At first the lion would not move and threatened them. Sanchez took his bottle of rum and threw it at the lion, hitting him on the rump. The lion let out a roar, and moved down the mountain. Sanchez checked the bottle and found out it wasn't broken and put it back in his pack.

The mountain got steeper, and Lee was concerned about their progress, he wanted to get to the top before dark.

Another hour went by and they broke out in a clearing and Sanchez said they were on top of the mountain. It was now dark and they couldn't see anything and Sergeant Lee told his men to pull out their sleeping bags and wait until day light. The men ate some sandwiches and went to bed exhausted.

A light rain was falling the next morning, and the clouds hung over the mountain and made it hard to see anything. Sergeant Lee and Sanchez went to the edge of a bluff and waited until the clouds lifted and they could see below.

After about an hour the sun came out and the clouds disappeared. Lee looked through his field glasses and saw a large house and a small shack with two men watching the valley below.

Lee made his plans; Sanchez and two of his men would go to the back of the shack and capture the two men, without firing a shot… he hoped.

Sergeant Lee and Rodney and the other three Marines would go to the back of the big house, and find a way inside while they were sleeping. The plan was good, but it didn't happen that way. When Lee and his men were at the back door, a shot rang out. One of the men at the guard shack got a shot off, and alerted the guard at the big house. Lee and his men rushed the house and killing the guard went inside. Two men came out of a room grabbing their guns, but Lee and his men shot them before they knew who was in the room.

Lee looked for a room that Gormay may be in and then knocked down the door. Gormay was standing in the room with a gun pointing at Lee. They both shot at the same time, a bullet hitting Gormay in the chest and knocking him against the wall. The other bullet hit Lee in his shoulder.

Rodney heard a cry and saw the young girl tied to the bed.

She had been molested. Corporal Rodney checked Lee and saw that it was not a serious wound and then went to the girl and untied her. Gormay lay on the floor dead. Two more men rushed the Marines and were shot dead. Lee had his men scout the area, but found no other Gormay gorillas.

Corporal Rodney put a bandage on Lee's shoulder and took the girl outside.

Sanchez and the two Marines, who took the shack, came back without a prisoner. Both of the guards had been killed.

Lee wanted to check the rooms and the office that Gormay had in the house, so he had the marines to split up. He and Rodney checked the office, and found a large safe.

He had Rod to go back and check Gormay's body for a key, or paper with the numbers of the safe.

When he got back he told Lee that he couldn't find anything. Then he had the men to spread out, and look for something to blow the safe.

About thirty minutes, one of the men came back with a stick of dynamite, and asked Lee if this might work?

"It might, if we can tape it to the door," said Lee looking for tape or a rope that they could put around the safe.

They found a rope, and wrapped it around the safe, tying the dynamite to the door. They lit the fuse and went into another room.

There was a loud explosion and when they came back, they found that the door was opened.

Money flew out in the room, but what Lee was looking at was six sacks in the back of the safe.

When he opened the sacks, they were filled with cocaine.

"The Captain will be please to see this. I bet these drugs where going to Miami."

They gathered the drugs and the money, buried the dead, and found a couple of rooms and went to sleep. They would leave the next morning.

Sergeant Lee and his men went down the mountain bringing the young girl with them. Sanchez got his case of rum and a six months supply of food. Lee made his report to Captain Blake and asked for a twenty four hour pass, saying he had some unfinished business at the town of Naha. Lulu would be waiting.

CHAPTER 3

San Diego

"CORPORAL! Come in here now." Captain Blake said, reading the papers one more time. "Damn, and just when I was getting used to being in Cuba."

"Corporal Chitty, where in the hell are you? I gave you an order. Doesn't anyone in this Marine Corps listen to me? I should have stayed at the Bank like my wife told me. But again, I would have had to listen to her every night when I got home. Hell, I have never seen a woman that nags like Linda. Now, I remember why I joined the Corps. "

"Corporal, if you don't get in here in five minutes, you will be peeling potatoes all night." the Captain said, looking at the papers one more time.

"Yes sir, Captain Blake, you want to see me?" Corporal Chitty said, holding a cup of coffee in his hand.

"Where have you been Corporal? I have been calling you for ten minutes"

"Getting you a cup of coffee sir. You did send me to get you a cup?"

"Yes, I forgot, put the coffee on my desk, and listen to me. Go and find Corporal Rodney and tell him I want to see him as quick as possible."

"Do I go sir, or do I send someone?"

"Please, just find him; I don't care how you do it, just go."

Corporal Billy Chitty saluted, and went out of the office, but had no sooner shut the door, when the Captain shouted again. "Corporal, come here a minute."

"Yes Sir, Captain?"

"Billy, you got any more of that cake that your mom sent you?"

"Yes sir, I think I do. Would you like a slice?"

"Bring me a big piece, Corporal. This coffee is strong I need something to help wash it down."

Billy went to his desk and took the cover off the cake that his mom had sent him. There was only one piece left, and he was saving that for his lunch. Damn, that's the last slice; I have only gotten one piece of my cake. He picked up the last slice and took it to the Captain saluted, and then went out the door to find Corporal Rodney.

He ran into Private Jimmy Reeves heading to the PX. "Private, where are you going?"

"The PX. Why, Corporal?"

"Jimmy I want you to go to the parade ground and find Corporal Rodney and tell him that the Captain wants to see him now."

"But Corporal, I was heading to the PX to pick up something for my wife, can't someone else go? That's all the way cross the base."

"Private, let me tell you how this works in the Marine Corps. You are the Private, and I'm the Corporal. That's makes me one rank higher than you. So I am giving you an order, go find Corporal Rodney, and if he is not there, go to his barracks, but find him."

"Gee's Billy, you don't have to pull rank on me. I thought we were friends."

Billy Chitty watched his friend go out of sight, and then he went to the PX and looked around, but Rodney wasn't there.

"Hi Shitty, what are you doing here?"

Billy turned around and saw Josie drinking a coke. "My name is Billy Chitty, Josie. That's spelled, C H I T T Y, not S H I T T Y. Please get my name right, or just call me Billy. Damn, I get tired of that."

"Ok Billy, don't get your bowels upset, I sometimes forget."

"Are you coming to the house tonight?"

"Yes, if you put those kids outside and keep the shades down in the bed room. Hell, Josie I don't like your kids looking in the window when I am making love. Don't you teach them anything, and why aren't they in school?"

"This is summer, and they don't go to school. And I tell them about the birds and the bugs." Josie said.

"That's the birds and the bees, don't you Cubans know anything, now get me a Coke."

Billy sat down at the table and drank his Coke, and told Josie he would be over tonight. "Josie, you reckon you could make me a cake? That damn Captain took my last piece."

When he had finished his Coke he looked at his watch, it had been an hour since he left the Captain's office. "Shit, the Capt will be climbing the walls; I guess I better get back. I hope Jimmy found Corporal Rodney, if he didn't then I am in big trouble."

Billy returned to Captain Blake's office and was relieved to find Rodney there. "Hi Rod, You been waiting long?"

"About thirty minutes, you said that the Captain wanted to see me. So tell him I'm here. "

"Good Morning Captain, Rod said, standing at attention and saluting. You wish to see me?"

"Yes Corporal Rodney I do. I want you to find Sergeant Lee and tell him I want to see him in my office as soon as possible."

"But he is in Naha sir; you gave him a three day pass. He has two more day's left." said Rod.

"I can count Corporal, but I want him here now, and I don't give a damn how many days he has left. Just find him and get him here, and that's an order, now get out of here. Any more questions or do I have to explain this to you again? "

"No Sir, I will leave right away," saluting, and then went out the door.

"Lulu this is like a vacation, just lying here on the beach, drinking beer and making love to my girl. What a great life, if I was home I would be at one of those 9 to 5 jobs. I will never be a civilian again; my home is in the Marines." Slapping Lulu on the butt he said, "Get me another beer honey, while I turn over and burn the other side."

She got another beer out of the cooler and looked down the road and saw a truck approaching them. As it got closer she saw Rodney at the wheel. She took the beer to Lee and said. "Rodney is on his way; maybe he wants to go for a swim. You do have couple days left, don't you honey?"

"Sergeant Lee, the Captain wants to see you."

"Hell Rod, you tell me that one more time and I will kick your butt" Lee said getting up. " I have two more days on my pass."

"That's what I told the Captain, but he said he didn't care, just put you in the truck and bring you back."

"What does he want me to do this time? Hell, I have killed Gomay and his men. Has he got another woman he wants me to rescue? I wish the Captain would find another Sergeant to do all his work."

"Get in the truck, please Sergeant Lee; the Captain is in a bad mood."

Lee put on his pants and shoes, while Lulu looked at him. "Are you going? I thought you were going to stay couple more days. What about your pass?"

"I know baby, but I am in the Marines and I have been ordered back. As soon as I can I will be back."

"This time I may not be waiting on you, I think. I just get me another fellow, maybe a sailor." Said Lulu.

"You do, and I will whip his butt, and kick you all the way down the beach. Now give me a kiss, I have got to go."

"No, go to your Captain. I don't care. "

Sergeant Lee and Rodney went over to the truck, and Lee stopped and looked at Rod. "Didn't you have a jeep the last time you came after me?"

"Yes Sergeant, but the Captain wanted to use it, and told

me to take the truck", and then he climbed in behind the wheel.

"Can we go now Lee, I 'm hungry and I can't face the Captain on an empty stomach?"

Lee looked at Lulu but she was looking out toward the ocean.

Rodney, open the door and we will go and see what the Captain wants, and Lee climbed in the truck, and then they made their way down the mountain. He looked back; Lulu was still looking at the ocean.

Lee looked at Rodney, and said. "Boy, she is pissed off, can't blame her though. We had the day planned."

Sergeant Lee and Corporal Rodney arrived at the base around noon, and both went into Captain Blake's office.

"Hi Shittie," Lee said as they entered. "Is the Captain in? If he is, tell him that Lee and Rod are here."

"The name is Chitty, hell, you know that Lee. Wait and I will tell him you both are here. He is not in a good mood. "

"When was he ever?" Lee replied

"He said to come in, and he heard that last remark. "

"Lee, I am sorry about your leave. I would not have called you if this wasn't important. But I have received an order here from the General. We are moving out and going to San Diego to form another Division. It will be called the 4th Division, and they may have enough men for a 5th. You two are going to be Drill Instructors and train these men. Are there any questions? "

"Yes Sir, Captain. Do we have a choice? Training a bunch of civilians is a bunch of crap." Lee said.

"I guess I didn't make myself clear. Did I ask you, or did I tell you what you two were to do? When we get back, you both will be D.I.'s to a bunch of recruits. Now am I clear? "

"Yes Sir, but one more question. When do we leave here? And what do you want us to do?"

"Go back to your barracks, assemble your men and tell them that all liberties are off, and to pack their gear. We will be leaving tomorrow, at 0700 and be at the C-dock at 0900. Our ship will leave at noon. Are there any more questions? "

Lee and Rod left the Captain's office and went back to the barracks informed the men, and started packing. Several hours later, Sergeant Lee went to Rodney's bunk. "Rod, I am all packed and ready to go, and I have a favor to ask. Will you make sure the men will get to the C-Dock on time tomorrow and see that my bags are on the dock? I am going to see Lulu tonight. I can still use my pass at the guard shack. "

"Lee, you know what the Captain said, all leaves are canceled. You are asking for a bunch of trouble. Do you like her that much? Maybe miss the ship or get in the brig? Hell Lee, she is not worth the risk."

"I got to let her know I am leaving. She loves me you know, and she will be heartbroken, if I don't."

"O.K. Lee, I will see that the men get to the ship, and your gear will be on the dock, but please don't be late tomorrow. I hope she is worth it."

Reveille was at 0600 and everyone was headed for the chow line that is everyone except Sergeant Lee. He was with Lulu. At 0700 everyone, (except one) was in the trucks heading to C-Dock.

Rodney made sure everyone was on time. They unloaded their gear on the dock and he then began looking for Sergeant Lee. At first he did not find him, but then he saw Lee limping down the road.

Corporal Rodney went to meet him. "At least you're on time; your bags are on the ship. Where did you get that black eye? And your lip is busted; did you get in a fight with Lulu?"

"No, not with Lulu. When I got there, she had a sailor in bed with her. Can you believe that? She ditched me for a swabby. What a letdown."

"What did you do Sergeant Lee?"

"I decked him, that's what I done."

"Then what happen?" Rod asked.

"He decked me back, and then beat the crap out of me. Let's get on the ship Rod, I hurt all over and don't wake me up until we get to San Diego."

CHAPTER 4

War

"Sergeant Lee, wake up." Rodney said shaking his friend. "We have docked in San Diego; the Captain has been asking about you, I told him you were sick."

"Thanks Rodney, how long have I been asleep? Damn I feel rough."

"You were pretty badly beaten up, had a broken rib but I had the Medic fix it and took care of some cuts. That must have been some sailor to beat you up that bad, as I remember you were pretty good in a fight. Was it one or two? "

"It felt like three was on me, but really only one, he was just that good." said Lee. "I think Lulu enjoyed the fight, damn bitch."

"I need to take a shower and then I will come on down to the lower deck, thanks' Rodney, for covering for me. "

Sergeant Lee went down to the lower deck met his men, and told them to get their gear ready to debark. He was feeling a little better after the shower, and took a couple of pain pills the Medic had given him.

"Sergeant Lee, I want to see you," a voice said that Lee knew only too well.

"Yes Captain," Lee said saluting. "You want to see me? "

The Captain looked him over, smiled and said. " Sergeant Lee, I understand you have been under the weather, are you feeling better now? "

"Yes Sir, much better sir. I must have had a touch of the flu."

Captain Blake again smiled, " Yes Lee there is a lot of it going around, think you feel like getting your men ready and let's get off this ship? "

"Yes Sir, Captain."

"Rodney get the men lined up and put them in the trucks. We are going to the San Diego Marine base" said Lee saluting the Captain.

They were met at the Marine Base by an MP who escorted Rodney and Lee to another area and showed them their tent, where they would stay for the next three months' and then the MP handed Lee some papers.

Lee read the orders to Rodney. They would have the weekend off, but Monday morning at 0900 they would meet a bus at the gate with fifty civilians, and they were supposed to make Marines out of them.

"Damn," said Lee," I guess we are DI's to a bunch of wet nose civilians, Rodney, let's go get drunk. "

Friday night they hit the bars in town and had a few drinks, but Lee stayed away from the ones that might be trouble, because he had his share of fighting, and didn't want any more. That night they got a room in town and both were soon sound asleep, they were exhausted.

Lee and Rodney slept until 0700 and then after eating breakfast and walking around for awhile, decided to go back to base; Lee had some more unpacking to do.

Lee said, "Rodney I need some shaving cream. There's a drug store across the street, let's go check it out."

They walked into the drug store and saw a beautiful lady standing on a ladder putting up stock. They both stood behind her and watched. She heard someone behind her, and came down the ladder.

"Can I help you?" she said smiling.

"Yes," Lee said. " We are new in town and don't know our way around, maybe you could help us. "

Again with a beautiful smile, she replied," how can I help you?"

"We were thinking about lunch, do you know of a good café in town? And my name is Sergeant Lee Robinson, and this is Corporal Rodney Sweeny. "

"Nice to meet you both, my name is Rosabella, and there is a good café down the street. It is called Francine, owned by a French lady. They have good food."

"Great", Lee said," I like French food. "

"It isn't French food, it's Chinese."

"Well that will be okay. Would you care to join us for lunch?"

"No thank you, I am married and you can find it without me, holding out her hand and showing a ring… now what was it you wanted?"

"That shaving cream you were stocking up on the shelf, can I have a can of that." Lee said

"It's in a jar, are you sure that's what you want? "

"Yes Rosemary, that's what I want."

"It's Rosabella, and I will get you a jar." Climbing back up on the ladder.

Lee and Rodney watched her climb back up the ladder, and come back down, Lee said, "Now that's beautiful, notice how she does that Rodney, so gracefully."

Rosabella said,"that will be two dollars; you want it in a bag?"

"Yes please, and are you sure…"

"Yes, I'm sure, and I have work to do," as she walked to the back room.

Lee and Rodney left the drug store with his shaving cream and walked down the street.

"Rodney why is it that all the pretty women are always married? I could have gone for a woman like that."

"Don't know, I think the young men marry the pretty ones, before they have the chance to meet the real men. Why did you have her climb that ladder again, there was shaving cream on the counter? "

"Rodney, if you don't know the answer to that, I better have a talk with you later."

"Lee, the shaving cream you bought, have you looked at it? "

"Rod, I know it's not my brand, but shaving cream is shaving cream. "

"Lee, look in the bag."

Lee opened the bag and pulled out the jar, and read it to Rod. "Lady Beth, shaving cream for women. Safe and can be used on the face. Under the arms, legs, and other private parts. Damn, she knew that, and never said a word."

"You told her to go up the ladder, that was what you wanted," said Rod.

Lee saw two nurses coming down the side walk and when they got near to him, he handed them the package and said," Merry Christmas from the Marines."

"But this is November" one of the nurses said.

"Then you will be ahead of everyone else. Rod let's go home. "

They walked down the street and headed toward the base. The two women stared at them, and one said, "Damn Bell Hops."

Monday morning Lee woke up at 0600 and shook Rodney. "Wake up sleepy head, today is the day we get to meet those wet nose civilians. So help the Marines."

Rod wiping the sleep from his eyes said, "We will have breakfast first, won't we Sarg? "

"Soon as we get dressed, I could never face those men on an empty stomach."

Lee and Rod ate some s.o.s. (hamburger gravy, on toast) and sat around drinking their second cup of coffee.

"Damn I hate this job Rod. I joined the Marines to fight, not to be nurse maids to a bunch of civilians, and as soon as I can I am transferring to another outfit." Then looking at his watch said," I guess it's time to go. "

"Lee you know we had to go through this same training. Hell, everybody had to when we enlisted. "

"I know Rod, but we don't have to do it now. Let's go and meet our future Marines. "

The bus was on time Rod and Lee watched as the recruits got off and moved to the sidewalk.

"Line them up," Lee said to Rodney," I want to see what we got."

Sergeant Lee approached the men, and went up to a recruit and asked,

"What is your name, and where are you from?"

"Jimmy Wilson Sir and I'm from Ohio."

"Charles Nelson Sir, from Alabama"

Lee then stepped back, and said. "The first thing that I want you to learn is that I am not a sir, it is Yes, Sergeant Lee, or Yes, Corporal Rodney. I know you men did not know that, and you will be given a Marine Corps Manual, It will be your Bible. Read and study it, because I will ask questions later on it."

"Now look at my arm, you will see three stripes, and two under. That means that I am a Platoon Sergeant. Look at this man; he has two stripes, so he is a Corporal. One stripe is a Private First Class, no stripes you are a private. And you all are Boots the lowest class that anyone could be. But so help me, I will make Marines out of you. "

"We are N.C.O. that stands for non commission, officers. But if the Marine has a bar, oak leaf or stars, then they are commission officers and deserve a salute and a Sir." And always stand at attention in front of an officer, until he tells you, At Ease. You will learn all of this from your manual."

"There will be no sweets coming from home for the next six weeks; there will be no smoking, cursing, or two in the bunks. You will "double time" everywhere you go, and no walking. Corporal Rodney and I will be your mommy and your papa. If you have a problem, come to one of us. Do you understand? "

"Yes Sergeant Lee," they shouted

"I don't think I heard that? I want it louder"

"Yes! Sergeant Lee. "

That's better and then Lee stepped up to a recruit who had an ear ring in his ear. He looked at him, and then said, "Are you a man or woman?"

"A man Sergeant," he said.

Lee reaches up and pulled the ear ring off, "If you are not a woman, then no man in my outfit will wear an ear ring, and don't let me catch it on you again."

Then he walked up to another man and asked, "What is your name and where are you from? "

"I am Joe Brown from Tennessee, Sergeant Lee."

"Mr. Brown, what did you do before you came here? "

"I was going to school, and worked as an usher at a Theater, Sergeant. "

"Did you see any good Marine movies?" Lee asked.

"Yes, Sergeant, "Pride of the Marines" with Wallace Berry, that's when I decided to join the Marines. "

Lee walked up to another recruit with long hair down to his shoulders. He looked at his hair and said. "How long did it take you to grow that hair?"

"Months Sergeant, I wash and brushed it twice a week."

" Well boot, it will take only five minutes to cut it off, and it better not be over an inch from now on. "

Lee stepped back and looked at the men. "Heaven help us, we are in big trouble. Rodney, take these Boots to their tent and then to the barber shop, and get them some new uniforms. I am getting sick at my stomach. It will take years to make Marines out of this bunch. "

"Will do, Sergeant. I will meet you in the mess hall for lunch."

Rodney looked at the men and said, "Make four lines, double time and follow me, and no talking. "

Lee watched Rod and the men leave and thought. *What in the hell did I do, to deserve this. I will make Marines out of them, even if I have to kill a couple.*

A month went by and it was December 5th 1941 and Sergeant Lee and Corporal Rodney had just come back from a three mile hike with their company of recruits.

"Corporal, dismissed the men, and have them to fall out for chow at 0600. I'm going down to the NCO Club. Join me for a beer later, if you care too."

Sergeant Lee arrived at the club looked around, and seeing a couple of friends at a table ordered his beer and set down with them.

"Hi Ray, George, how are things going in the Armory Company?"

"It stinks," George said." My Company is supposed to have six tanks, we have two. One of those is in the shop with a cracked motor. Hell, if we have a war, we are going to be in big trouble."

"It's not if we have war anymore, but when," Ray said

"I wonder which one it will be." Said Lee

"I wish to hell I was with a fighting division if war breaks out. Not a damn D.I. to a bunch of snotty nose boots" Lee said.

"Lee, wasn't you in Cuba with a Captain Blake?" Asked George

"Hell yes, that's the S. O. B. that gave me this job. Do you know him George?"

"Yes, I served with him in China; I understand he is at Camp Pendleton, putting together a rifle company with the First Division. I heard that he is a Major now. If war breaks out, maybe you can get your old job back. "

Lee finished his beer and went to the mess hall, thinking. *I will just go and see Major Blake tomorrow, all he can say is no.*

Saturday morning Lee got a ride to Camp Pendleton and asked to see Major Blake. He found his office and went to the Sergeant in charge to get permission to see him.

"Hello, Sergeant Lee. Good to see you again," the Marine at the desk said.

"Why, I be damn, It's Corporal Shittie," and Lee stuck out his hand.

"It's Sergeant Chittie, Lee. You want to see the Major? "

"Yes, please. Tell him Sergeant Lee would like permission to talk to him."

A deep voice said, "Come in Lee and tell me about your recruits, we will need them soon if war breaks out." Said the Major

Lee stood at attention and saluted. "Yes Sir. That is what I want to talk to you about, Sir."

The Major returned the salute, and said. "Well at least your job has taught you some protocol. What can I do for you Lee?"

"Sir, we are about to go to war soon, and I want to be in a fighting outfit, please transfer me. I hear you have a rifle company, and you know that I am qualified, I can take that company and make fighting Marines out of them"

The Major looked at Lee. "You want it bad, don't you? I see that you will never be a happy D.I. Yes, I could transfer you to my division, but we have a small problem. I have a good Platoon Sergeant, who served with me in China. I can't use another one, but I could use a line Sergeant, or Corporal, but you don't qualify. "

"Lee, go back to your D.I. job, and if war breaks out, come back and see me. On your way out, tell Sergeant Chittie I want to see him."

Lee was disappointed, caught a ride to Long Beach and made his way to all of the bars, until he knew he was drunk, and then got a ride back to the base, and then went to bed.

Lee was awakened by the bugler blowing reveille, and people shouting. "What's going on Rodney, this is Sunday. What the hell is going on? "

"We are at War Lee; the damn Japanese bombed Pearl Harbor, many of our ships are sunk and hundreds of people were killed."

Lee got up and put on his pants," Those S.O.B's. Let's go to the NCO Club and listen to the radio".

Wednesday, December 10th. Everyone was ordered to the parade ground, and was told to line up. The Commandant would be there with the other officers.

Sergeant Lee had his company at parade rest. He looked at the officers, and then at his men.

Then Sergeant Lee walked up to Hovack, the biggest Marine there, and said to him. "I will explain later, and buy you a beer… when I get out of the brig. " Then he hit him as hard as he could, and Hovack went down on the ground.

At first, no one believed what they had just seen. Then the Commandant looked at the Major, and said to him." Major Powell, have someone take that man to the Brig, and tell the MP's that I will stop by later and press charges."

Two Marines escorted Sergeant Lee to the brig, and on the way he saw George looking at him smiling. Lee smiled back and put up his hand in a victory sign.

Sergeant Lee got three days of jail time and was demoted to a Corporal.

CHAPTER 5

Guadalcanal

After three days in the brig, Sergeant Lee Robinson was escorted to the office of Captain Smart, the Officer of the Day. The unshaven Lee approached the Captain, gave him his best salute, and stood at attention.

"Lee, I have known you for five years, and I have never seen you do a stupid act like you did on the parade ground. I hope you had a good reason?"

"I did sir, I wanted to get out of the Boot Camp training program and join a fighting company. Hell, this war may not last over six months and I wanted part of the action."

Captain Smart looked at Lee, then reached into his desk and pulled out a large scissors, and tossed them to him. "Cut off those Sergeant stripes and you can put two back on. And then get out of my office, and I don't want to see you here again."

Lee cut his Platoon Sergeant stripes off, gave the scissors back to the Captain, saluted, and then was dismissed.

He walked the mile back to his tent, took a shower, shaved and pulled out a clean shirt. He found a couple of Corporal stripes and sewed them on his shirt. On his way out he saw Rodney, shook hands and told him he was going to see Major Blake at Camp Pendleton.

Corporal Rodney hated to see his friend go, but he understood. With five years in the Corps, Lee will now be in a fighting company.

Hell, maybe I should slug someone and join him. Corporal Rodney thought.

Corporal Lee walked out the gate of San Diego and never looked back. Reaching the highway to Frisco, he started walking and hitchhiking at the first car he saw. After about thirty minutes a car stopped with a couple of sailors.

"How far you going, Marine?" one of the men said.

"Camp Pendleton, Sailor. Can you take me that far?"

"Sure, hop in the back. We got a three day pass and heading for Frisco to wine and dine some beautiful women."

Lee got in the car, introduced himself and then the three of them talked about the war, and the S.O.B. Japs that bombed Pearl Harbor. After about an hour they arrived at the entrance of Camp Pendleton.

"It's about three miles up to the base. You are planning on walking?"

"Yes, unless a car comes by, it's a busy road," said Lee getting out of the car.

It wasn't long before a 6/4 truck came by loaded with Marines and picked him up. " You know all of this land and the base belongs to Gene Autry, the movie star, said one of the Marines. He leased it to the government several years ago."

Getting out of the truck, Lee headed for headquarters where he knew Major Blake would be.

"Stop there Marine," a voice demanded. "You can't just walk into the Major's office."

"Hello Shittie," Lee said

"Damn if it isn't Corporal Lee, and the name is Sergeant Chittie. Whatc'h wants to see the Major fer?"

"None of your damn business. Is he in his office?" Lee said walking toward the door.

"Just hold on a minute, I need to see if he wants to see you. He has Platoon Sergeant Bama with him." Sergeant Chitty said blocking Lee.

"What's the racket out there? Lee is that you?" said a deep voice behind the door.

"Yes Major, Corporal Lee, can I see you?"

"Just open the door and come in. I have someone I want you to meet."

Lee opened the door, saluted the Major, and looked over in the corner and saw the biggest Marine he had ever seen. At least 6'5 and 250 pounds.

"Corporal Lee, this is Platoon Sergeant Major, Bill Hitchcock, but we call him Bama, born and raised in Alabama. Bama was with me in China when I was a young 2nd Lieutenant. He stayed in China when I left, and came to the states about six months ago. I heard he was back and had him transferred to my outfit."

"What can I do for you Lee? I heard about you decking one of your men in front of the General. That was a stupid thing to do. You're lucky he didn't give you six months in the brig or a discharge. If we didn't have a war on, he would have."

"Major, you told me several months ago that you couldn't use another Platoon Sergeant, but you could use a Corporal or a plain Sergeant. So here I am Corporal Lee Robinson."

"O.K. You have earned it. You will be my new line Sergeant. You and Bama will make a good team, but it was a hell of a way to do it. Glad to have you aboard, Lee."

"Lee you will be in Baker Company, the second platoon under Platoon Sergeant Bill Hitchcock," the Major said shaking his hands

"Bama, fill him in on what his job will be." said the Major

"Sergeant Lee, you will have 12 men. All are trained but need a little more polishing. Two 30 cal machine gunners, two ammunition carriers, two mortar launchers, and six good rifle men. They are ready for a fight."

"The machine guns Bama. Are they water cooled or air cooled?"

"Water cooled; the air barrels get's too hot. Standard mortar launchers. And we use the new M1 Gerang rifles. One man still has the 03, and he would make a good sniper if needed. They are all good men, but we got a disgruntled Marine in the bunch that may challenge you. He was passed over for promotion, and is angry about it. If you have any trouble with him, let me know."

"If I have any trouble with him, I will handle it myself," said Lee

The Major looked over at Bama and winked. "You don't have to worry about Sergeant Lee. He took on almost a dozen gorillas in Cuba who had kidnapped the niece of the town's mayor."

After their meeting Bama took Lee to the PX and bought him a beer and then to his barracks and told him meet at the mess hall for breakfast. And then he would introduce him to the company and his men.

At 0900 they had breakfast and walked over to the parade ground. Lee met the platoon and after several marches, double time, and field exercises Bama dismissed the company, all but Lee's squad. Lee then took his 12 men and double time them to the other side of the grounds and had them to fall out.

Again he introduced himself, said he was a five year Marine and had served in China and in Cuba. He was fair, but he went by the book. We are at war, and I don't have time to baby anyone. If you can't take the heat now's the time for a transfer, because I'm going to work the hell out of you. Any questions?

And for the next couple weeks the training was rough, but Lee had no trouble out of them and was amazed with their firing and physical condition.

The war wasn't going well for America; we had lost the Philippines, Wake Island and Guam. The Major called for a meeting of his officers, and Sergeants.

"Men our Division may call for us at any time. The Japanese are building an air strip down close to New Guinea, and from there they will bomb Australia. They will have to be stopped. I know you have some good men, but push them harder; the Japanese will have us outnumbered. Their training will mean the difference between life and death. Thank you men, now take the time we have left, and push them to the edge."

The next morning Lee had his men to fall out. "Men, do you see that tree up there on the hill? That's one mile. I want you go and get your field packs, carry your fighting equipment, and double time up the hill and back. Do I make myself clear?"

"Yes, Sergeant."

"What! I don't hear you?"

"Yes, Sergeant,

"Hell Yes! Sergeant Lee."

He knew it would be rough on the machine gunners. The gun weighs 40 pounds and the bullet sleeves for the gun were even heavier. But they may have to do this in battle.

One of his gunners was named Al Schmidt and was from up north. The other marine was Ace McCord, the one that was turned down for promotion. He was the one Bama told him to watch out for.

They made the run up the hill, and after a thirty minutes rest, Lee told them to do it again. This time Ace McCord said, "Lee, go to hell. I'm not going up that hill again."

Saturday morning the Major called for a company review. Bama assembled the men and had them to do a right face and stand at attention. He went down the line inspecting each man. Then he came to Sergeant Lee's men, and saw one man with a black eye and a busted lip.

"What happen to your face Marine?"

"I fell Sir going up the hill," Corporal Ace McCord said.

Then the Major looked at Sergeant Lee. "You fall too, Sergeant?"

"Yes Sir, the hill was a little rocky."

"Well you two try to be a little more careful. We can't have you in sick bay, we have a war to fight," looking at Lee smiling.

A month later the 1st Division got their orders to get combat ready, they started packing their equipment in crates, greasing their guns and writing letters. All leaves were canceled, and they were on Ready Standby.

The order was given the next day, to load their sea bags on the trucks, and for the men to climb onto the trucks behind. Sergeant Lee waited until all of his men were aboard, and then handed his rifle to Corporal McCord and he climbed up into the truck.

It was a three hour ride to San Diego, and as they pulled into the ship yard, Lee could see several troop ships tied up to the dock. The order was given to climb out of the trucks march to the gang planks, and get on the ship.

Two decks down they found their beds for the next month, and Lee was lucky he found a bottom bunk. After finding their sea bags, he and most of the other men flopped on the bed and were soon fast asleep.

Lee woke up with the smell of vomit, felt the ship's roll from side to side, and knew they were on their way. He looked at his men, some were almost green with sea sickness, but all of them were ready to meet the Japanese and avenge Pearl Harbor.

Two days out, they found out where they were going. Guadalcanal, a small island in the South Pacific. The Japanese's were building an air strip on the island to bomb Australia and other islands in the area. The Marines had to move them off, and then hold the island until the Marines and Air Force planes could come in. This would be the first offence of the United States, and they had to make the stand here.

Lee was awakened by the sounds of gun fire; going up on the top deck he saw that the sea was full of ships. One of our troop ships had been hit and men were trying to swim to shore, and then he saw black fins heading from man to man. Next to Lee's ship was a U.S. Cruiser engaged in a fight with two Japanese Destroyers. Everywhere he looked, U.S. ships were in heavy fighting with the Japs.

The order was given to disembark, and Lee gathered his men and went to the side of the ship. They climbed down the cargo nets and into the Higgins boats that were waiting for them. Jap Zero planes were strafing his men, many falling off the nets and into the sea. He thought, *What the hell did I volunteer for?*

August 7th, 1943 the battle of Guadalcanal began, and the 1st Marines landed on the beach in the middle of Japanese fire. Hundreds of the Marines never made it to the beach, and were lunch for the sharks lying off shore. Bodies were in the sea, and lying in the sand, ½ mile in both directions.

Sergeant Lee and Platoon Sergeant Bama gathered their men and made their way over to Major Blake's Company. Then they formed a giant V and made their way into the jungles and to Henderson Air Field. The firing was light; the Japs had pulled back to the Tenaru River past Henderson field. But on the way, a Marine would fall, and then another. Lee wondered where the sniper was firing from, and after another Marine fell, he saw a Jap tied to the top of coconut trees. After warning his men, they turned their guns up into the trees.

The Division made their way to the air strip and started digging fox holes, where they would spend their nights for the next months. Lee checked his men, and one of his Marines, Al Schmidt had a bad infection on his foot. Lee ordered him to go back to the sick bay and have it treated. (Al never did, and the foot got worse.) That night as Al would say, "The fireworks began."

Every night they were shelled by the Japanese ships, and every Marine was thankful for their fox holes, and during the shelling they would dig a little deeper. The next day they fought a fierce battle pushing the Japs to the other side of the Tenaru River.

Bama and Lee would take patrols across the river and saw

that the Japanese were preparing for an attack to cross the river and retake Henderson field. The next night Major Blake had Bama and Lee place their two machine guns and mortar men this side of the river, and for the other Marines to spread out along the bank.

Al, Lee and a Marine, named Coons were sitting there about ten o'clock, shooting the breeze, when they heard the pop-pop-pop of the Jap rifles in back of them. They had just started digging a new hole; Lee and Coons dived into it, but it was too shallow for Al to get in. He sat crouched up on the edge with his head bent down and his feet in the hole, ducking tracer bullets as best he could. They were hitting all around him; he wondered why in hell the Japs were firing his way so much.

The Japs hung around most of the night firing at his position until daylight, and then sneaked away again to the other side of the river. Lee came around to check on his men, and found Al leaning against a coconut tree. He looked up at the tree, and saw what the Japs had been firing at. A Marine had hung a roll of toilet paper on a branch above Al's head; there were four bullet holes in the white roll. When Al saw that, his heart took a dive down to the bottom of his shoes.

The Japs planned to crash through the Marines lines and grab the air field before the Marines could regroup. There were eight hundred to a thousand Japs on the bank of the Tenaru River when the battle started. And across the river there were about two hundred Marines, with two machines guns and two 37 millimeter antitank guns.

About 0100 a.m. the Japs started coming across. It looked

like a bunch of cows coming down to drink. They had not spotted the gun placements. Lee stood up and began pushing sandbags away from around the front of the gun. He wanted to get clear so they could tilt the gun straight down and fire into the water if they had to. He said "Fire!" and Johnny opened up. McCord's gun, a hundred yards to the right, opened up at the same time.

Now the Japs had both Marine guns spotted and plastered them with everything they had. Bullets whizzed into the nest and threw chips of wood and dirt down the back of their shirt. Nobody was crouching down any more; they were standing up and firing their guns. Lee would punch Al on the arm and Al would punch Johnny, and point to where he should fire next. Then McCord's gun stopped, and then Johnny got it. A string of slugs tore into his face and the blood spurted out as though someone had turned on a faucet. He fell back in the trench without making a sound. Al moved over and took the gun and Lee got in position to load. They didn't have to say anything. They were trained for this too.

The Japs must have gotten rattled because they started coming over right where the moon was shining on the river; we could see the buttons on their jackets. We waited till they were only fifty yards away, and then we mowed them down like sitting ducks. Lee was loading and helping direct the fire. Al would be shooting across the river to the left, and he would feel Lee hitting him on the arm really hitting him, and pointing upstream.

A Jap machine gunner had gotten set up on the other side, and put a string of bullets through the water jacket of

Al's gun, about three inches in front of his nose; the water spurted out over his lap and chest. The gun got red-hot, but for some reason it didn't jam the way it was supposed to when it didn't have water. Lee spotted the Jap gunner, who had done it, and Al swung his gun around to his right and let go with a burst, and that was all they heard from him. A Jap bullet caught Lee on the shoulder and knocked him down; he fell across Al's feet. Schmidt went on firing and loading for himself. He would look at the belt every few seconds, and when it got close to the end he would fire a short burst, rip open the magazine, and stick in a new belt. He kept it up for more than four hours, without help, until heavy Marine reinforcements came and stopped the Japs cold at the Tenaru River that night.

Then one of the Japs got through. There was a blinding flash and explosion and something hit Al a terrific wallop in the face. It was a hand grenade that had exploded. He put his hand up and all he could feel was a wet sticky pulp, and warm blood pouring down through his fingers. It felt like somebody had cut off the front of his face with a hatchet. He went down on his back in the trench, Lee was laying across his legs. Al heard himself say," Damn, they got me in the eyes."

The Japs were still pouring bullets into the nest, and Al reached around to his holster and took out his 45. Lee heard him fussing with it and yelled. "Don't do it Smitty, don't shoot yourself."

Al said. "Hell, don't worry about that, I'm going to get the first Jap that tries to come in here."

"But you can't see," Lee told him.

"That's all right," Al said. "Just tell me which way he's coming and I'll get him."

This is a true story

Al Schmidt was almost the sole survivor of his squad at a point on the Tenaru River, and suffering from a previously infected foot, fought through to the finish. Of the 800 or more Japs who tried to cross the Tenaru, fourteen were picked up wounded after the fight and one was captured. The rest were killed. The number of bodies counted within range of Schmidt's machine gun ran into the hundreds; he was credited by other Marines who were there with killing at least 200 Japs.

Al Schmidt was awarded the Navy Cross "for extraordinary heroism and outstanding courage in action." He got his stripes as a Sergeant. But he did not fully recover the use of the one eye, and it was removed. He married his fiancee, shortly after his returned to the United States.

CHAPTER 6

The Bloody Battle of Tarawa— November 20th 1943

Tarawa is an atoll located approximately 2,500 miles southwest of Hawaii. The military importance of Tarawa lay in its strategic location at the gateway of the US drive through the central Pacific towards the Philippines.

Here, the Japanese built an airstrip defended by 4,700 troops dug in pillboxes and bunkers. Interconnected by tunnels and defended by wire and mines. The task of dislodging this force fell to the Marines of the 2nd Division. The resulting struggle produced one of the fiercest and bloodiest battles in Marine Corps history.

Coming in at low tide, the assault boats were forced to disgorge their men far from shore. Wading through waist-deep water over piercing, razor-sharp coral, many were cut down by merciless enemy gunfire yards from the beach. Those who made it ashore huddled in the sand, hemmed in by the sea on one side and the Japanese to the other.

The cost of victory was high for the Marines who suffered 3,000 casualties. The toll was even higher for the Japanese. Of the 4,700 defenders, only 17 survived.

SAN DIEGO

Sergeant Lee Robinson was put on a hospital ship and sent back to San Diego; his fighting on Guadalcanal was over.

December 9th 1942 General Vandergrift turned over command of Guadalcanal to the Army.

Nurse Patricia Mason or Pat as she preferred to be called pushed her hair back, straightened her uniform and unsnapped a button in front showing part of her breast, now she was ready. She opened the door to the room where seven wounded Marines were lying in bed. "Good Morning heroes, it's time to get a shot for Malaria and some blood."

"Aw Hell!" The Marines that were awakened hollered out. " We already gave our blood on Guadalcanal. Now you want more blood?"

"Sorry boys, Doctor's orders. You wouldn't want me to get fired, would you?"

"Baby, if you got fired, you can come and live with me," said a couple of Marines.

She approached Sergeant Lee's bed, with the needle pointing to his hip. "Turn over Sergeant, I haven't got all day."

"Why the hip nurse, you just want to look at my butt?"

"I've seen better looking butts in the nursing homes," she said plunging the needle into his hip.

Then the nurse bent over and stuck a thermometer in Lee's

mouth, while he looked at her beautiful breast. She smiled and said, "Take a good look Sergeant; you will be here several more weeks." Then she removed the thermometer, and went to the next Marine.

Lee had been in the hospital for a couple days, when the nurse came in and said he had a visitor. "Hello Sergeant, I heard you were back, and in the hospital. How are you feeling?"

"Rodney! And a Sergeant too. Damn, it's good to see you again." Lee stuck out his hand.

Lee bought him up to date about his days on the island and about his wounds. Then Rodney filled him in about the drill instructor's school at the base. The two old friends talked about an hour, before the nurse came in and told Rod he had to leave.

The next day Sergeant Lee Robinson had another visitor, this time it was Major Blake. The Major pinned a Purple Heart on Lee and saluted him.

"Lee, have you heard about TARAWA?" "We got the hell beat out of us, and had 3,000 casualties. We didn't know about the coral beaches at low tide, and the Jap's had a field day. That won't happen again."

"I've been called to Washington to form a new outfit. When you get out of here, I want you to go back to Boot Camp and be a Drill Instructor with Sergeant Rodney. I know you don't want to, but I promised you it will only be a short time. I want that shoulder to heal, because I will need you, maybe Sergeant Rodney too."

"Get well and work out on your swimming; I will get back to you in a couple months." The Major saluted Lee and left the room.

Lee watched the Major leave. "I wonder what the hell he's up too. It sounds like I may see some more action. But anything is better than being a nurse maid to a bunch of civilian boots."

"Nurse, bring me a bed pan, unless you want your bed messed up?"

Couple of weeks had passed and the doctor examined Lee's shoulder and told him he was releasing him for active service. The nurse changed his bandages, and gave him an instruction list.

"Pat, now that I've been released. What about your telephone number, and where you live. All that I know about you is that your first name is Pat"

"Sorry about that Marine. But I'm married to a wonderful sailor."

Lee dropped his instruction list and looked at her. "A Swabby?"

"You mean you have been teasing me all along, on purpose leaning over me, and getting me all worked up?"

"Sorry about that Lee, but I have been a nurse for a long time, and I know about Marines."

"I thought if you got your mind on something else, you would forget about your shoulder and get well quicker. I'm happily married Lee, sorry if I gave you the wrong impression."

"Hell Pat, it's been six months since I have held a woman's hand or kissed a woman."

Pat took Lee's hand and then bent over and kissed him. "Thanks for what you and the other Marines did, and you will find a nice girl."

"Now get dressed, your friend Rodney is outside to take you back to your base." She left the room, looked back and threw him a kiss.

Rodney walked into the room, seeing Lee getting dressed, said."I will get your things, and I will buy you a beer before we go back to the base." They got into the jeep and Rodney took Lee to the PX and had a couple of beers. It was two good friends back together again.

"Hup, two, three, four. Get in step George, the war will be over before you learn to march. Bill, wipe that grin off your face, Lantz get that rifle straight on your shoulder. Hell, what did I do to deserved you bunch of recruits?"

The day finally came to an end, and Sergeant Lee dismissed his company and went to his tent and took a shower. Rodney came in when he was getting dressed.

"Where you going, Lee?"

"I've got to get out of here before I hit somebody. Going to town Rod, and get drunk. Will you go with me?"

"Can't. Unless. I have a date with Sue, maybe she can get a friend and we can go out together. Will you go with us Lee, if she can find a friend?"

"Hell yes, I haven't been with a woman in three months. Think Sue could get me a date?"

"You finish getting dressed, and I will go to the office and call Sue, she would be glad to see you again, like old times."

Rod came back smiling ear to ear. " Sue got you a good looking date. She's around twenty, brunette, and likes to have fun. We will pick them up at Denny's restaurant at six p.m."

They met the girls at Denny's, and Lee's date was a beauty. She said her name was Joy Smith, and she loved Marines. She took his hand and they went inside.

After a good meal, Rod suggested they go to the bar down the street and have a beer. But Joy said, "Let's go to my place, I have some beer in the fridge, and I just made a chocolate cake this morning."

They got a taxi, and Joy gave the driver the address, and it wasn't far across town. Lee paid the cab fare, and the four went upstairs to the third apartment.

Joy cut the cake, and gave Lee the biggest slice. After they had eaten, she turned the radio on and asked Lee if he could dance. The four of them began to dance to the tune of "Blue Moon." They had one song after another, and then they sat on the couch, and Joy went to the cabinet and pulled out a bottle of scotch, and made everyone a drink.

After a couple hours, everyone was happy. Joy moved over to Lee, put her arms around him and gave him a big kiss. He looked for Rod and Sue, but they had disappeared to the bed room.

"Honey, you fix yourself another drink. I'm going to the bedroom and take a shower. I will knock on the door three times, and then you can come in." said Joy kissing him again.

Lee was fixing another drink when Joy came running out of the bedroom with only a slip on. "You and Rod got to get out of here, my husband is getting out of his car, and he has a General with him. Please leave now."

Lee dropped his drink and looked at her."You're married?"

"Yes, he's a Major in the Marines. He is coming up the steps. You will have to leave by the window."

"Hell Lady, we are on the third floor, and you expect me to go out the window? I ought to throw you out."

"Yes, it's the only way. You will run into them in the hall way."

Lee knocked on the other bedroom, "Rod put your pants on and get out here now. And don't leave any of your clothes."

Rod came out carrying his shoes, looked at Lee and said."What's going on?"

"Joy is married to a Marine Major, and he is coming up the steps with a General. We have got to go out the window. Now!"

"But Lee, we are on the third floor."

"You want broken bones, or spend the rest of your life in Fort Leavenworth? I will take the broken bones," Lee said, as he went to the window.

Lee looked outside, and saw a ledge leading to the corner of the building and a drain pipe going down to the ground, it was their only chance. He took Rod's shoes and threw them out the window, and then grabbed and pushed him out the window onto the ledge.

Rod was hugging the wall as close as he could, and Lee was right behind him. They reached the drain pipe, and Rod grabbed it and started climbing down. He was half way down when Lee reached the drain pipe, and with both of their weight the drain pulled from the side of the building, and they both went tumbling down and landed into a water fountain.

"Lee, you hurt?"

"No, but you are going to be. Why didn't you tell me she was married, and to a Major?"

"Rod if you weren't my best friend, I would kill you. We were lucky to get out of there."

"Honey, why are you looking out the window?" Joy asked. "What do you see?"

"A couple of drunken Marines, sitting in the fish pond."

"Hey you Marines down there. Get out of the pond and go back to your base, or I will call the Military Police."

Lee looked up at the Major, saluted and said," Yes sir, we were just leaving."

Lee found Rodney's shoes and tossed them to him." Put those damn shoes on and let's go back to the base."

"We can't get a ride looking like this, we are soaked," Rod said pulling a gold fish out of his pocket.

"Then we will walk, we will be dry by the time we get to the gate," he said climbing out of the pool, and shaking the water out of his ears.

Two wet Marines walked back to the base avoiding the M P saying very little to each other. When they got to the gate, they showed their wet pass to the sentry. He looked at the pass, then at them, and grinned.

"Sentry if you say a word, I will knock the hell out of you, I've had enough crap for today." Lee said looking at the private.

When they got to their tent and went inside, there was a letter on the table. Lee picked it up, and after reading it, said to Rodney." Take a shower and change clothes. We are to report to the Captain at Headquarters."

"Sergeant Robinson and Sergeant Sweeny reporting, sir." Lee said saluting the Captain.

"Where in the hell have you two been, we have had Marines out looking for you"

"On liberty sir. We just got back and found your letter, sir."

"Well you two are flying to Kauai, Hawaii tomorrow at 0800 on a B-24 bomber from Miramar Air Station. Here's your orders, and when you arrive, get a ride to this address." The Captain said giving Lee the papers.

Sergeant Lee and Rodney landed at Kauai, took a taxi to the address on their orders, and found an old building with a sign in the yard. UDT...Underwater Demolition Team.

CHAPTER 7

Battle for the Marshall Islands

January-February 1944

The capture of the Marshall Islands moved American reconnaissance and land-based strike aircraft within range of both the Carolinas and the Marianas, and opened new bases for the U.S. Navy.

The rapid victories in the Marshalls gave added momentum to the Central Pacific drive. The low number of casualties---fewer than 3,000 combined for Marines and Army---shows that the lessons that the Marine 2nd Division paid such a high price for at Tarawa were put to good use. Surface and air bombardment and naval gunnery improved in strength and accuracy. Tactics against heavily defended atolls had been changed and improved. The Marshalls assault forces had more and better transportation to the beach.

"In the seizure of the northern portion of the Kwajalein Atoll, Marine 4th Division casualties were 313 killed and 502 wounded. They defeated an estimated 3,563 Japanese garrison forces, taking only 90 prisoners."

UNDERWATER DEMOLITION TEAM

When Sergeant Lee and Sergeant Rodney landed at Kauai, Hawaii they were met by two MP (military police) and were escorted to a truck parked off the air strip. There were at least 20 Marines in the truck, and they were told to climb aboard.

When the last man entered, the MP pulled the canvas together and no one could see out. The Marines looked at each other, and then one said, "What the hell did we volunteer for?"

Two trucks full of Marines went speeding down the road, they had no idea where they were going and what they would do when they got there. After about an hour the trucks pulled up and stopped. The MP pulled the cover back and they were parked in front of an old school house which had been deserted years ago. There were two more buildings, but no houses in view. Rod pointed out to Lee, the ocean that was within a hundred yards.

"Get out of the truck Marines; this will be your home for the next three months, no phone calls and no liberty." Said one of the MP's

In the front of the building was a small sign. U.D.T. Underwater Demolition Team.

The MP lined the men up and they were marched inside. When the last man was inside, the MP closed the door and stood in front of it. There was a Sergeant sitting at a desk.

"Glad to have you aboard men, now one at a time step up to the desk, and give me your orders."

Lee was third in line, and when the Marines in front of

him left he approached the Sergeant. He handed him his papers, and waited while he looked at his orders, and then at him. After five minutes, the Sergeant smiled and asked Lee to stick out his hands, and then stamped it UDT and then motion Lee to sit down while he checked each person out.

When the Sergeant finished with the last man, he asked the twenty men to follow him. "Men I did not address you as Marines, you are now recruits, regardless of your branch of service or your rank. There are a couple of sailors, and one Army. You are now known as the UDT team; you will live, and fight together as a team, so get to know your buddies. Some of you are officers, and all of you will still be paid what your rank calls for. Here you will be judged not by rank, but by your job abilities."

They left the room and went into the hallway. "Look up at the top of the door, the letter M stands for Mess Hall. A bugler will sound one note for breakfast, two for lunch and three for supper. Since we are close to supper you will eat and then have the rest of the day off, to look around or write letters. Now let's go to the "B" room, this is where you will sleep."

"Going outside you will see room G for the gym, and an inside Olympic Pool. Now as we pass through the G room and back outside you will see the ocean. You are one mile to the beach, pass that you will see a buoy at one mile, two miles, and three miles. We expect you to go the three miles before you graduate; if you can't you will be washed out of UDT."

"Now you can wait for supper, with the rest of the day off, Breakfast, one note at 0700. At 0900 a.m. we will be a meeting in the C room, where you will meet your officer in charge of this little operation"

Lee found Rodney and they went toward the bunk house to find a bunk to sleep in. Actually the buildings were close together and they would have no trouble finding their way around. As they approached building B, Rod pointed out to Lee the ten foot high fence surrounding the buildings and the guard shacks.

"Rod, I don't know what we got ourselves into, but I'm sure we are going to see some action."

After supper they went back to their bunks. Lee hit the sack while Rod wrote a letter to Sue. It had been a long day.

Lee was awake before the bugler sounded reveille, and hit Rod on the butt.

"Wake up sleepy-head and quit dreaming of Sue. It will be a long time before you will see her again."

After the bugler call, a great big Marine came inside the room, saying. "Get out of those sacks; don't let me have to pull you out, his deep voice drifting through the hall. Remember after you eat, you will meet in room C at 0900 a.m."

Lee looked at Rod. "I know that voice."

"Bama, is that you?" "I thought you got killed on Guadalcanal?"

"Sergeant Lee. You're the one that got shot at the river with Al Schmidt. I saw them carrying you off on a stretcher." Bama came forward holding out his hand. "Damn it's good to know you're still alive, and you volunteered for this outfit."

"Major Blake didn't tell me you were joining his outfit, but then he doesn't tell his Sergeants everything." Bama said smiling.

"I got some things to do; after you eat I will see you in the meeting room. Damn it's good to see you again," as Bama walked out of the barracks.

After a good breakfast of ham, eggs, redeye gravy, and pancakes Rod and Lee made their way to the meeting room. They saw Major Blake going over some maps.

"Good morning Major."

"Lee, Rodney, glad to see you both. I was hoping you two would volunteer. We are building a brand new outfit, and this job goes all the way to the top. Have a seat and when the others get inside, I will tell you all about it."

After Bama had the men stand at attention, Major Blake walked into the room, and then he had roll call. There were sixty men who were present.

Everyone got quiet as the Major stood and looked at his men. "Men, all of you are volunteers, and were picked by me and my staff. You are the best in your branch of service. Some of you are from the Navy, Army, and Marines, and with difference in rank. But today you are recruits, and I have three months to make you into a fighting machine. You will be the finest service men in the U.S. Armed Forces. The President and Admiral Chester Nimitz has asked for your service. I need forty good men. That leaves twenty that won't make it, don't be in that twenty."

"I can't tell you where you're going, or when? But we start

today. After three months you will run five miles, swim three miles, and will know ten ways to kill the enemy with your knife and bare hands. Our fighting will be close combat. Anytime someone wants out, come to my office. There is no shame in quitting, and no one will know about it. You will be put in another outfit, and not the one you came from."

The Major continued, "On Nov 23rd, 1943 the U.S. Marines took a beating at Tarawa Atoll. That emphasized the need for hydrographic reconnaissance and underwater demolition of obstacles prior to any amphibious landing."

"Admiral Nimitz has asked for a central Pacific operation requiring an efficient amphibious force. Many of the targeted islands are coral obstacles to our landing forces. If we get forty good men, twenty will go to Europe under Eisenhower. The other twenty men will stay under me. The men that don't make it will be sworn to secrecy, and transferred to another outfit."

"It's very important that you can swim three miles, you will be required to do it on graduation. We will go to an island before the invasion by submarine, swim to the island in teams. If it's a small island, we look for the best landing places. Then we look for the underwater obstacles. If it is fence, then we put mines on it, and blow it up the day of our landing. There may be some mines under the water; we have to take care of those too. We destroy anything that may harm our men in their landing. We will plant mines on the bottom of enemy ships. We may be called on to rescue our downed pilots and I'm sure the Admiral will ask for a few more things.

Now, does that give you men enough excitement? You will

work out five days a week. Saturday you will meet here in this room, where you will learn sign languages and Japanese. After lunch you will have the rest of the week off, but you cannot leave the base. Anyone wants out come to my office, or follow Bama to the gym. "

Lee looked at Rod and said," WOW "

"Rod you're planning on marrying Sue, why don't you get out. I have no one in mind, so I'm staying."

"Lee, we have always stuck together, if you are going to stay, then I'm staying with you. Hell, I will probably get washed out anyway. I know I can't swim three miles and stay afloat for two hours. I've never expected to live forever, beside it might be fun."

Lee grabbed Rod's hand and said. "OK, good buddy, we are in this together, you watch my back, and I will watch yours. Now let's go find Bama."

They walked to the gym where Bama was doing some hand to hand combat with one of the recruits. They watched for a few minutes before he spotted them.

"Hello Lee glad you came, you're next." Throwing his man over his shoulder and unto the pad.

"Can't I just watch, I will learn more that way?" Lee said as he watched the man getting up from the pad shaking his head.

"Sorry Lee, everyone has to pass by me, until I say he's ready."

In the next two hours Lee learned how to disarm a man cut his throat or break his neck, in less than five minutes. Then he was given to another instructor who would show him exercises to build up his arms and legs for swimming. And that was Day 1, with many more to come.

Day 2, they were taken to the running track and ran the course twice which would be two miles. After a thirty minute rest they were told to run to the beach, and swim out to the platform to the first buoy, which was one mile. Lee looked for Rodney, who was the third person in line. After a ten minute rest, they were ordered to get back in the water, stay afloat without swimming for ten minutes, and could use any method to stay afloat, to accomplish their objective.

That afternoon they went to the Olympia pool and Lee, Rod, and another recruit got in the water. They were told to swim and tread water for an hour. Lee looked at Rod and said, "This is fun, I could do this all day."

But Rod was looking at an underwater gate that was slowly opening, and then he saw two large sharks coming out.

"Crap! Look what's coming out Lee, we got company."

The two sharks were at least twenty feet long and slowly made their way toward the men. One of the instructors jumped into the water with a spear gun, but only motioned the men to stay still. The sharks would only attack if they smell blood, or the swimmers panic or try to swim away fast. The three men had to stay calm, while the instructor watched each man for fear. This would be important if they were at an island alone, where there may be sharks. After the standoff, the sharks ignored the swimmers. But Rod and Lee never took their eyes off of them. The instructor told the men they would be armed with a large knife, and couple package of shark repellent, and they would swim in pairs. They could not talk, but use sign language. Any noise or conversation would give their position away.

Each day that followed, something new was added. After the first month ten men had dropped out, those that were left were getting stronger and swimming further out each day. Lee and Rod were now at the 2 mile buoy. Boot Camp was a snap compared to the training they were now getting. They were the elite of the elite. The best of the American Fighting Forces.

Two months had gone by and there were 45 men left, and all had qualified for the three mile buoy. Now they were working with rubber suits, face masks, and fins, staying under the water for a maximum of three minutes, while working with explosives. Sometimes they would let the sharks out of their cages while they were working.

They had been training for two months when Major Blake was called to Admiral Nimitz's flag ship station in the Pacific.

After two days he was back and called a meeting of his men.

"Men we are going to be put to the test. I will need ten volunteers and their names will be posted on the door tomorrow. If you are one of those men, pack your ditty bag and leave most of your stuff here. We will only be gone a week, take only what you will need."

The next day Lee saw his name and Rodney's on the list, and they went back to pack their ditty bag with the necessary toilet items, and one change of clothing. They waited for their transportation at 0600 a.m.

At the exact time a covered truck pulled up and the ten men climbed into the back, then the covers were pulled down, still not knowing where they were would be stationed. They rode about thirty minutes and got out at a Navy base, where they boarded a Catalina. (Sea Plane)

After two hours of flying, the plane landed on the water and waited.

Rod and Lee kept looking out the window; they were in the middle of the sea, with nothing but water around them. Then suddenly Lee saw a big black submarine emerging from the water. He hoped it was one of theirs. When it got to the top of the water, the coning tower opened and American sailors rushed out, and untied a rubber raft and came toward the plane. Lee and the other men climbed into the raft and were taken to the sub. Once the men were inside, the submarine went back under the water.

Major Blake was on the submarine and he greeted his men, and they were taken to the galley, and he asked everyone but his men to leave, and then he shut the door. He pulled a curtain back and exposed a large map.

"Men this is the Kwajalein Atoll, known as the Marshall Islands. We are only interested in four of them. We want to know the best landing beach, the depth, and what we are facing on shore. We have aerial photographs, but we don't know what they have prepared for us under the water. And that is your job. The sub will take you men two miles from the shore. Then you will get into rubber rafts, and they will take you within a mile of the beach. They will sit there for three hours, while you men will swim as close as you can to do the job, you are assigned to do. Study and memorize the map."

"You will be equipped with a rubber suit, face mask with a two foot air tube, fins and a belt with a Bowie knife, flashlight, heavy shears, shark repellent, and a beeper. On your left arm will be your compass, and on the right arm will be your depth gage. And that men, I hope will be enough. The Navy is working on a Lung machine, where you can stay under water for an hour, but it's not ready yet."

"Any questions? Be aware of the undertow near the shore, and check the distance, we don't want any of our Marines drowning before they get to the beach."

The men took the small map of the places they were to check out on the beach. Then they took a tour of the submarine.

They were awakened at 0300 a.m. and told to put their suits on; the submarine had already risen to the top of the water. Lee looked over at Rod and gave him the victory sign, and then the men climbed into the rubber rafts. They were paddled within a mile of the beach, and getting in the water headed for shore, setting their compass to the location where the men would wait on them.

Rod and Lee headed to the beach of Roi and Namur, splitting up, but keeping track of each other. They found nothing under the water but a smooth beach. Since it was a dark night, Lee got a little closer and took some pictures of gun emplacements. He could hear talking and laughing on the beach, but was careful not to get too close. After finding out they would not need explosives, he waited for Rod. They used hand signals to talk, and agreeing they returned to their boats. After swimming a mile, Lee flashed his signal light, and made contact with the raft. They climbed inside and waited for the others.

When everyone got back, they rowed to the spot where the submarine would pick them up. Everyone made it back safely, and the sub went back under the sea.

After a couple hours, the submarine rose to the top of the water again, and the sea plane was waiting for Major Blake. As his plane few away, they went back under the water, and waited for another sea plane to take the UDT team back to their base on Hawaii. The mission was a success.

"A week later, on June 15th, 1944 the Marines landed on Saipan."

CHAPTER 8

The Battle of Saipan

Saipan is one of the islands in the Marianas chain, about 1,300 miles south of the Japanese home islands. It is a small, pistol-shaped island about 5 miles wide and 18 miles long, which had tremendous strategic value for the United States.

First, Saipan straddled the major supply routes between the Japanese home islands and the Japanese garrisons in the Central Pacific; second, its airfields provided a major staging area for Japanese air attacks on the American fleet operating in the Central Pacific; and third, its occupation by the Americans would provide a base from which to launch air attacks against Tokyo and the Japanese home islands.

The nearby island of Tinian would later serve as the base of operations for the planes that dropped atomic bombs on Hiroshima and Nagasaki in August 1945.

"The Battle of Saipan was a battle of the Pacific campaign of World War II, from 15 June 1944 to July 9th 1944. The 2nd Marine Division, 4th Marine Division and the 27th Infantry

Division, commanded by Lieutenant General Holland Smith defeated the 43rd Division of the Imperial Japanese Army, commanded by Lieutenant General Yoshitsugu Saito."

June 10th 1944

Lee woke up with the humming sound of the two big engines of the submarine. He watched as the sailors tended to their gages, and did their work. His nose was stopped up, and he had a headache, he wondered how deep the sub was under the water.

A sailor was going to the bunks of the UD Team waking each man up. He came to Lee's bunk. "Time to get up sir, chow (breakfast) will be ready in thirty minutes."

He looked over at Rodney and gave him the victory sign. The other men slowly got out of their bunks, and went to the head while Lee was putting his pants on, and looking at the bulkhead on the side of the submarine, he saw a calendar. It was the 10th of June, 1944. He had been onboard for three days. The U.D.Team would swim to an island, with 30,000 Japanese soldiers, an island called "Saipan" A place he had never heard of before until four days ago. Would this mission be a success, and would- they all get back?

After getting dressed they went to the galley and had a light breakfast, while Captain Sands went over their mission. Lee felt a vibration and the submarine rose to the top of the sea and cut the engines. Immediately the doors opened and the crew unloaded the rubber rafts.

At 0200 a.m. Sunday morning, Lee and Rodney got into

one raft with a sailor, while two other UD men got in the second raft with a sailor pushing them off and then jumped into the boat. Then the crew rowed them a mile from the beach. It was a dark and misty morning, and Lee could not see, but heard the surf washing up on the beach. They used sign language to talk, set their compass to the boat location, and he and the men slid into the water. Two of the men went to the east beach, and Lee and Rodney went to the west beach, swimming to an island called Saipan.

When they could see the beach, Lee and Rodney split up, going under the water and checking for wire, mines, or anything that would give the landing troops problems. They checked the water and the beach, a mile in each direction; they would not be in contact with each other until they got back to the raft.

Lee found nothing in the water, so he crawled up on the beach and looked through his infrared glasses, studied the beach and surrounding area. He spotted two large 5 inch guns pointing out to sea. He took pictures of the guns, and then saw a large building several yards past the beach. He had to find out what it was. He had forty-five minutes left, plenty of time to check it out. Staying in the thick grass he approached the building.

He crouched close and watching for a sentry. In ten minutes he spotted one walking around the building checking the doors and the beach. Lee timed the sentry's pace around the building. He would have plenty of time to check the front, while the sentry was in the back. He needed to know what was inside.

After the guard went around the back, Lee jumped up and went to one of the windows, and looked inside. At first he couldn't see anything, but he heard a noise. Looking through another window, he saw Japanese soldiers sleeping, must be at least a hundred. This would make a good target for our guns on D-Day.

Excited, he had stayed too long. He felt a rifle barrel stuck in the middle of his back, cold chills went through his body… he had blown the mission. Speaking in Japanese, he grabbed his knife and turned. The sentry surprised that the intruder was speaking his language hesitated just long enough for Lee to slash his throat.

He cut off one of the pants leg then tied it around the soldier's neck to stop the bleeding. Satisfied he took sand and covered up the blood that had spilled to the ground. Then he picked him up and carried him into the bushes and headed for the cliff. After about ten minutes he came to an edge with about a fifty foot drop to the sea with rocks below. He threw him over and then looked at his watch. He had used up most of his time, but he could make it if nothing else happened. The men in the raft would wait thirty minutes if one of the men wasn't back, but after that time, they would leave.

Lee hurried to the beach, and washed the blood off his wet suit, making sure he did not have any blood on him to attract the sharks. Then he looked back, and seeing no activities, slipped into the water. He checked his compass, and saw he was way off course. He slipped under the water and headed out to sea. After about quarter mile, he came to the top, looked to see that he wasn't spotted and began to swim north, to align himself with the raft. Later stopping again, he was only a few yards off course. He rolled over on his back, to rest and regained his strength.

Suddenly he was hit in the back, knocking him out of the water. Then he saw a gray fin circling him. Reaching back to his belt he removed a shark repellent, and placed it in the water. He stayed still for five minutes, and then slowly began to swim away. After about a hundred yards, he lined up with the raft and started swimming again.

Again he was hit, and rolled him over. He took a deep breath, reached for his flashlight and dove down to twenty feet, making sure his light wouldn't be seen from shore. Looking around he nearly choked with fear. Twenty yards ahead of him was a large fish, at least ten feet long, coming toward him. Putting his flash light in his left hand, he pulled his bowie knife out and waited.

Okay Mr. Shark, It's either you or me. Pointing his knife toward the fish. When he got closer, he shined the flashlight in his face.

Well I be dammed. You're not a shark, turning his knife sideways, and slapping him on the nose as he came pass him. It was a large Dolphin and after being hit, turned and went out to sea.

Lee was late, but he hoped they would wait on him. After swimming out about a mile, he pulled his infrared light from his belt and flashed it two times. No answer he became worried, had they left? He flashed his light again, waited, and then he saw one red flash. They were still there, and he began swimming as fast as he could. He saw the raft, and then

The Adventures of Lee Robinson

Rodney holding his hands out.

"Lee, where in hell have you been? We were only going to stay ten more minutes. I thought about coming after you, but that would have hurt our mission. Damn we were worried about you, what happened?"

"I had a big Dolphin who wanted to play beach ball with me. I was the beach ball, and he flipped me over a couple times. Boy! Does my butt hurt."

"Sorry Lee, but you can't get a purple heart from a Dolphin wound; now climb into the raft we're running late. I hope the submarine is still there, I saw couple of Japanese cruisers moving around, our sub may have company."

The crew paddled as fast as they could, and reached the area where the submarine should have been waiting, but there was nothing but open sea. The navy crew man looked at his compass, Lee and others looked at theirs. They all agreed that this was the place, and in a couple hours it would be daylight, and they would be seen from the shore.

The two rafts sat there for about an hour, and it was beginning to get daylight, when Rod saw waves and ripples in the water, then about two hundred yards away, a periscope appeared in the water. Rod was ready to cheer, but Lee put his hand over his mouth. After the periscope moved in all directions, the submarine emerged from the sea.

The crewmen rowed the rafts over to the submarine where by now sailors on the deck were waiting. Once the men were all inside, the submarine went back under the water at a fast pace.

Lee and the UD Team gave their report to Captain Sands,

and he was happy with the pictures of the 5 inch guns. Their aerial maps had not showed the guns. He was also pleased with what the team had found out, and as soon as they had gotten out of enemy waters, a plane would be waiting for him to take the information to Admiral Chester Nimitz.

They gave the team a sandwich and coffee, and before Lee could take a bite, the buzzer went off, and the speaker came on."Every man to his battle station, Dive, Dive, Dive." Every crewman went to his station, and then Lee lost his coffee as the submarine went into a frontal deep dive. The team members grabbed anything they could reach to keep from falling.

Lee looked at the gauges as they went from 50, 75, 100, and he could feel the pressure. At 200 feet, the submarine leveled off, and the team members felt a moment of relief, as fear left their faces.

Captain Sands came back into the room and said to them." A plane spotted their submarine, and now a couple of Japanese cruisers had begun the chase. Everyone be quiet, the navy crew has been through this before. Just hold on to something, it may get a little rough when they start dropping their bombs."

He told the men, that the plane would drop a few bombs, and then go on his way. But the Japanese cruisers would hang around for a while dropping their cans (explosives) so they were going to set on the bottom, until they thought it would be safe to restart the engines.

Lee could hear the bombs going off, but then the sounds trailed off in the distance. Then it got quiet about for thirty minutes, and then all hell broke loose. A can fell on the sub, but rolled off and exploded shaking the men inside. It was followed by other cans, dropping close by. Water leaked from the pipe above, spilling hot water on one of the crew, burning him. Two other sailors raced forward, and with wrenches stopped the leak. For the next hour they were pounded with can explosives, and they had two more water leaks. Then finally they heard the explosive going away in the distance, the cruisers had lost them.

The Submarine Captain waited another hour, and getting no more beeps that the Jap cruiser was no longer around, started the engines, and slowly began to move forward and raised the submarine to 100 feet. After another hour, with no cruisers on their chart, he leveled the ship off at 50 feet, opened the throttle and headed for Hawaii. They were late and had to make up lost time.

Now that they could talk, Lee looked at Rodney and said. "I would take the front line fighting anytime. These Submarine men are the real heroes"

Sometime the next morning, the sub rose to the top, and Lee and his men got some fresh air. Then they saw a Catalina (sea plane) landing close by. Captain Sands shook hands with the men and thanked them for their mission. Then after getting on the plane the Captain flew away.

The submarine then headed for Honolulu, where Lee and his team would have a three day leave, before reporting back to base. The mission was a success.

"Battle of Saipan began on June 15—July 9, 1944
U.S. Killed was 2,949—wounded 10, 364 -- Japanese killed was 30,000- Civilians 22,000 "

3 miles from Saipan

"Battle of Tinian began July 24th---August 1st, 1944
U.S. Killed was 328 –wounded 1,571 ---Japanese Killed 8,110- wounded 313 "

* From Wikipedia, the Free Encyclopedia *

CHAPTER 9

Honolulu- Three Days of Rest

After two more days their submarine landed at the Honolulu Naval Base, it had been three days and the battle of Saipan had begun. Lee and Rodney were given a three day leave, their first in six months, and they were dry and thirsty. They checked with the Marine Paymaster and received three months pay.

"I'm rich," said Rodney. "I haven't had this much money at one time since I was a civilian, and that was a long time ago."

"Where are we going to spend it, Lee?"

"Well, first we are going to wet our whistle at that bar across the street, then if we aren't too drunk, we are going to find us the biggest steak in town."

The two Marines made their way across the street and entered the bar. Each ordering two beers, and got a table in the back. "Rod old buddy, we are going to get drunk." Lee said putting the bottle to his mouth." But remember we can't say where we have been."

"Wonder how the battle is going? I'm going to turn that radio on, over by the bar." Lee said getting up.

Lee went to the bar, reached across the counter and switched the station over to get some news.

"Hey," a young lady said," I was listening to the music."

"Turn that station back marine, my girl wants to hear some music." The big, muscular sailor sitting at the bar said.

Lee looked at him, and then said. "There's a war on Sailor, it's the battle of Saipan. Some of our buddies are fighting on the island."

The lady leaned over to the sailor and kissed him," I don't want to hear about the old war honey. I want to hear music and dance."

"Marine, I'm telling you one more time. Turn the radio back to my girl's station, or I'm going to deck you and throw you out of here."

"Swabby, I think that would be a bigger job that you can handle." Lee said, backing away from the bar.

The sailor got off his stool and swung a fist at Lee's face. He blocked it, and drove his fist in the sailor's stomach. Then as he got up, Lee hit him again in the jaw. By now two of the sailors buddies came up and approached Lee, one had a broken beer bottle, and swung it at Lee's face. Lee put his hands up to block it, but the glass cut his hand. He kicked the sailor in the groin, and with his left hand gave him a judo chop in the neck.

By now Rodney had reached one of the men. "Lee, its looks like you're having all the fun." Spinning one of the sailors around and hitting him in the face and the stomach at the same time. Two other sailors joined the fight, then a couple Marines came in saying, "Let's make this a fair fight, we don't like the odds."

Now the floor was full of Marines and Sailors, while the bartender was trying to save the beer and the mirror on the wall. The young lady watched, and turned the radio back to her music. Then she grabbed a sailor and began to dance between the fighting men.

Lee and Rodney stood back to back, hitting every sailor that came by, and sometimes another Marine by mistake. "Lee, all that training we took was a big help, this is fun." Just then someone hit him with a beer bottle and he slid to the floor.

Someone hollered MP and Lee picked up Rodney and they went out the back door.

"Rodney, you hurt anywhere?"

"No, I'm fine, but I will be sore tomorrow. Let me look at that cut hand Lee."

"That's a bad cut Lee. You need to have it sewed up. There's a hospital cross the street. You need to go and have some stitches put in your hand."

"Hell Rodney, all I need is a band aid."

"Lee that's a bad cut, and it could get infected. And if it does, Major Blake won't let you go on the next mission, and you wouldn't like that."

"OK, but you go back and get us a room at the 'Sea Breeze,' I will go across the street and have it sewn up. Then I will come over later, shower and we will have that big steak for supper."

They parted and Lee went across the street to the small hospital, and walked up to the reception lady. He showed her his hand, and asked if they had a nurse or doctor who could put stitches in the cut. Looking at his hand, she told him to wait until she could find a nurse.

She came back and said that a nurse would see him. Going into another room, Lee only saw the back of the nurse, as she was getting her gloves on, and then picked up a needle to numb the hand while she sewed up the cut." That is a very bad cut marine. How did it happen?"

He told her about the fight, and the broken beer bottle. She looked at the wound, then at him. "Lee, you must be more careful. He could have cut your neck."

"How do know my first name?" And then looking up at her. "Pat!"

"Yes Lee, I'm Pat. The last time I saw you it was in San Diego, you had gotten wounded on Guadalcanal."

"But Pat, how did you get here?"

"The war seemed to be going in this direction, so I asked to be transferred to Honolulu, I've been here about three months, and I love it here."

"You probably can't tell me, but have you seen more action?"

"Yes, and No. I have seen a little action, and no, I can't tell you about it."

"Ouch! That hurt. Are you taking it out on me, because I tried to get your phone number, and asked for a date?"

"Really no, I was flattered, and if things were different I would have been glad to go out with you."

"I know, you told me you were happily married, to a sailor I believed you said."

"Sometimes we have to tell little white lies to keep our jobs." Pat said looking into Lee's eyes.

"I don't understand," he said." What little white lie did you tell me?"

"My name is Miss Patricia Mason but they call me Pat, and I am not married, and never have been, sorry I told you a little white lie. We were told to tell the service men that we were married, so they wouldn't make propositions to us. Our boss was a lady in her 60's and said that she knew men. I think she's been married five times. She said that the Marines were the worst. Said she would fire us if we went out with one of our patients. "

"What did she have against the Marines?"

"Said that she had married three, and they were all alike."

Lee looked at her." Since you're not married, would you have a beer with me?"

"I don't drink beer or any alcohol drinks. But if you wish, I will have a cup of coffee with you. I do owe you for my little lies. I will be off in about an hour; can you meet me in the front?"

"Pat in one hour, I will be waiting at the door steps," Lee said smiling.

Lee went to the Sea Breeze hotel and asked at the front desk, what room was he and Rod in. After getting the key he went up to the room and found Rod sleeping on the bed. He let him sleep, took a shower and changed to his one clean uniform. The shower woke Rod up, and he looked at Lee.

"Sure took you long enough to get your hand sewed up, when we going to eat?"

"How about 0700 p.m." Lee said." I got to meet a girl at 0500."

"You got a date? With who, the doctor?"

"No, a nurse. Remember the nurse at San Diego when I was in the hospital, name Pat?"

"Yes, and I also remember you told me she was married. You are not getting involved with a married woman are you? Remember what happen the last time; you blamed my Sue for that."

"No, Pat isn't married; she just said that because of her boss. And she is working here in Honolulu. I'm just having coffee with her at 0500. I should be back at 0700, and then we will go and get us a big steak."

Lee combed his hair three times, and looked at Rod. "I guess I better am going. "

"Lee it's only about a twenty minutes walk to the hospital. She must be some girl."

"She is Rod, and I don't want to be late. I will see you at 1700, walking out the door."

Lee was at the steps of the hospital by 1400. He sat down and watched the people go by. Then an hour later Pat walked out, and asked him. "Where did he want to go?"

"Since we don't have lots of time, let's go to that coffee shop down the street."

They entered the café and found a table. After ordering the coffee, she looked at Lee. "How long will you be here, or will you be shipped out soon?"

"Pat I have two more days, then I will have to leave and go to another island, but I can't tell you where or when I will come back." Now that I have met you again, I wish I would never leave here."

"Will you have supper with me tomorrow night?"

"What about your friend Rod?"

"He will understand. I could pick you up at 1700 or maybe later?"

"I had planned to do some shopping when I left work. But yes, I will have supper with you, if you don't keep me out too late. Where do you want to go?"

"I will eat steak with Rod tonight. Do you know of a good sea food place?"

"Yes, I know a good place on Gay Street, you know where that is?"

"Gay Street? Yes, I believe I do."

"I thought you would. Every service man knows about the cat houses (Prostitution) on Gay Street. But this restaurant is a mile down the street. We will need to take a bus; I'm not walking down the street in front of the cat houses."

"How do I find your house?" asked Lee

"Pat wrote down her address and gave it to him. I usually take the bus, but I have to walk a block. If you get a taxi, it doesn't cost much more and you won't get lost. Now I have to go, and you have a date with Rodney. If you can't make it, call me at this number at the hospital." Then she got up and went to the bus stop. Lee stayed with her until the bus came.

After Pat got on the bus, he walked back to the hotel. Rodney was ready and they looked for a good steak house. They found one next to the Hilton Mall, and ordered the biggest steak on the menu. Lee couldn't stop talking about Pat.

Rod looked at him and said," Lee my friend, you have been bitten. I think you are in love?"

"Don't know about that, but she's the only woman that I would like to marry. And I only have tomorrow night to be with her."

"If you feel that way about her, tell her. She might feel the same way; it's not the first time two people fall in love at first sight."

"I can't Rod, after tomorrow we may never see each other again. With our job, we can't ask a girl to marry us. We may never live through this war, what we are doing; the odds are stacked against us. We have been lucky so far."

They finished their steaks, drank couple beers and went back to their room.

The two marines slept until ten o'clock. Lee was the first one to get up, and took a shower. He slapped Rod on the butt saying. "Get up buddy, let's go down to Pearl Harbor, and see the damages what the Jap's did to our fleet."

So the two marines toured Pearl Harbor, ate lunch, had a few beers and went back to their room, and took a nap.

At 1500 p.m. Lee took another shower, but complained that he did not have another clean shirt. They had told them to dress light, but he didn't know he was having lunch with a beautiful girl.

At 1700 p.m. Lee went outside and found a taxi, he was

early, but he wanted to see where she lived. He could always wait down at the corner. The traffic was heavy, so since he was almost on time, he asked the taxi to wait.

Forty five minutes later Lee went up to a white house, where there were several apartments. He looked for apartment 5 and knocked on the door. Pat opened the door, and invited him in. I will be another ten minutes."Would you like a Coke?"

"No thanks Pat, just take your time, I'm a little early."

She came back into the room, and Lee had never seen her in a dress before.

"Pat you're beautiful, that dress was made for you."

"Thanks Lee, I get tired of wearing a uniform every day, sometimes I like to dress up. I'm glad you asked me out."

"If I wasn't in the Marines, I would ask you out every night."

"Thanks, you're sweet, but I'm afraid we are both committed to the war. Maybe one day it will be over and we can go back to our normal life. Now let's go find that restaurant, I'm hungry."

The taxi was still there, so they got in and Pat told him where to go.

They went down Gay Street, and Pat smiled at Lee as they passed the long lines to the cat houses. He looked out the other window like he had not seen the line. At the end of the street the lines disappeared and they saw several restaurants, and one that said fresh fish and oyster bar. Then Pat told the driver to stop.

The place wasn't crowded, and Lee picked a table in the

back, where they would have more privacy.

Looking at the menu they both ordered the sword fish, and Lee couldn't keep his eyes off of Pat. He slipped his hand on hers, and said, "I want to thank you for going out with me tonight. I haven't had supper with a pretty girl in a long time."

"Thank you Lee, I have enjoyed our time together, I'm sorry now that I didn't go out with you in San Diego, boss or no boss. "

"What time do you leave tomorrow?" Pat said holding his hand.

"I've got to be at the Pearl Harbor Naval base at 1600 p.m., wished I had more time."

"Lee, I have asked for tomorrow off, it's been a light week."

"We could have breakfast together around ten o'clock, and then go to the beach, that's if you and Rodney hadn't planned anything?"

"That would be great, no we haven't any plans, and I'm sure Rod would understand. I will be at your apartment around nine.

They finished eating and then looked around in the shops.

"Lee , since we are going to be together tomorrow, would you take me home? I have got some washing to do tonight?"

The next morning Lee was dressed and ready to go at 0800 a.m.

Rodney, still in bed, looked at Lee. "Yep, you're in love.

I can see that puppy love all over your face. I'm glad for you Lee."

Lee knocked on the door around 0900 and Pat came to the door and kissed him.

"I'm ready Lee; I fixed couple of sandwiches to take to the beach. We can't go to Waikiki Beach, it is fenced in with barb wire, but I know of another small beach. It's so small they wouldn't expect a landing there, but they do patrol the waters."

They took a bus to the beach, but still had to walk a couple of blocks. At the entrance, was a small café, where they stopped and ate breakfast? Then they walked down to the beach.

They held hands and walked in the sand, neither saying anything but each in their own thoughts. A small coast guard boat came by, and they waved to the couple, a reminder that that the war was still on. Lee wondered where he would be tomorrow.

Lee stopped, put his arms around Pat and kissed her." I have no right to say this now, but I love you, and to hell with the war."

"And I love you Lee, and no matter where you go, I will wait for you."

They kissed each other, and then sat down on the sand and he made love with her. Two wonderful people that loved each other, but with the war, would they ever see each other again?

Lee woke up and looked at his watch; he had only an hour to be at the base. Both he and Pat had fallen asleep.

He kissed her. "Wake up, I've got to call a taxi and be at the base within the hour. Let's stop at the café, I can call a taxi from there."

The taxi pulled up in front of the café, Lee still had time to make it. "Can I ride with you to the gate?" Pat said.

"Yes, I don't have time to take you home, after I get there, you can take the taxi back."

The taxi drove to the Pearl Harbor Base and pulled up to the gate. Lee looked down at the water, and saw the 'Merry B' the submarine that was used for their missions sitting in her slip with the engines running. He grabbed Pat, and hugged her, then with a broken voice said. "When we meet again. Will you marry me?"

"Yes, Yes, and I will wait on you, no matter how long it is." She kissed him, saying. "Please hurry back, I will always love you."

Lee removed his arms, and walked slowly down the gang plank, and stopped at the bottom, looking at the submarine.

CHAPTER 10

Iwo Jima

Iwo Jima is a part of the Bonins island group. It is four miles long, shaped like a pork chop, and covers eight square miles. It has no front lines, no rear, and every inch is a battleground. Captain of the 3rd Marines later said. "We were confronted with defenses having been built for years."

"At great cost, you'd take a hill only to find the same enemy suddenly on your flank or rear. The Japanese were not on Iwo Jima, they were in it."

Major General Harry Schmitt led the 4th and 5th Marine Division, with the 3rd held in reserved. Iwo Jima had 3 airfields, with planes that attacked our B-29s going and coming back from Japan. We had to have that island.

"February 19th, 1945, the Marines' left flank almost touched the beginning of the slope of Mount Suribachie, the 556 foot high extinct volcano. They were in ankle-deep black sand. One regiment of the 28th Marines reached the summit the morning of Feb 23rd. The flag went up and the world-famous picture was taken."

<u>February 19th to March 26, 1945</u>
Marines: Killed 6000....Wounded 17,000
Japanese: Killed 23,000....Wounded unknown
"From Wikipedia, the Free Encyclopedia"

Lee reached the end of the gang plank, turned and looked at Pat with tears in his eyes. "I will be back, please wait on me. I love you." Then he stepped on the Merry B and went down below.

"Glad you made it Lee, we were worried about you." Rodney said, closing the hatch behind his friend Lee.

The submarine made a roar, as the sailors untied the ropes and the Merry B left its slip… like a race horse wanting to begin the race and a new adventure.

The Major asked Lee and the men to assembly in the galley to go over their plans for the next mission. Men looked at the map on the bulkhead. The Major commented: "You will see a small volcanic island. It is covered with black ash, but has three airfields that we need. From there we can fly to Tokyo and back. Our planes can also use it for our next invasion, which will be soon."

Lighting a cigar, He continued: "They have had years to prepare for us, and I'm sure the waters surrounding the island are full of barbed wire, spears, and mines. We have taken aerial photos, but we're not sure what they have prepared for us under the waters near the beach. We have enough men to check every foot of the beach. Plant your explosive, check for rip tides, and try not to be spotted. Find the best place for a landing. Are there any questions?"

After the meeting he walked over to Lee and said. "Let me look at your hand. That's a nasty cut, and could be infected. I'm scrubbing you for this mission. You can't go with the men, but stay on the sub." Major Blake said.

"But Major?"

"No buts' Lee, that's an order."

"If there are no more questions, get out of here, study your maps, and come back in an hour for chow." After the men had eaten, some went back to their bunks and played cards; others studied their maps and then took a nap.

"Sorry Lee," as Rod gave him a couple cards. "The Major was right, that hand looks like it could be infected."

"Hell, I know that. But this is the first time we haven't been together on the same mission. Who's going to watch out for you?"

"Aw, Lee, you treat me like a kid. Hell, I can take care of myself. You being in puppy love, you wouldn't be much protection anyway. Are you going to marry Pat when we get back?"

"I want to Rod, but with the war going on, I'm not sure we should. Maybe we should wait, or I could transfer to a shore job. We will talk about it when we get back."

For the next two days, the submarine, Merry B made its way to the shores of Iwo Jima only coming up to the surface at night to recharge its batteries.

Lee woke up. The engines had stopped and Rodney was putting on his rubber swim suit while other UDT men stood by the door, leading to the top side.

Slowly the Merry B ascended to the surface, the door opened, and sailors ran to the deck, some manning the guns, while others went to the rubber rafts.

Lee put on his rain gear, and went to the top, helping with the rafts. He looked for Rod, then shook his hands and hugged him.

"Watch your ass old buddy, do your job and get back here in one piece."

The UD Team climbed into the boats, along with two sailors who would paddle the rafts and wait for the men to return.

Lee watched Rodney and the men disappear into the black night and said a little prayer for their safe return.

Since it was a dark night the submarine did not submerge, but sat low in the water. Major Blake and Lee waited on the deck for the men to return.

"Lee for years I have tried to get you to go to OCS to become an officer. You never did, so now I'm giving you a 'battlefield commission.' Beginning tonight, you are a First Lieutenant. Now maybe you will and know how it feels to send men into a hazardous situation, while you stay behind. It's not an easy job, but I think you can handle it."

"But sir, I never wanted to be an officer. I like being a Sergeant."

"Lee, the other reason I'm doing it now, is because Rodney said that you found a girl and would like to get married. As a First Lieutenant you will make more money and it's easier to get a housing allowance. You will need both."

"Thank you sir. I will try to do my best and not let you down." Lee said, and saluted him.

Major Blake held out his hand. "Lee you have never let me down, and our friendship goes back ten years when we were in China together."

"Tell me about your girl. Rodney said she was a nurse."

"Yes sir, she was at the San Diego hospital when I first met her. Then I saw her again at the Honolulu hospital. She is attached to the Red Cross, and asked to be transferred here. She is a lovely girl, sir."

"I'm sure she is, and I want to be invited to the wedding," Major Blake said, standing up. "Lee did you hear some gun fire?"

"Yes sir, I did. Look sir, there's some lights coming from the beach. Our men must have been spotted."

They watched and listened then they heard a boat engine, then more firing. They saw a searchlight moving back and forth, and heard more firing.

Then everything got quiet, only a light was shining in the water.

Lee and the Major were standing on the deck, when the Captain of the Merry B came toward them.

"Major you and Lee may have to come below. If your mission has been discovered, we may have to make a fast dive. If they found the rafts they will look for a submarine."

"Captain please wait. We have some good men out there, and I want to give them all the time that we can give them." Major Blake said.

The officers listened and one of the crew manned the gun.

All eyes were looking at the shore watching for a signal light.

After about ten minutes, Lee saw a light from a signal gun. "That's one of them sir, maybe they are okay." He and the Major continued to look, but didn't see the light again.

Then the men saw several spotlights, and heard motors running from a large ship. "That's it." the Captain said. "They're sending out a destroyer, we got to dive."

Just then Lee heard Rodney call. "Help Lee, I'm hurt, please help me."

"He's over there Major, I'm going after him."

"But Lee we don't have time to find him." But his words fell on deaf ears because he had already dived into the water.

"Rod where are you? Send me a signal. Or just keep talking."

"Over here Lee, just keep coming. I think I hear you. Now I see you. More to your left. Hurry Lee, I can't stay afloat much longer. Hurry Lee."

Lee found him. Rod was floating on his back, and blood was coming from his hip. He wrapped his arms around Rod's head. "Just kick good buddy, I will do the swimming." Then they made their way to the submarine.

After about five minutes a rubber raft approached them. Two sailors pulled them into the boat and headed back to the Merry B.

After the Major and the crew pulled them on board, the Captain said. "All hands below deck: Dive! Dive!" They locked the hatch, and the submarine went down to 100 ft. and leveled off.

The crew listened and they heard the Jap destroyer heading

The Adventures of Lee Robinson

for them. The ship's explosives in cans started pinging around the submarine. Again they were lucky. No hits.

Rodney was taken to the medical room where a doctor looked at his wounds. He had been shot in the hip and had lost lots of blood. They must have been spotted from shore, because a small enemy boat came out and started shooting at them. Johnson was killed, and he and Sam dove under the water. The boat turned their spotlight on them. He saw Sam's head explode and then he was hit. He went under the water and stayed until the enemy lost him.

The boat kept running around using their spotlight, but he managed to stay hidden. Then he slowly moved toward the Merry B. The motor boat went back to the dock, as Rodney swam toward the submarine.

The doctor said that his hip bone was shattered, and he would have to have extensive surgery when they got back to Honolulu. Lee stayed with Rodney, until they gave him a shot and he went to sleep.

You could still hear the explosion on the surface, but the submarine whined and groaned, making its way back to Pearl Harbor.

The next day the submarine made its way to the top; where a seaplane was waiting for them. Major Blake got on board and flew to Admiral Chester Nimitz's flag ship to give his report.

After recharging the batteries the Merry B descended to 100 feet and continued on to Pearl Harbor.

An ambulance was waiting at the dock when they arrived, and Rodney was put inside. "I will see you later Rod. As soon as I have filled out my reports and can get a leave." Said Lee.

He made out his reports then headed for the Marine Headquarters. He was issued new officers' uniforms and a silver bar. Looking in the mirror he saluted himself, and said. "I can live with this, it might come in handy."

He got a 24 hour pass and flagged down a taxi. "Honolulu Hospital and hurry."

At the hospital he found Pat who was working on her charts. Lee kissed her on the back of the neck. Jumping up she swung her hand to slap him, then looked at him. "Lee, what are you doing in an officer's uniform?"

"I have been promoted. The Major said that if I was going to get married, I might need a bigger salary."

"You would have been fine as a Sergeant. But you do look handsome in an officer's uniform," she said kissing him.

Then together they went to see Rodney. When they got to the room, he was asleep. Lee took his hand, and he woke up. He tried to stand up and salute, before he recognized him. "Lee. Where are your Sergeant stripes?"

"I've been promoted; Major Blake gave me a battlefield promotion. But you don't have to salute me; I'm still Sergeant

Lee to you. How's the hip coming?"

"Doing fine, with a few weeks of therapy, I will be back on the job."

Lee introduced him to Pat, saying. "This is the woman I'm going to marry, and you will be the best man, when you get out of here. So hurry up and get well."

"I will be there if I've got to crawl. Pat, you're getting a good man."

"Haven't got him to the preacher yet, but I'm working on it." She said kissing him.

"Pat, what time can you get off? I would like to take you to supper, or do you have to go home first?"

"Don't have to go home, but I have about an hour of paperwork to do, before I can leave. Talk to Rodney, I'll hurry."

Pat left the room and Lee pulled up a chair beside Rod's bed.

"Lee I don't understand, you always told me that you did not want to be an officer, you wanted to stay a Sergeant. Why did you change your mind?"

"What I did not want was to go to OCS for three months, then be a Second Lieutenant. As a Master Sergeant I make about as much as a Second Lieutenant now. Major Blake gave me a 'battlefield' promotion. He said since I was getting married, that was his present to me, and I would skip OCS and the gold bars, but as a First Lieutenant, I would have silver bars, and a bigger pay check. It doesn't change anything with us Rodney. Of course if we are around other Marines, you may have to salute me."

"I couldn't think of a better officer to salute." Rodney said smiling.

"Now Lee let's talk about Pat. I think she is beautiful, and would make you a good wife. I like her. When are you going to marry her?"

Lee looked at Rod with a worried look. "I would have married her before I got on the Merry B, but now I'm having second thoughts. On our last mission, two of our friends were killed, and you got shot in the hip. I should have been on that mission, maybe the one that got killed. What if I had married her and then she would have been a widow after just two weeks. Rod, for the first time in my life, I have found the woman I want to marry, but now, I'm afraid to do so."

Rod clasped Lee's hand. "My good friend, we don't know when our time is up. But we can't quit living, we have to find happiness where and when we can. I think Pat would prefer a few days with you, than wait and never have loved as husband and wife. Ask her which she prefers."

Pat came back into the room, and told Lee she was ready. "I told the cook to give you extra portions, and they have chocolate cake for dessert," she said to Rod.

"Thanks. Now I know why Lee wants to marry you."

Lee took Pat by the arm, telling Rod he would see him later. As they got to the door, Rod hollered to Lee. "Pat, don't let him talk you out of it."

They walked down the street to a nice restaurant that was famous for its country cooking. They went inside and got a table in the back. After sitting down, Pat looked at Lee. "What did Rodney mean, don't let you talk me out of it? What is it you want to tell me? Lee, I love you and I think you love me.... Do you not want to get married?"

"Honey, you're the only woman that I would want to marry and yes, I love you very much... but I'm scared. The mission that Rodney was on... it could have been me who got shot. Two of my friends were killed; I should have been one of them. I was scrubbed because of my hand, one of my friends took my place and now he is dead, instead of me. I have no right to ask you to be my wife. My friend had a wife and two children, now she is a widow."

"Lee, I understand your feelings, and I'm sorry for his wife and family. But I bet if she had it to do over, she would not change anything. She had many happy years together as his wife."

"Pat I love you, but I'm worried about this next mission. Can we wait until I get back, and then get married?"

"Lee I love you, and would gladly marry you now, but if you want to postpone it, I will be there at the dock when you return. But please don't ask me to wait too long." With tears in her eyes, they ate and then she asked him to take her home.

CHAPTER 11

Okinawa—The Last Battle of WW II

The land battle took place over 81 days, beginning April 1st, 1945.

The first Americans ashore were soldiers of the 77th Infantry Division, who landed in the Kerama islands (Kerama Retto), 15 miles west of Okinawa on March 26, 1945. Subsidiary landings followed, and the Kerama group was secured over the next five days. The operation provided a protected anchorage for the fleet and eliminated the threat from suicide boats.

Marines of the Fleet Marine Amphibious Corps landed on the western coast of Okinawa on L-Day, April 1st, which was both Easter Sunday and April fool's Day in 1945. The tenth Army swept across the south-central part of the island, capturing the Kadena and the Yomitan airbases. In light of the weak opposition, General Buckner proceeds immediately with Phase 2 of his plan, the seizure of northern Okinawa.

When northern Okinawa was cleared, the 1st, 2nd, and 6th Marine Divisions wheeled south across the narrow waist of Okinawa. The 1st and 6th divisions encountered fierce resistance from Japanese troops holding fortified positions on high ground and engage in desperate hand to hand combat along 'Cactus Ridge' northwest of Shuri. By April 8th the Marines had cleared these and several other strongly fortified positions. They suffered over 1,500 battle casualties, while killing or capturing about 4,500 Japanese, yet the battle had only just begun, for it was now realized they were merely outposts guarding the Shuri Line.

KERAMA RETTO

Lee took Pat home, kissed her and said good night. Neither was in the mood to talk, everything had already been said. He heard her crying as she shut the door. He got into the taxi and went to the Navy Base, then walked down to the submarine Merry B.

"Lieutenant Lee," the Captain of the submarine said," I'm glad your back. All leaves have been canceled; we are to join a Sub Pack tomorrow off Iwo Jima. Where we go from there, only God and Admiral Chester Nimitz know?"

"Major Blake wants to talk to all your team tomorrow at 0900 so get some sleep"

Lee didn't get much sleep, he kept thinking about Pat. But he got up, put on his uniform and went to the galley for breakfast. He missed Rodney; this would be only few times that they weren't on a mission together, and he would have told him to marry Pat. But Lee had a premonition of danger on this next mission, and he couldn't shake it off.

At 0900 he and several of the U. D. Team met in the galley

after the crew had cleaned it up. Captain Sands was there along with Major Blake and Captain Evans, the commander of the Merry B. The door was closed, and Major Blake pointed to the map on the wall, and then drew in the name.

"OKINAWA was only 300 miles from Japan. A staging area for our planes and the invasion of Japan. The island is 60 miles long and 16 miles wide surrounded by two islands called IZENA SHIMA and IE SHIMA, plus several smaller islands. The two islands next to Okinawa will be taken first. The estimate was about 7,000 Jap soldiers. This would be our largest invasion, and then to JAPAN. Three submarines would be used and twenty of our UD Teams. We have lots of beaches to check out. At the Kerama Retto, there is a natural harbor for our ships, hundreds of suicide P.T. boats that would have to be knocked out before the invasion. That will be the job of the Merry B and ten UD Teams."

No one left the Merry B and around 1500 p.m. the submarine left the dock, heading out to sea. Major Blake said; "Lee I want you to take three men and plant as many mines that you can on the freighters, we might be able to stop a few of the supplies before they unload them. We will have another team to check the beaches around Kadena Airfield. "

Major Blake continued, "The harbor is full of supply ships, and suicide boats. We need to blow up and sink as many as we can, so they won't damage our fleet. The Merry B will block the entrance, and stop any boats that may try to leave. Our map does not show any cruisers or destroyers at the harbor, so the Merry B will stay afloat, and knock out as many as we can with our 40 m.m. guns." He said pointing to the map.

"What kind of explosive will we use, Sir?" Lee asked

"The plastic stick-on, with a two hour timer. And Lee makes sure you get your men out of the harbor within the hour. If they are not through with their mission, have them leave anyway, and get back to the sub."

The night of March 12, 1945 the submarine Merry B approached the harbor of Kerama Retto. She rose to one hundred feet, raised the periscope and looked around. Seeing no battle ships she came to the surface, and cut her engines, while the crew rushed out and manned the guns. Others that were that assigned to the rubber rafts started unloading three boats. There would be one crew member and three UD Teams in each boat. After paddling the rafts a mile to the entrance, Lieutenant Lee and the U D Marines made a last minute check, and then slid into the water. They split up and Lee spotted a large freighter and headed for it. He dove under the hull, and placed a plastic mine on the bottom, setting the timer for two hours.

Then he approached another freighter and attached a mine to the bottom of the hull. He watched his men do the same thing to four other ships. Now they needed to do something to the suicide boats, which were tied together in two's. He placed the mine on the inside of the boats. When it exploded, it would also blow a hole in the other boat. He finished with his mines, by attaching them to two freighters and eight P.T. or suicide boats. He looked for his men, one holding his fingers up for five more minutes. Lee waited until he was finished, then the three started swimming to the rubber rafts.

The three men made it back to the raft, when large spot lights came on and picked up their submarine and then all hell broke loose. Large five inch guns from shore fired on the Merry B, and then a Zero (Jap plane) flew over and dropped a bomb on the deck, and the submarine exploded, causing a concussion that knocked Lee's boat out of the water, and the three Marines in every direction. These three men never saw each other again.

Lee saw the sub burning, and then felt a hot searing pain in his shoulder, grabbing hold of a floating cushion, he then blacked out.

Lee woke up feeling the warmth of the sun on his face and the gently slapping of the waves. Looking around he saw nothing but sea in every direction. His arm was getting numb, where he had wrapped them in the straps of the floating cushion. He pulled his left arm out, only to feel a sharp pain in his shoulder. It was only then that he noticed that he had been shot. Looking at his bloody arm, he saw a hole where the bullet had gone through his arm. The salt water would be good for the wound, and he gently lowered his arm into the sea.

Where am I and what happened? then he remember seeing his submarine the Merry B exploding in the water, while he and his friends were trying to reach it. Looking around, he said. "Where are Sam and Eddie? Did they drown? Did they finish their mission?" But it was quiet, with only the slapping of the waves, and nothing but the sea around him.

The sun's rays began to get brighter and caused his eyes to burn. He pulled his hood up and put on his underwater glasses. Then he put his arms through the straps of the cushion sliding it down behind his back, and then flipped over. Now he could rest floating on his back. Several hours went by, and then he heard airplanes coming toward him, He wondered; *was it ours or the Japanese?* When they got closer, he saw they were Japanese. One of the planes veered off and came toward him for a closer look. Lee slid out of the cushion, and got under it. The plane came down several hundred feet, but seeing nothing but the cushion, made a short burst from his guns and then rejoined his squadron.

After the planes left Lee moved back up onto his cushion, and lay on his back with his feet dangling in the water. He was getting hungry and thirsty; it had been almost two days since their mission. He looked at his compass, and saw that he was drifting North West of Okinawa. He wondered when the battle would begin, maybe then an American plane may spot him. If not, he had no idea where he would end up, he figured he was drifting two or three miles a day.

He dosed off and then was awakening by something hitting his foot. The water had numbed it, but when he pulled them up, he saw blood on his leg. Looking around he saw a gray fish about ten feet long. *This was no Dolphin, but a shark checking him out.* He reached to his belt, and pulled out a shark repellent, and threw them around him, hoping they would work, because it was all that he had.

A couple hours passed, and he was drifting out of range of the repellent. Again about dark, he saw a fin coming toward him. He didn't rush, but the ten-foot body breaking the surface of the water was in a steady direct line, effortless and deadly. Lee kicked and splashed the water, and this time the shark veered off past him, not frightened, not hurrying. He followed him with his eyes. He went out about twenty feet and swam back and forth.

The shark was going to come in again. Every muscle in Lee's body tensed for the attack. He reached back and pulled out his big bowie knife, and waited.

Then the shark turned to make the attack. He came in straight toward him, slowly, and he could see those large teeth. Lee began to splash the water and held his knife up in the air. When the shark was almost on him, he swung the broad side of the knife hitting him on the nose, as fast and hard as he could. The shark swam by, turned and waited. Lee saw blood coming to the top of the water; the fin of the shark had cut through his suit, and cut his hip. Now he would never leave, because he would smell the blood, it was either the shark or him.

Lee realized that he would have to save his strength. If the shark was going to keep on attacking, he was going to have to rest between the attacks; so that he could hit him hard enough at the right moment. He turned his knife blade up where he could cut the shark when he came by. And then he put his head on the cushion, and watched as the two stared at each other waiting.

About fifteen minutes passed, and then the shark started to come in at the same angle as before. When he was almost on him, Lee raised his knife and cut down on his head and his nose and as many times that he could. Lee felt the flesh torn from his left arm, and he could feel the movement of his great body against him as he swam by.

His whole mind and body now centered on the battle against annihilation, as if he was an animal fighting off a stronger, larger beast. At intervals of ten or fifteen minutes the shark would ease off from its slow swimming and come directly toward him. Only twice did it go beneath him. Helpless against this type of attack, he feared it the most, but because he was floating on top of the water, the shark seemed unable to get at him from below.

Each time he attacked on the surface, he would cut him with his knife, but the shark would take another nip out of him. After an attack, Lee would look at his legs and feet. He saw that the big toe on his left foot was dangling. His left calf was torn. If it did not actually sink his teeth into him, his rough hide would scrape off pieces of skin. He was not conscious of great pain. The physical shock of the encounter served to keep that in check for a while.

Time was endless; he knew he was slowly losing the battle. His concentration never wavered, but his strength was being depleted. The constant hitting the shark with his large knife made the muscular ache in his arm more painful than his wounds. As he watched, he saw two other fins approaching the now bleeding shark. Then with a great splash, the two attacked the wounded shark.

Lee started paddling away from the fight as fast as he could. Then as if God ordained it, a storm came up with winds pushing him further and faster away.... where he did not care.

It was getting dark, and now he was feeling the pain. The salt water stopped his bleeding, so maybe the blood wouldn't attract any more sharks. It began to rain and the waves got bigger; he slipped his arms inside the cushion, wrapping them twice so he wouldn't slide out. He thought he saw land when the lightning flashed, but he was too exhausted to care. He wondered when he had anything to drink, or eat. *How many days has it been? Would I ever see Pat again?* Then he drifted off into a deep sleep.

Chan was only ten years old, but his father let him walk down the beach after a storm. Sometimes he would find many things they could use, maybe a large turtle washed up on the beach. But this morning he saw something strange lying in the sand. Running fast... it looked like a man. Was he dead? What kind of man is this? He has on a rubber suit, with many holes where something had bitten him. He turned him over; he wasn't an Okinawan, but of another country. Then he saw him breathe, he was still alive.

Chan ran to his house shouting," Father come, and look what I found."

Mr. Gee heard his son shouting and was almost to the beach, where his son was pointing. He also was amazed at the body of the man; he was dressed in a rubber suit, and must be from far away. But he was barely alive so Chan ran back to the house, and gathered a couple blankets, and he and his father rolled him over on the blanket and dragged him to their house.

CHAPTER 12

The Last Battle -Victory

Rodney was discharged from the hospital and went back to his base on limited duty. It was there that he heard about the submarine Merry B and that all of the crew was missing or dead. He couldn't believe that his friend Lee was dead. The report came from one of the other submarines that were on the same mission, that they had received a distress call, saying they were being attacked, and were unable to dive. Three of their UDT men were still out and trying to get back to the submarine, and Major Blake wanted to wait for the men. Lieutenant Lee, Sam and Eddie never made it back before the submarine exploded and sunk.

The other two mission submarines stayed in the area for another day, but did not find or hear from the Merry B. She was considered missing in action, with all hands dead, and they returned back to base.

It had been two weeks since anyone had heard from the Merry B and Rodney just couldn't wait any longer. He had to go to the hospital and tell Pat. He got a 24 hour pass and went to Honolulu.

He found Pat at her desk, and when he approached her, she screamed. "No! I don't want to hear it. He's not dead?"

"Maybe not Pat, but he is listed as missing. It's been two weeks and we haven't heard anything. We know all the other crew was drowned."

Pat looked at Rod with tears in her eyes. "Can you tell me about it?"

"Very little, it's classified. He was on a mission to Okinawa. That I can tell you, because we are fighting on the island now. It's on the radio. He was on a submarine and it was sunk. Lee and the crew are missing. That is all we know, I'm sorry."

"I wanted to get married, but he was concerned about this mission." Pat said crying. "Rod I loved him so much, and now you tell me that he is dead."

"Pat if it's any comfort to you. I don't believe that Lee is dead. Missing … yes. Let's just wait and pray."

"I have to go and I will let you know if I hear anything. Please don't give up hope and keep praying." He kissed her and started out the door.

"Rodney how's your hip doing, are you back on active duty?" she asked.

"No, I'm still on limited duty. Got a couple more months of therapy."

Rodney walked down to the Navy yard where the Merry B was usually berthed, but there was only an empty slip. A navy Captain was standing on the dock, looking at the same open space.

"Good evening Sir," Rod said saluting. " Have you heard anything about the submarine Merry B?"

The Captain returned the salute."Did you have friends on the submarine?"

"Yes sir, I did. That was my submarine, and all of the crew was my friends."

"Major Blake and I were classmates at San Diego. I understand the submarine was sunk, and there were no survivors."

"Yes Sir that was the report I got too, sir. I was hoping that it wasn't true," Rodney said wiping a tear from his eyes. – The Captain saluted the open slip, and then walked up the gang plank.

ISLAND OF ZAMAMI

Lee opened his eyes and looked around the room. It was small, with a couple of chairs, table, and another room that he could see that had one bed and a pallet on the floor. He raised the cover and looked at his body. All of his rubber suit and under clothes had been removed, only a small padding covered his private parts. Then he saw bandages on his foot, hip and arm. A wooden box sat next to his bed, with a jar of water and some fruit. Thirsty and hungry, he drank the water and ate some of the fruit.

He looked out the open door, but couldn't see any one.

No sound came from outside. He tried to get up, but fell back down on the bed. Where was he? The last thing he remembered he was on a life cushion floating in the sea. The shark, what happen to him? He remembered a storm had come up. He put his arms in the straps, so he wouldn't slide out. It was dark, and the waves kept pushing him. Did he go to sleep, or did he pass out? How did he get here, and who put the bandages on him?

Voices, I hear someone. Their talking, but I have never heard that language before. Where in the hell am I?

An old man, woman and a boy about ten walked in the door. Seeing him awake the old man said something and smiled. Lee not understanding shook his head. The woman came over and looked at his arm, saying something in Japanese. Lee grinned and said."I can understand and speak Japanese. I'm an American he said, but I know their languages."

In Japanese, the old man said."I'm Gee, wife Rookie, son Chan. We are Okinawa people. "You come from the sky, or from the sea?"

"From the sea, I am a Marine. My ship sunk, and I floated on a life cushion, had a fight with a shark. How did I get here? Where am I?"

"Chan, my son found you on the beach, he thought you were dead. He called for me, and I saw you were barely alive. We took you to my house, and Chan went for a doctor, Dr Soo sewed your toe up, and bandaged the hole where the bullet went out of your arm, and patched up the shark bites. You are lucky to be alive."

"I thank you for all that you have done, but I have no money to pay you or the doctor. Are there any Japanese soldiers on this island?"

"No pay. No Japanese on island. We don't like Japanese soldiers. They came two months ago and took all our children age 14, and young men. Said that the children were men, and would be put in the home guard, and the young girls would be trained to be nurses. Now just old women, and old men live here."

"I'm sorry; did you have a son or daughter?"

"Two sons, 14 and 16, and one daughter age 13. I may never see them again," looking at his wife Rookie, who was crying.

"What about the doctor, they didn't take him?" Lee asked

"Doctor too old. He used to live on Okinawa, but when he retired he came here. He is 85 years old; he fixed you up good, yes?"

"Yes I think so. How long have I been here?"

"Three days, doctor sat with you all night. He thinks you will be okay now, but you need rest for a few days. He will come back tomorrow."

"How many people live here on this island, and how far are we from Okinawa?"

"This island is called Zamami, sixty miles from big island. We number about two hundred now. They took about sixty of our young people. We are farmers and fishermen."

"Do you have a boat that I can get back to Okinawa, I'm a soldier and I need to get back to my outfit?"

"No boat, the Japs took all our big boats. Only little fishing boats that can't make it to big island. We used to have a ferry that came by every week, but the Japanese stopped that too."

"Can I have some more water?"

"Give water, little of Rook's soup, then you go back to sleep. We talk more later."

Lee took another drink of water and ate the soup that Rookie made, then fell back to sleep.

He was awakened by someone pouring alcohol on his arm, and the burning pain went through his body. "Hey! That hurts."

When he looked, he saw a white headed and white bearded old man kneeling beside him, and putting on fresh bandages. "You must be the doctor. Thank you for patching me up. "

Lee looked at his big toe. It had been sewn back on, his side had a big hole and you could see the ribs. The doctor washed the wound out, put on another pad and then taped it to his chest. "You do fine now," he said.

"Thank you, but I don't have any money to pay you." Lee said.

"Don't want money; you just kill lots of Japs."

"I would like to, if I can get off this island. Do you know where I can get a boat?"

"No big boats on island, and the ferry from the big island has stopped coming by since the Japanese soldiers came and took all of our young children. Me like to cut the tongue out of the soldiers."

After the doctor left he sat up in the bed, and saw a newly cut walking stick in the corner. Lee then stood up, feeling dizzy at first, but made it over to the cane and walked to the front door. When he looked outside he spotted a chair and sat down. Hearing a shout he looked toward the garden and saw Chan and Gee smiling and waving at him. Mrs. Rookie Moon bought him a fresh peeled turnip, and motioned for him to eat.

Lee sat there by the house watching his new friends work in the garden; it was a beautiful day with a slight wind blowing in from the sea. War seemed so far away, yet American Marines would invade their islands and many of their friends and relatives would die on the big island of Okinawa. What would they think of him then, would he be their enemy? He remembered Saipan, where they thought that the Marines would rape their women and kill their children. Hundreds threw their babies over the cliff and then they would jump.

These were poor, simple farmers who wouldn't hurt anyone, yet the Japanese soldiers took their children away. And Lee knew that they would put them on the front lines to slow the Marines down, and most of them would die.

He knew that it must be close to April, and that would be the month that Okinawa would be taken, he must keep track of the days and months. Chan said that he had been here for five days. That would make it March 17th, 1945. He went back into the house, finding a small knife he cut a ring around his walking cane, now he could keep up with the days.

That night they had cooked turnips, beans and dry fish. Rookie had made a rice pudding, and Mr.Gee brought out a bottle of Awamori (rice wine). Lee asked Gee if there was an old empty house nearby that he could fix up and live in. He did not want to be a burden to them. Chan had given him his bed and was sleeping on the floor. They looked at him and said he was welcome in their house, but they understood and would look for a place tomorrow.

After supper Gee and Lee went out to the porch and drank the rice wine. It was a day to celebrate for he felt much better, and he could now walk with the help of the cane that Gee had made for him.

Two days later Gee came to him and said that they had found a house. Needed some work, but that they could do. It wasn't too far away, and Gee and Chan pulled him in the cart. Arriving at the house, he saw that it needed a roof, a door, and a good cleaning because animals had been living in it. Gee said tomorrow they would go to town and buy some nails and some tin for the roof. Rookie Moon and Chan would clean inside the house, and put something in the door to keep the goats out.

The next morning Gee hooked the cart up to his old mule and asked Lee to get in. It was about two miles to town, and he was looking forward to seeing it. When they arrived he saw a dozen or more stores. There was a café, two grocery stores and a hardware and feed store. Going inside the hardware store, Gee asked for some nails and tin sheets for the roof. As Gee started to pay the man, Lee pushed him aside and showed the owner his watch. "Will you take my watch for the bill?" he said in Japanese.

The owner looked at the watch, then at Gee and nodded yes. But Gee shook his head, and said in their native language. " More." Lee not understanding stood aside and watched. Then the owner went over and picked up a big bag of rice and carried it outside and put it in the cart, along with the nails and roofing materials. Then he looked at Lee, and pointed to the watch.

As they started to leave, two men came up to them, and talked to Gee in their native language, pointing at him. They motioned that they all go to the café, have some sake (rice whiskey) and talk.

Gee told the two men that Lee understood Japanese, and would they talk in their language. They introduced themselves to him, saying that he was the Mayor of the island, and the large man was the town policeman.

"What country are you from, and how did you get here?" the Mayor asked.

"I'm an American, I was shipwrecked at sea, and was washed up on your island, and Chan and Gee found me, and took care of my wounds. I had been bitten by a shark.

"Are you a soldier, and why were you close to our islands?"

"Yes sir, I am a Marine. I was on a submarine that sunk, and was the only survivor, and during a storm I was washed up on your island."

"Does your country intend to attack Okinawa, kill our people and live on our island?" said the town policeman.

"No sir that is not our intention. We are only at war with the Japanese they bombed our homeland, and killed thousands of our people. They started this war, but we aim to finish it. If we invade Okinawa, we will fight the Japanese, not your people. And when it is over, your island will be given back to you. I wished we didn't have to fight on your island, because many of your people may be killed, but we have too, in able to get to Japan.

"When will this be?" said the Mayor

"I do not know sir. Sometime this year."

"I am part Japanese, part Okinawa. I do not like what my countrymen have done. They came to this island and took away my only son. He was just fourteen. I may never see him again. I have heard what they did to your country, and it was wrong. I have no grievance with you, or your country. You are welcome to stay on our island."

The meeting was over Gee and Lee got in their cart and went back to his new home. When they got there they found a small group of farmers cleaning and working on the house. Some had brought food, fruits, and clothing. One farmer about Lee's size gave him some wooden shoes. He was amazed, and grateful for their kindness. Chan gave him a large sack, saying it was for starting a fire and to be used for cooking. Lee looked inside and saw it was dry goat manure.

They passed the bottle of awamori (rice wine) around, and everyone wanted to shake his hands. Looking at his new friends, he wondered how they would feel, when their island would be attacked, and many of their friends and family would be killed. He knew that it would be soon.

That night Lee slept in his new house for the first time. The bed that Rookie had made with goat skin was as comfortable as any bed he had ever slept on. In the morning the sun shined warmly through his one window, and he slowly got out of bed. He looked to see what time it was, but had forgotten that he had traded his watch for the materials to build his house. That would be one thing that he would miss. But he could still tell what day it was, by his walking cane. Picking it up, he carved another notch on it. It should be March 18th 1945.

He picked up the sack that Chan had given him, and put two dry goat manure balls in his small wood stove. After the fire began to burn, he rubbed the skillet with goat butter and placed two rice cakes in, and browned them. And then topped them off with Rookie's homemade syrup. Someone had given him some coffee, so finding another pot he added some water and poured in the coffee, grounds and all.

After breakfast he went outside and saw Gee and Chan coming up the hill pushing their cart.

"Good morning men," Lee said walking toward them.

"Morning Lee. You spoke those words in our language, you no speak Japanese?"

"I'm trying to learn, by your talking. I'm beginning to pick up a few words. What are you two up to?"

"Chan and I are going to plow up some of your ground and then we will plant potatoes, turnips, onions, cabbage and a little wheat. You need a rice paddy, but your ground is too dry, and too far away for water. But rice is cheap we can trade potatoes for it. You have two banana trees, and a breadfruit tree, you will have a good farm, and not go hungry."

Then Gee looked at him and said. "You know how to milk a goat?"

"No, I never had to, why?"

"Rookie is bringing you a goat, she will show you how."

Two weeks had gone by, the potatoes had begun to sprout, and Lee had learned to milk a goat, after being butted couple times. He was turning into a good farmer. After big storms, Chan would come by and they would go to the beach and see what had washed ashore. He would pick up all wooden boards, and when he found enough he would build a shed, to keep his garden vegetables.

Gee came by and brought some rice pudding that Rookie had made, and a bottle of rice wine. "Mr. Lee, we need to talk. You are getting to be a good farmer. But you need a woman, and she will give you children. I and Rookie have seen them. Many good women would be glad to be your wife. Do you want us to find a good one for you?"

"Thanks Gee, but I have a woman back in Hawaii, I planned to marry her if I ever get back. "

"We were hoping you wouldn't go back, we would like you to stay here. Chan would be heartbroken if you left."

The two men drank their wine and talked. About dark, Gee said goodnight and left. Lee threw the empty wine bottle away, went to the outhouse and went to bed.

Lee was awakened by loud booms. At first he thought it was a storm coming up, but the sounds were continuous, not like thunder. Then he heard planes, lots of planes. There was only one answer. Okinawa was being invaded. Getting out of bed he looked at his walking stick. Today was April 1st, 1945.

Putting on his pants he went outside and looked toward the big island of Okinawa. He now could see the bright flashes, as well as the booms of big guns, that could only come from battleships. As the sky got brighter, he could see planes, hundreds of them, diving and dropping their bombs.

Later Gee, Rookie and Chan came up and watched. To Lee it was like the 4th of July, they had never seen anything like this before. It went all day and into the night, for three days and nights. It was the greatest moment of history, and Lee was standing on the side lines, and could only watch.

CHAPTER 13

The Bomb is Dropped-W.W.II is Over

Rodney was at his desk when the news came over the radio, the battle of Okinawa was won. It began April 1st, and after almost three months later of hard fighting, on June 21st, 1945, it was over. He ran into G room to tell his friend Bama the news.

When he got to the gym, he laughed as he saw his friend flip a much larger man over his shoulder. "Bama, the battle is over on Okinawa, now I guess we will be going to Japan. I wished Lee was here, and could go with us."

They were at the training base somewhere on the island of Kauai, and the home of the UDT unit. Rodney had been wounded on their last mission, and was now assigned to a desk job. "I'm sure the Major will be recruiting some more men to go to Japan. I'm going to ask if I can go, my hip has healed, and I don't like a desk job." Said Rodney.

More men had joined the team, but Rodney didn't make it. His bad hip had failed him on the swimming course. But for the next two months the new men trained, and trained. They would need every man, for this next mission. Scouting out the beaches of Japan, would be their most challenging, and dangerous job, that was ever given to a soldier.

On August 6th 1945 an Atomic Bomb was dropped on Hiroshima, two days later another Atomic Bomb was dropped on Nagasaki, and on August 14th 1945, Japan surrenders.

Rodney received the news with mixed emotions. He was glad that the war was over, but after ten years as a Marine he would now be a civilian. He would go to San Diego and if Sue would have him, they would get married and have a bunch of kids. He would miss the excitement and adventures of a Marine, but with his friend Lee killed, it didn't seem the same.

Two weeks later their unit would be shut down, and they would go back to the states to be discharged from the Marine Corps. At the end of the week he went to see Bama, and they hugged each other and promised to stay in touch. Then with a two day pass, he went to Honolulu with the dreaded task of seeing Pat.

Pat was at her desk when Rodney walked in. With tears in her eyes, she said." You don't have any good news to tell me?"

"I'm sorry, but it's been almost a year, and now that the war is over they have closed their records and listed Lee as 'dead in action.' I know you loved him, and he was my best friend, we both will miss him."

"What are your plans now Pat, that the war is over?"

"As you can see, I'm carrying his baby. I'm going back home to Ohio, have our baby and then I may work as a nurse in the local hospital. After that, I have no other plans."

"What are you going to do Rod, stay in the Marines?"

"First I'm going to find Sue. And if she will have me, we are going to get married and have a flock of kids. It will be up to her if she wants to live a Marine life, or I will leave the services."

"Pat, give me your address in Ohio. Later when Sue and I are married, we will try to come up. We want to see you and Lee's baby. Do you know if it is a boy or girl?"

"Not sure, but if It's a boy, his name will be Leland, but I will call him Lee."

Island of Zamani

Lee watched the planes as they fought the Japanese in the sky, and heard the rumbling of the big guns from the battleships. Every once in a while an American plane would fly over his island, he would wave and the plane would dip his wings and fly by. He wondered how the battle was going, and wished he were there.

After a week or two the loud firing stopped, now the ground war would begin. He could no longer see or hear the big guns. Gee and Chan had quit watching the war and went back to their farming. Lee went back to his little house, and took a nap. He dreamed of Pat and wondered if she was waiting, he had never met a girl like her before, and loved her so much.

He was awakened by someone throwing rocks against his house. Looking out he saw two men and a woman running down the path. He thought. *Everyone is not happy about the fighting on Okinawa. I'm sure many of their relatives would be killed, but it cannot be helped, this was war.* He got up fixed some fried potatoes and ate some dry fish. "Boy! I wished I had a good hamburger."

That night a storm came up, and tomorrow he and Chan would go to the beach, and see what they could find. The next morning, they went to the beach and looked at the things that had been washed up. He found life jackets, part of an airplane, and then they spotted a Japanese pilot, who was dead. He asked Chan to go get the cart and they would bury him.

The family buried the Japanese pilot up on the hill, and Lee put up a marker saying Unknown Soldier.

After the burial Lee went to Gee's and Rookie's house ate supper and drank rice wine. Then he went home and cut another day on his walking stick, it had now been three months.

With the lumber he and Chan found on the beach, he decided to build a small shed to put his vegetables and tools in. He didn't go to town anymore since the battle begun, because he didn't know how some of the town folks felt about the Americans. Gee had told him that the hardware store was closed, since they could no longer get supplies from Okinawa or Japan.

He took a large nail that was in a board he had found on the beach, built a fire and placed the nail in the fire, getting it red hot. Then picking it up with his shears he burned holes in the end of the boards. When he had several boards with holes, he found some hard wood limbs and with his bowie knife made some wooden pegs. Placing the wooden pegs in the boards, he built his small shed.

Several more months had passed, and he had no more trouble with rocks. They had heard nothing about the battle on Okinawa. Only occasionally he would see a plane fly overhead. Since it was an American plane, he felt sure they had won. Looking at his garden the potatoes were ready to gather.

Chan came over and helped him dig the potatoes, the turnips, and pick the cabbage. He had made some wooden boxes, and filled them up with the vegetables, and stored them in the garage. Gee was amazed with him building a garage without nails. They finished about dark, and Gee looked at the sky and said to Lee. "It is good we got this work done. From the look of the sky, we are going to have a big storm, maybe a Typhoon."

The next day it was still dark and Lee heard a bell ringing. Chan came running up, saying 'Typhoon, Typhoon coming. Papa said to tie everything down, lock the door and come over to his house. The wind was beginning to increase, and then the rain came. When they finished, they ran to Gee's house.

"Lee we have to go, big storm coming."

He hitched up his mule, put Rookie in the cart, turned the goats out and they took off down the road. After going a couple miles they arrived at a big cave in the side of a hill. Several people were already there, but they made room for everyone. Gee tied the mule behind the cave.

The storm hit with a fury, with wind knocking down trees, and the rain came in sheets. It would be known as the great Typhoon that hit the islands with winds of over 150 miles.

The day became night, and everyone stayed close together. When the lighting lit up the sky, Lee could see trees, houses, and goats flying through the sky. The storm lasted throughout the day and most of the night.

Finally, the rain and the wind stopped, they stepped out of the cave and saw total destruction. Gee found his mule dead, a tree had fallen on him. His cart was gone, but they were still alive. Thinking that the storm was over they walked back toward home, or what was left of it. Gee had seen many such storms in his 60 years, and they would build back. They would gather the pieces and rebuild.

Lee looked at his place, the walls were still standing, but he would have to build another roof. The garage was caved in but he could fix it. But first he would help Gee and his family, and then he would work on his. Rookie picked up her plates and furniture while the men went out to look for the goats.

After several hours, all the goats were found but three. Two were dead, but the others may show up the next day or two. The men fixed a shelter that would keep the rain out, until they could repair the house. That night Chan dug some turnips and they found some dry fish, ate and then they went to bed exhausted.

Gee went into town and found out many of his friends had been killed, or injured. He was given a bag of rice from the mayor, and walked the long way back.

In the next three days they fixed up the house, where they could live in it again. Then they all went to Lee's place and began the work to put on another roof. There was no problem finding lumber, the fields were filled with it. The roof of the garage had caved in, but the boxes with the vegetables were still in tack.

This was Lee's first Typhoon, but he hoped he would never see another one. The next day he and Chan would go to the beach and see what the storm blew in.

The sun came out the next day and a perfect day for walking the beach. Lee collected the boards and put them in a pile to be picked up later. Chan found some clothing and a pair of shoes. Lee saw a box floating in the water and waded out and pulled it in. It was full of k-rations, this they could use.

He heard Chan shout and he ran to see what the trouble was. Around the bend he saw him chasing a large sea turtle. Look Lee! A big one, he will be good to cook for supper tonight. He helped corner the turtle and they turned him over on his back. Lee found a wide board and rolled the turtle on it keeping him on his back. Then he and Chan carried him back to Gees house.

They killed and cleaned the turtle, and cut the meat up in small portions. It would be enough for supper and once salted down, would last for weeks. Lee had eaten turtle before, and it was delicious.

After eating a big supper of boiled turnips, cooked potatoes, and fried turtle, Gee pulled out a bottle of awrmori (rice wine). After the meal, the men went back to the beach and carried the boards back to the house.

"Gee we have enough boards to build you a shed, to put your crop and tools in. I think some of the boards have nails in them, so we won't have to use wooden pegs." Lee said prying some of the nails out with his bowie knife.

The next morning of fried strips of turtle, eggs, and tea, Lee went down to Gee's house and they started on the shed.

Around ten o'clock an American Navy plane flew over. They watched it as it flew around the entire island. Coming back toward Gee's house, he dropped down to about thousand feet, and dipped his wings.

Lee thought that he must be looking for any Japanese soldiers on the island.

After making another circle around the island, the plane flew back toward Okinawa.

The next day, Chan came running up to Lee's house all excited, "Lee, Mr.Lee, big boat coming up to our island."

He grabbed another cup of tea, and ran outside and looked where Chan was pointing. He saw about a mile from their island a LST (landing ship troops) and it was coming to the town's dock. Part of the dock had been damaged from the storm, but the LST would probably pull up on the beach anyway.

Everyone was running toward the beach and waving at the ship. Then the same plane flew back over the Island, and made a big circle, again dropping down low.

It would be a good walk, so Lee went inside his house and picked up his walking cane. Then he and Chan started walking toward the beach where the ship was headed.

When they arrived, the ship had already beached itself, next to the damaged pier, and a company of Marines in full battle dress had exited the ship. A Captain got off, and wanted to talk to the Mayor, or 'who was in charge.'

Mayor Soo stepped forward and told the Captain that he represented the people on the island.

"Are there any Japanese soldiers on the island?" the Captain asked.

"No sir," he spoke in Japanese language

"Are there anyone here who speaks English?"

Lee stepped forward and said. "I do sir, I'm an American," and saluted the Captain.

The Captain looked at him, dressed in peasant's clothes, and a big wide brim hat.

"You are an American, what are you doing here? Are you a deserter?"

"No sir, I am First Lieutenant Lee Robinson, U.S. Marines. I was shipwreck, bitten by a shark, and washed up on the beach. I was almost dead when these good people" pointing toward Gee and Chan." Found me and patched me up."

"How long have you been here, Lieutenant?"

Looking at his cane and counting the notches said. "eight months and three days sir."

"Do you know that the war is over?" said the Captain

"You mean Okinawa?"

"That too, but I mean the big war, World War II?"

"No I didn't sir. Did we go to Japan?"

"Didn't have too. We dropped a big bomb, called an Atomic Bomb. After two cities were destroyed, they surrendered. No one on this island had a radio?"

"No sir, not that I know of. You are the first people that have come to this island since I have been here. A few planes have flown over, but we have heard nothing about Okinawa. Seeing American planes, I assumed we won the battle on the island."

Then the Captain looked at the crowd that now had gathered. "How bad was the Typhoon, and do you need any food?"

"Pretty bad sir, the Mayor knows how many died or injured in the storm." Then Lee asked him in Japanese.

Turning back to the Captain, "he said they have ten deaths, and twenty or thirty injured."

Tell the injured to come to the ship; we have a doctor on board. And we brought plenty of food."

The Captain looked at his Sergeant," tell the men to start unloading."

They unloaded tons of food and water on the dock, and the Captain pointed to the Mayor for him to be in charge. Then they unloaded plywood, nails, tools, and blankets.

The Captain looked at Lee. "We will be leaving in a couple hours. Do you need to go back to your place for anything?"

"Yes, can I get someone in a jeep to drive me back? I still have trouble walking any distance. I would like to get a couple things."

"Sergeant, get a jeep and drive the Lieutenant where he wants to go. Be sure to be back here in a couple hours, we will be leaving before dark, after the doctor sees everyone."

Lee climbed into the jeep with the Sergeant, then looking at Chan said. "Get in, you can ride with us."

It didn't take long to reach Lee's house, the driver pulled up in the yard and stopped. "The house is not bad sir, did you build it?"

"Yes, with the help from Chan, and his father. They are a very generous people, I will be sorry to leave them. They taught me many things."

Lee went inside and picked up his bowie knife, and then gave it to Chan.

"Be careful with it, it's very sharp. Tell your folks to take all of this food, and anything else they want. "

"Where's Rookie?"

"In the house," Chan said.

Lee went to Gee's house, found Rookie and hugged her.

With tears in her eyes she said. "Will you come back?"

"Not sure Rookie, I would like too, but I'm a Marine and have to go where they send me. I thank you for patching me up, and taking care of me."

The three got back in the jeep, and drove down to the dock. They had finished unloading and the doctor had seen the injured ones, and then left them with some medicine.

Captain seeing the three had returned, looked at Lee and said." Say your goodbyes, we need to pull out."

Lee found Gee and Chan, hugged them and then said" Good bye. I hope I can come back some day."

After everyone had gotten on the ship, the LST left the shore and headed for the big island of Okinawa.

Underway, the Captain said to Lee. " I have a bottle in my cabin, let's go below and I want you to tell me everything."

CHAPTER 14

Killed in Action

On the way to Okinawa Lee had told his whole story about what happened to him. The Captain looked at Lee saying,"That is one amazing tale, if your story is true, then you will get eight or nine months back pay, a small fortune."

"It's all true Sir. Do you know if anyone else survived the sinking of the submarine Merry B?"

"Not that I'm aware of, but when we get back we can check our records. We should be docking in about an hour, and then I will have the Sergeant run you up to headquarters. I'm sure General Gates will be interested in your story."

The L.S.T. landed at the dock of Kerama Retto, and the Captain had a driver to take Lee to NAHA, and to Marine Headquarters. He was taken to the office of records. He gave his story again to Major Evans, who was in charge. He looked at Lee. " And you had no way to get back to the fighting, or did you want to?"

"No sir, there were no boats on the island that could make the trip. The Japanese took all the large boats, as well as all the young men and women. There was no one there, but the very young and old men and woman."

"Write down your full name, rank and outfit. Corporal, you take this information to the record room, and bring me his files."

After about thirty minutes, the Corporal returned, and gave the files to the Major. After looking at it for ten minutes, he looked at Lee. " Lieutenant, from these records you are dead, drowned on the Merry B nine months ago. All hands were drowned including Major Blake, a good friend of mine. What are you trying to pull?"

"Nothing sir, but I am First Lieutenant Lee Robinson, U.S. Marines attached to the UD Team in Hawaii. If you can call them, they will verify that. Talk to Major Sands."

"My records shows he is dead too. Do you have any live friends that will vouch for you?"

"Sir, I'm sure they have my finger prints on my records somewhere. Take my prints, and send them to Marine Headquarters in Washington. I would like to get back to my outfit at Kauai, Hawaii."

"Robinson, I can't let you go anyplace, until we prove who you are. You may be an imposter or a deserter. From my records, Lee Robinson is dead." Corporal Hays, take this man to a detaining room with a bed, and put a guard on the door. Lee, or whatever your name is, we will put your file on ASAP, and try to clear it up as fast as we can."

The detaining room wasn't bad, it had a library, bath with shower and a large window with a view of the ocean. A much nicer place *than* where he had come from. But he was getting restless, he wanted to get his records straighten out and then go see Pat. *Gosh, has it been nine months, has she heard that I was dead. If so, would she still be at the hospital, what if she got married?*

The next day he was served with a good breakfast. Ham, eggs, pancakes and real coffee. " I haven't had a breakfast like this in nine months. Wonder if it's for a condemned man. What will happen if I can't prove who I am?"

He went over to the book case and picked up a book called" Dominica, written by Ed Robinette." Lee remembered him from Honolulu; they had a few beers together.

That afternoon there was a knock on the door. When he opened it, the sentry stepped back and saluted him. " Lieutenant Robinson sir. The Major wishes to speak with you." Lee felt kind of silly in his island clothes and a wide brim straw hat, but he returned the salute.

"Lead the way Corporal… I hope he has some good news."

They went into the Major's office and Lee saluted him saying." "First Lieutenant Lee Robinson, Sir. Did you wish to see me?"

After the Major saluted him back, he asked him to sit down. "Lee I got information back from Washington. They matched your finger prints, and it seems that you're not dead, but who you claim to be. The clerk said that you have created lots of extra work for him, it would have been better if you were dead."

"That's his problem, I don't like being dead. Now where can I get out of these clothes, and get a Marine uniform?"

"I will have the Corporal drive you down to the Marine Base and you can stay there tonight, but come back and see me tomorrow. I hope to book you on a B-24 heading to Hawaii. I'm sorry for all the confusion, but I don't have cases like this very often," the Major said holding out his hand." Welcome back to the human race."

The Corporal drove Lee down town to the Marine Base. He was amazed how quickly the town was being restored. But you could still see the damages; our planes and ships guns did to the city. He would have liked to have seen it before the war; he bet it was a beautiful place.

The Corporal pulled in front of the Marine Base. "Do you want me to wait sir?"

"No, just pick me up tomorrow around noon, I don't want to miss that plane to Hawaii, I have a girl to see."

The quartermaster fitted Lee with three uniforms, shoes and a couple of fatigues, and looking in the mirror he was please with himself. Without the beard and a haircut, he looked like a Marine again. He had lost weight, but he was sure he would put it back on in the months to come.

That night he walked around town, stopped in a bar and had a beer, the first in almost a year. The Navy doctor had examined him and said that after a little rest, he would be fit for active duty again. Then he gave him a thirty day leave, and after that, he was to go back to his old unit.

The plane lowered the flaps and began to descend. Lee woke up and looked out the window, and saw the prettiest view he had seen in months. To his left was Diamond Head, and to the right was Pearl Harbor. The B-24 circled and came to a perfect landing.

He picked up his bags, hailed a taxi to the Honolulu hospital, looking at the famous Gay Street. But today, there were no lines, the war was over and the service men were going home.

Arriving at the hospital, he bought some flowers from a vendor and walked up the steps. He met an older woman at the front desk, and he asked to see Pat Mason.

The nurse looked at him and said. "The war is over and she went home to have her baby."

"Home! Baby, what are you talking about? Where's home, and who's baby?"

"Her parent's home in Ohio, I don't know what town. "

Lee could not believe what he had just heard.

He gave the flowers to the nurse, and then with tears streaming down from his eyes, he walked outside.

He got a taxi to the airport and checked on a flight to Kauai. By the time he read the paper, his plane was ready. The garden island is only about thirty minutes by air. Once landed, on the strip he took a taxi to the UDT base. The sign in the front yard had been removed, and the place looked deserted. He walked up the steps and knocked on the door.

After about ten minutes a Marine private came to the door. Stood there for five minutes, and then stood at attention and saluted. "Can I help you sir?'

"Yes you can Private, let me in. Where is the commandant officer?"

"Hey Mike, someone wants to see you?"

An unshaven Marine Sergeant came to the door."What'ch wants Roy?"

The Private was still standing at attention. "This Lieutenant wants to see someone in charge."

Then Mike saw the silver bars on Lee's shoulder, and stood at attention.

"Can I help you sir?"

"Who is in charge here Sergeant?"

"I guess I am sir. Can I help you?"

"Let me in, I want to see what the hell's going on here, is there anyone else here?"

"Just us two sir, was three, but Joe's gone to lunch."

"What is Joe's rank, and what does he do?"

"He's a Corporal Sir, I have the highest rank. What can I do for you sir?"

By now, Lee was getting upset. "Sergeant Mike, where are the men in the UDT?"

"They all went home, we would be too, if we hadn't been given this crummy job. We have to pack all this stuff up in boxes, so they can ship it out."

"Sergeant Mike, have you packed an address book of the teams' home addresses?"

"Yes sir, I believe it's in that big box, over yonder."Pointing to a big box.

"Mike, would you look and see. It's very important."

"Heck sir, we spent three hours packing it."

"Look Sergeant, I'm about to get mad. Now open that box and see if you can find an address book. I won't ask again."

Sergeant Mike and Roy went to the box, and opened it up. Mike said," I think I have found it sir."

"Good, bring it to me,"

"Don't know if I should sir, all of this stuff is classified." Mike said.

"Mike, just bring me the book, I will take full responsibility."

Once Lee had the book, he ran his fingers down the list of names. His finger stopped on Rodney Sweeny. Home address was 1410 Beech Dr, Cullman, Ala.

"Find what you was looking fer, sir?"

"Yes Mike I think so, now you can put it back, and I will leave. Thank you men, for your help."

"Sir, you have a higher rank. Do you think you could get us off this job? We sure would like to go home."

"Boy's I'm sorry I can't. I would like to go home myself, but we have to wait for orders. Just work harder and it will be done quicker."

"Yes sir," Mike said with a halfway salute.

Lee went back to Honolulu, and checked into the hotel that he and Rod had shared before. He went to the clerk and asked if he could make a long distance call to someone in the states. After much haggling, the manager agreed only after Lee slipped him a five dollar bill.

"Operator, I want to call this address in the U.S. I don't have a number, but it is very important."

"One minute please, I will see if I can find a number, whom do you want to speak to sir?"

"Mr. Sweeny or a member of his family." Five minutes passed then a voice came on the line.

"Hello, this is Sara Sweeny. Who is this?"

"Sara, this is Lee Robinson, a good friend of Rodney. Is he there?"

"Lee Robinson? Rodney told me that you were dead, killed on Okinawa."

"Yes M'am. Everyone tells me that, but I'm very much alive, and trying to find my girl, Pat."

"She isn't here, where did you see her last?"

"I didn't think that she would be there, but I thought Rod might know where she went. Do you know when Rod will be home?"

"We got a telegram from him, said he was in San Diego. He would be coming home in the next few days. Be home for Christmas."

"Mrs. Sweeny, are you his Mother?"

"Yes I am. Can I help you?"

"Get a pencil and write this number down. When Rod comes home have him to call this number. I will be staying with my younger brother on his farm in Hixson, Tn. Please tell him to call, it's very important."

Lee then called the Marine Base, and asked if he could get a ride to the states on one of the navy planes? He was in luck; a B-17 would be going to Texas tomorrow at 0900 a.m. From there he could rent a car and drive to Tennessee.

He made arrangements to stay the night; he would go one

more time to the hospital and see if someone else knew where Pat had gone.

He took a shower, and went to the hospital, and then to the front desk. It was a different lady this time. "Yes, she knew Pat, but all that she knew was that it was somewhere in Ohio. She was going to stay with her sister until the baby was born. "

She then looked at Lee." Are you the father? She told me that she was in love with a Marine name Lee Roberts. She said he was killed."

"Lee Robinson, and yes, I think that I'm the father of her baby. Everybody thought I was killed. But as you can see, I'm very much alive and I want to find her. Please do you know anyone that knows where she went in Ohio? That's a big state; I need to know the city?"

The nurse got up from her desk, talked to several other nurses, then went to the office and checked the record books. Only one address was listed, and that was the one in her apartment in Honolulu.

"I'm sorry Marine, but that's the only address that I came up with."

Lee left and walked the sidewalks of Honolulu, he couldn't think of anything else he could do. His only hope was that Rod would call and know the address. To kill time he went into a bar and had a couple drinks.

Two hours later he went to a restaurant and ordered a steak, finished supper and went back to his room. Tomorrow he would be flying to the states. That night was something he hadn't been doing, he said a prayer that somehow he would find Pat.

The plane had been on time, and he slept most of the way. When he looked down he saw the Lackland Airport at San Antonio, Texas. For the first time in three years he was walking on US ground. He hailed a cab and went to town, and booked a room. Tomorrow he would rent a car and drive to Tennessee.

It was a long drive, he stopped several times to eat and rest. He was too tired to go all the way, so he stopped in Alabama to spend the night. He called the operator and asked about "Bama Wilson," then he remembered, he didn't know his first name. She couldn't help him, so he ate supper and went to bed.

The next day he arrived in Chattanooga, and then drove to Hixson and to a farm where he was born. As he pulled in the driveway, he saw that it hadn't changed much, in seven years. That was the last time he was there, it was for his father's funeral. Couple of small children came running out to the car. That would be his younger brother's children. His brother Carl and his wife Lucy came out and met him.

It was a good reunion, with lots of hugs and laughter. Carl was four years younger than him, and was too young for the war. And after his father and mother had died, Carl stayed home and took care of the farm.

Lee was introduced to all the kids, four boys, and two girls. Lee thought, *when did his brother have time to farm?*

Carl wanted to know all about his adventures, and yes they got a telegram saying that he had been killed. Lucy prepared a big supper, Lee had bought presents for the kids, and they spent the next three hours talking, then Lee said that he was tired, and they all went to bed. He said a prayer that tomorrow he would hear from Rod and find Pat, and then he fell asleep.

Lee woke up hearing cows mooing, and chickens clucking. Looking out the window he saw his brother Carl feeding the stock. He looked at the clock, it was only 5 o'clock. He got up and put his pants on, but was convinced he did not *want* to be a farmer.

"Carl, do you get up at this time every day?"

"No, I sleep until 6 a.m. on Saturday and Sunday. I'm sorry if I woke you up. Lucy will have breakfast on the table at 7 a.m. I hope you're hungry, she is having eggs, bacon and pancakes."

"Carl give me that bucket, and I will feed the chickens." Lee said reaching for the bucket.

The chickens, cows and six pigs got fed, and the two brothers went to an outside pump and washed up for breakfast.

"Lee you going to stay in the Marines? Half of this farm is yours you know."

"I'm not sure, I have fifteen years, and with another five I can retire with a good service pay."

"We have plenty of room in the bunk house, we and the kids wish you would stay. Are you planning on marrying, you told us about Pat, have you seen her yet?"

"No Carl that's why I'm here. We were going to get married, but I got shipwrecked, and by the time they found me the war was over, and she had went back home, somewhere in Ohio. I understand she has my kid too."

"What are you going to do now?"

"Well I'm hoping a friend of mine may know where she lives. His mother said he was coming home in a couple days, and I gave her this number."

"I hope he knows where she lives. It's about time you're getting married and settling down," said Carl.

CHAPTER 15

Christmas of 1945

"Carl, it's been nine days since I called Rod's mother, and I haven't heard anything. I may never find Pat, but I wish her happiness, and that my kid grows up to be a fine man. I have used up two weeks of my thirty days leave. If I'm going to be a farmer, I need to get out of this uniform and get me some work clothes."

Lee went to town and bought two pairs of blue jeans, and three flannel shirts. He also purchased a leather jacket." Now I look like a farmer," he said to Lucy, " and I bought some presents for the kids."

"Thank you Lee, it's hard to believe that Christmas will be in two weeks."

"Yes, and the war has been over for four months, and that puts me out of a job. I would like to get out if I can stay in the Marine Reserves. I could still build my time up, and when I total twenty years I would have a full retirement."

"We would love to have you stay here. Carl could use some help. The kids do what they can, but during school days they have their homework."

"Lee I hope you can find Pat, Carl said that you two had planned on getting married before you were washed up on an island. I wished you would tell us more about it. Nine months Carl said, and you didn't know that the war was over."

"Yes, and I was listed as killed in action. I'm sure it was hard on Pat, and she was carrying my kid. I have got to find her, I love her very much."

"I wish I could hear from Rodney, but then again he may not know where she went. "

Lee got up early drank a cup of coffee, and went outside to help Carl with the cattle. After the cows and chickens were fed, they went inside and had a good breakfast.

"Lucy, if I stay here I will gain ten pounds with your cooking. Marine's food was never like this. I lost twenty pounds, but at this rate I will get it back in a few weeks."

"Lee the weather man said we may have some snow this week-end. We need to get some feed from the silo, and throw some hay in the garage for the young cows. I'm leaving the older cattle out in the pasture, but we need to take some bales of hay out near their watering trough."

"Sure thing Carl, you are going to make a farmer out of me yet," winking at Lucy.

Six days passed and there was about two inches of snow on the ground, and a week before Christmas. Carl and Lee were repairing the pig fence, when Lucy sent little Carl to find Lee. "Mom said for me to tell you that your friend is on the phone, and wants to talk to you."

"Could it be Rodney? Tell her that I will right there."

Lee handed the hammer to Carl," this is the call I have been waiting for, I will be right back." Then he started walking to the house.

"This is Lee, am I talking to Rod?"

"Yes, and am I talking to a ghost? I heard that you were killed about a year ago. Damn, I'm glad that you're alive, and later I want to hear all about it. But mother said you had something real important to ask me. Is it about Pat?"

"Yes it is Rod; I have got to find her. Do you know where she might be? I was told she was in Ohio someplace, and with my child. Please tell me that you know the address?"

"Well, as a matter of fact, I think I do. This is the address she gave me. It's her Sister's place, her mother and father is dead. When are you going up?"

"Today, if I can rent a car. Rodney when I get back we are going to get together, have a beer and I will tell you all about it. Thanks old buddy for this information, maybe I can have my baby and Pat with me when I get back."

"Lucy I'm going to take a shower and pack a few things, could you drive me to town, where I can rent a car."

Carl came in and seeing his brother packing said. "I hope that was the news you been waiting for. Did you find the town in Ohio? When do you think you will be back?"

"It's Hamilton, Ohio;" Rod said he thought it was outside the city. She is staying with her sister, and I have the address. I'm not sure when I will get back, but I hope to bring her and the baby with me. I will try to get back before Christmas, and then I will have to check into the Marine base at Camp Lejeune.

"Is it okay for Lucy to drive me to town, I can rent a car there."

"Sure, if I didn't have to finish that fence, I would take

you" shaking his brother's hand. " Find her, marry her, and get back here for Christmas."

Lee took a shower while Lucy put his bag in the car. "Are you wearing your uniform?"

"Yes, she has never seen me without my uniform; she may not know me in civilian clothes. I will get her used to that later, I'm thinking about getting out of the Marines"

Lucy drove to Chattanooga, and found a car rental agency, Lee kissed her and said. "Wish me luck, I will get a room for tonight, and try to find the house tomorrow."

"Call us Lee and try to get back for Christmas, the boys will be disappointed if you don't make it."

Lee waved to her, and then he pulled out of the parking lot.

He arrived in Hamilton, Ohio about dark, drove to the Holiday Inn and booked a room. Laid his bags on the bed, and then called downstairs and asked for a good place to eat. He should have known, they recommended the restaurant downstairs. That was okay, he wanted to look at the city map, and he then went downstairs and ate supper.

He slept late, because the address wasn't too far away, and he didn't want to get there too early. Around ten a.m. he got in his car and drove the five miles to the address that Rod had given him.

As he got out of his car, he began to feel nervous." What if this was the wrong address or maybe she wouldn't want to see him. After all, it's been about a year. Would she still want him?"

He rang the bell, and a beautiful lady came to the door, holding a cup of coffee. "Pat I'm Lee; I have been looking for you." As he pushed the screen door open.

Pat looked at him and said, "Oh my God! Lee I was told that you were dead," dropping her coffee, and reaching for a chair.

Hearing the commotion, her sister Sara came running into the room."What's wrong, who is he Pat?"

She said. "I'm alright. This is Lee Robinson, the Marine that I have told you about. The Daddy of little Lee. I have told you about that, remember?"

"Sara go back into the kitchen, I need to talk to Lee," now getting composed in the chair.

"Lee where have you been, I waited, then Rod said you were missing. I still waited, then the war was over, and he said that you were listed as dead. I cried all night, but then I thought of the baby. You were gone almost a year, and I was going to have your baby. So after a month, I wired Sara and told her that I was going to have a baby, and the father was dead. She sent me a wire to come home, and she would take care of me."

"I'm sorry", he said," I know it had to been rough. But everything is okay now," reaching over and taking her into his arms and kissing her.

When he kissed her, every motion and excitement traveled through her body, she wanted to respond, and hold him tight, and telling him how much she loved him. He made her feel like a real woman, something she hadn't felt in a long time. But reality stepped in, and she pushed him away. "Please don't."

He reached for her again, but this time she pushed him away. "Lee, I love you, and I waited, I wanted you so bad, and I cried every day… Lee, I'm married."

The words went through every muscle in his body; he never thought that she might marry someone else, *she kidding me, isn't she?*

"When? Does he know about the baby? Do you love him?"

"Yes Lee, I have told him about you, and I was carrying your baby, but he still wanted to marry me and give the baby a name."

Lee still shocked, looked into the living room and saw baby toys and clothing under the tree.

Sara walked back into the room."Pat you okay? Your husband will be coming home in ten or fifteen minutes. You better get all you're talking done."

"Pat, there are so many things that I want to say to you, why I couldn't come back." "Would you meet me at McDonald's restaurant tomorrow, I need to talk to you; I have looked for you for so long. Please?"

"I will meet you there at ten o'clock. But please don't expect anything."

He tried to kiss her again, but she pushed him away. I will see you tomorrow, and went into the kitchen.

Sara held the door open for him, " I'm sorry, but she did wait for you."

For the rest of the day he walked the streets, Christmas music was playing in the doors of every store. He ate supper then went back to his room and read himself to sleep.

The next morning he got up and showered, put on a clean shirt and went downstairs and drank two cups coffee, until nine a.m. Then he drove to McDonald's, and found a table in the back.

Would she divorce her husband? What would she do, I know that she still loves me, is it wrong to want her back?

At nine thirty Pat walked in the door. He could smell her perfume five feet away; he never knew she was so beautiful. I can't let her get away again. Lee stood up and gave her a chair, then held her hands and said. "Pat I love you, I know you are married, but it hasn't changed a thing about the way I feel about you."

"Lee don't, I'm having a hard time holding my feelings, but we must get this said. I going to say this once, then we will forget about it, and never bring it up again, okay?"

"But first, I want to hear all about your adventure, what happened, and why you couldn't come back. Why did they say that you were dead? I would have waited."

For the next hour, Lee told her everything that happened. She listened and held his hand.

"Now it's my time, I came home with a baby of eight months; at times I didn't think I would make it. Sara took me in, and helped with the baby. After the baby was born, I met Ralph. We had met before in high school. He is older than me, I didn't love him, but I knew he was a good man. He offered to marry me, and give my baby a last name. He knows about you, and that it is your baby."

"Lee, I love you, but I will not break up my marriage and hurt Ralph. So I'm asking you if you love me, please get out of my life." Then with tears in her eyes, she stood up and walked out the door.

Lee sat there until she drove away. He felt like he had been hit by a 2x4, he couldn't believe what he had just heard. We both love each other, how could it end like this?

He set there thinking that she might come back, but then he relized it was over, and he had a son who he would never see.

Lee started walking back toward town, it was early but he wanted to get drunk, dead drunk. After several hours he found a bar open and went inside, ordered two beers, and when they were gone, he ordered two more. The bartender tried to get him to go home. "It was Christmas," he said.

Now he felt better, but he didn't like the big Army Sergeant drinking next to him.

"I don't like you doggie soldier, and Lee threw a bottle at him, almost hitting him."

The big soldier looked at him and then threw a punch to Lee's face knocking him across the room. "I'm not supposed to hit an officer, but what the hell… the war is over."

Lee rubbed his jaw, and went after him swinging. "I won't pull rank on you; let's see if you can hit me again."

This time, Lee was hit in the stomach, and he gasped for breath, he didn't realize he was out of shape. It must have been the easy living on the island; then again he had gotten a little older. The soldier waited until he got his breath back, then he swung at Lee hitting him in the jaw, and he hit the floor.

"Go out the back, the police are coming." Said the bartender.

The soldier picked up Lee and dragged him outside. Then he took him to a bench, and set him down. "Marine, I don't know what your problem is, but I don't like hitting a fellow soldier. But next time pick on a smaller guy, someone you can lick. Hell Mate, this is Christmas and we shouldn't be fighting."

"Sorry soldier, but I just lost my girl."

"Ha, you wanted to get beat up. No woman is worth it. Like a street car, if you miss one, another one will come by. Where are you staying? I'm hailing you a taxi to take you to your room, and get some sleep, and Merry Christmas my friend."

The next day Lee couldn't remember why his face was red and bruised, but after breakfast it all came back to him. His head was killing him; he must have had too much to drink. Then he thought of Pat, she wanted him out of her life, well he would just do that." Hell, I will re-enlist, and stay in the Marines, They never let you down."

Lee found his car and drove to Camp LeJeune Marine base. He called Carl, and told him things just didn't work out, and he was going back in the Marines, and asked for oversea duty. He hoped they all would have a good Christmas, and he would write to them later. P.S. "The hell with women."

He turned down his discharge and signed up for Active Reserves, but would have to go to Japan for a year. After that he could get out, but stay in the Reserves and his time would count. He would have twenty years in the service and would draw a good pension. Then he called Rodney, and filled him in about Pat, and his re-enlistment.

"Lee I have another two years to go, reckon we could go to Japan together? Sue said she wouldn't wait, unless we got married, but she doesn't mind being a Marine wife, if she could go with me. Think they would let her go?"

"Rod, with the war over, they don't get many volunteers, yes I think you both can go. If you're going to get married, I want to be best man."

"Lee, you will always be my best man, and I won't marry without you being there."

He only had two weeks left, so he called Rodney and said."Rod old friend, I have been made Captain, and I have pulled a few strings. You now are Master Sergeant Rodney Sweeny, and we both will be going to Japan and join the 4th Marine Division. We will be helping to disarm the Japanese. If you're married, she can join you in two months. So let me know when and where the wedding will be?"

Three days later Lee received a telegram. "My wedding will be January 2nd at the little 'White Oak Baptist Church' in Cullman, Alabama at two p.m. Come early, you are the best man."

On January 2nd 1946 a wedding was perform at a little church in Cullman, Alabama. Captain Lee Robinson was best man, and Master Sergeant Rodney, and Sue Sweeny were united in marriage.

Lee kissed the bride, hugged his friend Rodney and said

goodbye. He was to report back to the base, at Camp Lejeune, North Caroline, the next day. And the Sweeny's took their honeymoon at an unknown location.

Captain Lee was given C- Company and began to train his men. Most were first year reserves, but many were veterans, that had re -enlisted. Master Sergeant Sweeny was still on leave, and would report in two weeks.

He called his brother Carl, and hoped that they had a good Christmas, and talked to all the kids. He told him that he would be leaving for Japan soon, and would stay a year, then he would leave the Marines, but his time would continue until he got his twenty years in. This mission won't be fighting, but a peaceful trip, he hoped.

February, 19, 1946 the 3rd Amphibious Corps lands at Tokyo Bay, Japan.

Since Rodney was a non-commission enlisted man, he didn't see Captain Lee on board ship very often. But they would make up for that later.

"Rod, come over to the jeep, you can ride with Captain Burns and me to the base." Lee was watching for him when he got off the ship. He introduced Rod to the Captain, and told him that they had been together for over ten years.

Tokyo City was crowded, and they could see the damages done by our bombers, the Japanese citizens would look at them when they drove by, but would not smile or wave.

Captain Lee said to Captain Burns, and Rod. "I don't think they are happy to see us. Can't blame them. If we didn't drop the bomb they would still be fighting us. Thousands on both sides would have been killed."

Rod looking at the unhappy citizens and said, "Where is our base, I hope it's not inside the city?"

"No Sergeant, our base is ten miles outside the city. But still, we have a heavy guard around us. Many of the citizens and soldiers are not willing to quit fighting, and that's why we have a full division here, plus the 3rd Corps."

"Our job is to disarm them, and it may not be easy. There's a couple of large islands close by, and I understand thousands of Japanese soldiers." Captain Burns said. They drove through the city and into the country, but it too showed the damages our bombs had done. After another ten miles, they could see their base with Marines guarding the front gate. "Marines, this is your new home."

CHAPTER 16

Japan

When they went into the base, Captain Burns dropped Rodney off at the non-enlisted Marines' quarters, then after saying good-by, he took Captain Lee to his quarters and dropped him off. Lee carried his bags to his room, and dropped them on the floor. He was ready for a nap, but seeing a note on the table he picked it up.

"Captain Lee Robinson, Welcome to our little base, hope you will enjoy your stay here. When you get rested, come by my office at 0200 and we will discuss your duties. Sincerely, Major Sam Hatfield.

Lee didn't have time for a nap, so he unpacked his bag and then went to the officer's mess, met a few of the other officers and had a light lunch.

At 0200 he walked over to Major Hatfield's office where another officer was waiting. Lee saluted the officer and spoke."Lieutenant, I am Captain Lee Robinson, shaking the Marines hand.

"Lieutenant Ed Brown, Sir. I think we will be working together Sir," standing at attention.

"Hell, relax Brown. If we are going to be working together, you can call me Captain or Lee."

Lee told the Corporal at the desk."Inform the Major that we are here." The two officers walked in the office of Major Hatfield, stood at attention and saluted. "Captain Robinson and Lieutenant Brown, Sir."

The Major saluted back and said, "At ease men," then they shook hands. "Did you two get a chance to get know each other?"

"We met outside Sir," said Lieutenant Brown." I told him that we would be working together, that's was about it Sir."

"Men, come over to the wall, and look at this map. This is the map of Japan. You will see several places where a Japanese flag is on a pin. These are the places where some of the Japanese soldiers are still holding out. Some may not have heard that the war is over; others may not give a damn. It is your job to convince them to lay down their guns and come into the city, or go back to their homes.

They can no longer have any weapons in their possessions. When you finish inside Japan, you will go to islands where there are still Japanese troops. When you've covered the area, replace the pin with an American flag. Any questions?"

"Yes sir, how many Marines will we take with us, and will they be combat troops?" Lee asked.

"We have ten thousand Marines at this camp and other bases. But you will take a company of Combat Marines, two Corpsman's, sometimes a doctor, and three Japanese interpreters. One will drive the front truck; he knows where all these places are. You, Captain Robinson, will be in charge and use your judgment, to how many troops you will need. You will carry food, two empty trucks to bring back the Japanese soldiers and civilians. But by all means, tell your men not to use their weapons; we don't want to restart this war over."

"Sir, what if they fire on us, and like on Saipan they will not surrender?" said Lieutenant Brown.

"Lieutenant, that will be a call that Captain Robinson will have to make. We will have the interpreters and they have a copy of the Peace Agreement, signed by Tojo himself. If they still won't come in, leave them some food, patch up their wounds, and leave. Do not force them, but when you get back, report it to me. "

"It will not be an easy job. But whoever said that a job for the Marines was easy."

"If there are no more questions, you start tomorrow. This job has never being done in our life time. We have to learn as we go. Captain report to me after each mission and at once if there is a firefight, but protect your men. We don't want anyone killed on either side. Now good luck and, draw the men you will need."

"Major Sir, I came over here with a friend of mine. He is a Master Sergeant; I would like to add him to my company."

"You are in charge Lee, choose the men that you will need. If there are no more questions, you are dismissed."

After the meeting, Lee met a Corporal outside and ordered him to find Master Sergeant Rodney Sweeney and have him report to his office immediately.

Then he asked Lieutenant Brown to join him in his office.

"Ed, when Sergeant Sweeney gets here, I want the two of you to pick the men that will be going with us. The Sergeant has been in combat many times, and he's a good Marine to have around." On their first mission Lee guess that they would see about fifteen Japanese soldiers and five women. "Pick a total of twenty or thirty men, and if they can be counted on, we will keep them for our entire missions. We will only use ten marines for this trip, but have the others to stay in stand-by mode. "

"I'm not sure where the Japanese interpreters will be, but get us two for this mission. Again Sergeant, Rodney will be a big help to us, he understands and speaks Japanese. One Navy Corpsman or Doctor, and the last thing we will need is a jeep, and three 2/4 trucks and load one with c-rations."

One hour later, Lee heard Rod talking to the orderly in the front office. "Sergeant, please come into my office."

"Rod, I'm going to need you, but first I want you to meet Lieutenant Ed Brown, the three of us will be working together for a long time. Lieutenant Brown will fill you in on what we need, and plan on meeting tomorrow, at 0900."

The next morning when Lee walked outside, there were a jeep and three trucks waiting. Rodney had the men fall out of the truck, and stand at attention, while Captain Lee shook each man's hand. He asked," How many of you have been in combat? All raised their hands. Then he explained their duty, and orders not to shoot unless ordered, or unexpected danger came up, and was forced to."

A Japanese interpreter was driving the jeep with Rodney

sitting beside him; Captain Lee and Lieutenant Brown were in the back seat. Captain Lee gave orders to move out.

They drove about ten miles out in the country and came to a small cave. "This is the place," the Japanese interpreter said. They got out of the jeep, Lee asked his Marines to get out of the truck and line up on each side of the cave. Then he asked his interpreter to go inside and call them out.

After about twenty minutes, ten soldiers, and five women came out with one carrying a baby.

"Tell them if they have any weapons to lay them on the ground." Lee said.

They looked at him and shook their heads.

"When have you last eating?"

One of the women spoke up. "Not for three days, and my baby is hungry."

Captain Lee asked the corpsman to check the mother and baby out, and then asked one of his men to get some milk and food out of the truck, and give it to them. While they were eating, he told the interpreter to tell them he would take them to town, give them more food, blankets, and later they could go home. Everyone had been searched again for weapons, and then they got on the truck. Lee asked Rodney and several Marines to search the cave.

After about thirty minutes, Rodney and his men came back out with two more women. "Is that all of them?" Lee asked.

When they were sure that everyone was accounted for, they drove back to town and the base. Again a doctor checked the woman and baby out, and they would be taken to a Japanese camp, and later to their home.

Captain Lee dismissed his men, and told them to be ready for tomorrow. And then he went to see Major Hatfield, where they discussed today's mission.

After meeting with the Major, Lee went back to his room, took the Japanese pin off the map, and replaced it with an American pin. Then he showered and went to supper. Tomorrow would be another mission.

For the next two weeks, they covered the map, replacing the pins with American flags.

Captain Lee was ordered again to see Major Hatfield. "Captain, you and your men have done a good job, but now come the hard part. Starting tomorrow, I want you and your men to go to the islands surrounding Japan. We know that there are Japanese soldiers there. Many may not come in or lay down their weapons. This time take a company of Marines and be careful. On Shima there are at least a hundred soldiers. The word we get from our interpreters they will fight to death, and will not lay down their weapons or surrender." Captain Lee, You and your Marines please be careful."

"Yes Sir, and if we have a fire fight?"

"If it cannot be avoided, try not getting any of your men killed. I'm hoping they will surrender. But it will be your decision."

That night Captain Lee had a meeting with the Marines

that he would take with him, a hundred men, two corpsmen, and three interpreters. They would meet at the dock and go in a LST. The next morning everyone was at the dock, and with an armored S. U. V. and three trucks. Again, Captain Lee briefed his men and for them to be extra careful.

Shima was a small island about a hundred miles from Japan and was used as a radar station, watching for U.S. planes heading for Tokyo. It was mountainous with a small civilian population of about two hundred.

They arrived around noon, debarked, and headed the two miles to town. People came out of their houses and stores staring and shouting, "Death to the Americans". Two men came up to them with a white flag. In Japanese language they approached Captain Lee and Lieutenant Brown saying "They are in that cave up on the mountain, we told them that the war was over, but they said they would never stop fighting, Japan had been disgraced."

"How many are there, and do they have any big guns?" Lee asked in Japanese.

"No big guns, but they have many guns. You kill them?"

"I hope we don't have too. Are there anyone here in town they may respect and trust?"

"Some of our family has talked to them, but they say, they will fight to the death, for the honor of Japan."

Lee looked at Brown and Rodney, "Well this is what the Marines pay us for. Let's go and earn our money. Rod, tell the Marines to lock and load, and form in two's." Then they began the three miles up the mountain trail, each man thinking. *What a hell of a time to get killed, with the war over.*

The mountain trail was steep with heavy underbrush. Lee could see why it was ideal for a radar lookout station. It took them two hours to reach the top.

He saw the radar tower, and a small bunk house where the men slept. It was quiet, with the exception of sea gulls flying overhead. He gave the bull horn to one of the interpreter, and asked him to tell the Japanese soldiers to come out and talk.

"Come out my fellow countrymen, the war is over. You will not be hurt, and we will give you food, then you can go home."

He was answered by a volley of shots, and the interpreter fell over dead.

Lee had his men to unlock their guns, spread out, and look for cover. Then a hail of shots was fired from the bunk house and from the cave. A trumpet sounded, and Japanese soldiers rushed out in a Bonsai attack, and then it was hand to hand fighting. The fighting lasted for only about thirty minutes, three of Lee's men were killed, and ten wounded and Japanese bodies lay on the ground. This was not what he wanted to happen.

Lieutenant Brown had been shot in the hip, Rod had a cut on his arm from a bayonet, but Lee escaped injury. The two corpsmen were busy taking care of the wounded. All of the hundred or more Japanese were dead. Lee looked at the bodies and shook his head.

"What good did this do? The war was over and they could have gone home, this is senseless. What do I tell the mothers and wives about their sons and husbands, that their men died after the war was over? For what?"

They put the dead men on the trucks, and asked the town

people if any of the dead were related to them. Then they unloaded the food and gave it to the town.

When they got back to the Marine base, the men that were wounded were taken to the hospital. The dead Marines would be shipped back home. Captain Lee went to see Major Hatfield and told him what happened.

"Captain Lee, I'm sorry. But it was out of your hands, there was nothing else you could have done. I know you are upset about your men. If you wish, I will write the letters to the family of the three Marines that were killed. You and your men take couple days off, maybe see the city."

With Lieutenant Brown still in the hospital, Lee and Rod went downtown to see Tokyo. They walked the streets and went in most of the bars. Nothing helped Lee to forget the good Marines that were killed. "Rod, we were set up. Someone from town told them that we were coming up. They were waiting for us, damn good Marines getting killed after the war. "

"Forget it Lee, get it out of your head. There was nothing that we could do. Marines know the risk they take, war or peace."

"Lee, let's take a bus and go see Hiroshima, They said that the Atomic Bomb destroyed the whole town."

When they got off the bus, they saw miles of rubble; you wouldn't believe that a town was once there. There wasn't one building standing, an eerie feeling ran through the two men. *Is this what future wars will be like?*

Now both men were more depressed than before. Lee said." Rod lets go back to town and get drunk. When we get back, I'm getting out of the Marines; I'm tired of wars and killing."

After what happened at Shima, General MacArthur stopped all the other missions. Years later, a Japanese soldier would be found. But many starved and didn't know that the war was over.

For the rest of Lee's tour he was assigned to a desk and paper work, then the year passed, and soon he would be sent to Camp LeJeune, North Carolina.

He only had a few weeks before he would leave and go back to the states. He thought of Gee, Rookie and their son Chan, he was going to leave from Okinawa, and then to the states. Maybe he could visit them on Zamami Island, before he left Okinawa? He called Major Hatfield and asked if he could see him.

On arrival he went to the Major's office. "Major Hatfield sir, I would like to tell you a story, and then see if you could help me?"

Captain Lee Robinson told Major Hatfield the whole story of being shipwrecks, fighting the shark, and then washed up on the beach on Zamami Island. He was found by Chan, the son of Gee, almost dead. They carried him to their house, found a doctor and took care of his wounds. He lived with them for eight months. He did not know the war was over until some Marines came to the island bringing food after the big typhoon hit the island. When he went back to Okinawa, he was listed as dead and drowned on the submarine Merry B.

After several weeks, and from his finger prints in Washington, he proved he wasn't dead, and sent back to the states. Where he re-enlisted and was sent to Japan.

The Major listened to his story. "Captain Robinson that was some adventure, part of it is on your record, and I have been curious about it. Now, how can I help you?"

"Major, I would like to leave a week early from Japan and fly to Okinawa. Then I would have a week before I would fly to the states. In that extra week, I would like to take some gifts and visit my friends on Zamami Island."

Major Hatfield smiled. "Yes, I think I can take care of that, and it's a good thing that you want to do. Could you leave tomorrow morning? I know of a B-24 going to Okinawa tomorrow. You pack, see your friends here, and I will have the Sergeant start on the paper work. He stuck out his hand; we will miss you, but have a good trip."

He went to see Rodney and his wife Sue, and told them of his plans. Lee gave him his brother's address and phone number. That was where Lee would now live, once out of the Marines.

The plane touched down at Yonton airfield, on the Island of Okinawa. Lee caught a ride to the Marine base and reported in. That afternoon he went to the P.X. and started shopping.

He bought a watch and a bike for Chan. Then he found a manual washing machine, because they had no electric power on the Island. Then after looking in the gardening section, and hardware stores, he found a garden tiller for Gee.

Then he made arrangement to have it sent to the ferry at the dock. After getting ready, he went to the Marine base, ate and spent the night. It would be two days before the ferry went to the island of Zamami.

He did some sightseeing for the next two days, seeing places where his Marine friend Ed Robinette had fought the Japanese. It must have been some hard fought battles. History Books say it was the largest Air, Ship, and Land battle in American History.

As soon as the ferry landed, he rented a truck and loaded up the tiller, washing machine, and bike. Then he drove to the farm owned by Gee Moon.

When he reached the house, Gee was plowing with a homemade plow, pulled by his mule. Chan was hoeing with a forked stick. He did not see Rookie; she must be in the house cooking.

Lee blew his truck horn, Chan saw him first, and came running. When Gee came from his garden, the three men hugged and cried. Rookie hearing the commotion came running out. It was a great reunion among friends. Then he showed them their gifts, and they hugged him again. Chan jumped on his bike and went about twenty feet and fell. Everyone had a big laugh.

Lee stayed for three days; they drank the rice wine, sung and had a great time. But then on the fourth day Lee had to say goodbye. Looking at his friends, he realized he would never see them again. They went with him to the ferry, and waved until the boat was out of sight. Lee had taken a picture of the family, and he would always keep it, and remember them.

CHAPTER 17

Home

Captain Lee Robinson landed back on Okinawa, and immediately went to the Headquarters of the Marine base. He wanted to make sure that all of his papers were in order for the flight to the States tomorrow.

His plane would leave at 0900 a.m. from the Yonton airfield. He arrived early and had a cup of coffee in the pilot's lunch room. Looking outside he saw a B-24 warming up on the strip. Checked his pass, and confirmed that would be his plane.

Twenty minutes later, a crew member came in and said that the plane was ready to load, and would fly to San Diego, California. From there he would have to get a plane to Quantico, Virginia and be discharged from the Marines.

It was a smooth flight to the states, and the B-24 landed on time. He got his bags, thanked the pilot and crew, and then checked on his flight to Virginia. It would be tomorrow before he could get a plane so he checked in the Marine base in San Diego for a place to stay. He looked for his friends George and Ray, but both had been discharged and went home. Going out that night to the parade ground, only a few Marines were walking around. It was sad; it will never be the place it once was during the war. He would miss being a Marine.

The next morning he got a ride to the Miramar air field, and found the plane that would take him to Quantico. This time it was an A-20, a small fighter that he had never flown on before.

Again the flight was smooth, but not the comfort of the B-24. He landed on the airstrip, and found a ride to take him to the Marine base.

He got his rupture duck (discharged papers) but would be in the Inactive Reserves for four more years. This would be added to his retirement. This would be okay, because there won't be any more wars. He went to the P.X. and bought presents for his brother Carl and his family.

Captain Lee Robinson, now Civilian Robinson bought a bus ticket to Chattanooga, and then looked for a good used car. He found a Hudson, with low mileage. Throwing his bags and presents in the back seat, he headed for Hixson, and his brother's farm.

When he pulled in the driveway, he saw Carl next to the barn, milking one of the cows. Stopping the car, he walked over to the barn, and the two brothers hugged each other.

"Brother, are you home to stay? I see you have the ruptured duck on your uniform that means you are out of the Marines, am I right?"

"Yes Carl, I am no longer an active Marine. But as the saying goes, once a Marine, always a Marine. So I guess that I will always be a Marine. But now I am a civilian, tell me where to put my things, I will change clothes, and help you milk the cows."

When they got near the house, Lucy and the kids came running up, and hugged him. The kids took his bags to the bedroom.

"Carl later I want to fix up the old bunk house, and I will live there. I intend to stay here, and do my share of the work."

"That's great brother, and there's plenty of work to share. I have wanted to get ten more cows, but I couldn't handle them. Now we can, with your help."

For the next six months Lee fixed up the bunk house and moved in, he added an extra bedroom, another bathroom, and made a covered porch in the back, where he could watch the sun go down, and watch the cattle. Carl had purchased the other ten cows, which gave them a total of fifteen. The local Co-Op would take all their milk, and the local store would buy their eggs, and chickens. Things were going good for the Robinsons.

Lee got a telegram from Rodney in Japan. Said, that he was a father of an 8 pound boy. They would be coming home in a few more months. He asked. "How did Lee like civilian life?"

It was October, 1948 and the wind was bringing in the cold air from the north. It was time to gather in the hay and check the barn for storing the feed.

Lee and Carl were busy, getting everything ready for winter. Lucy was canning and storing food in the pantry. They hoped it wouldn't be as cold as last year.

Lee was storing the hay in the barn when Lucy came out to talk to him.

Looking at him she said. " Lee, there is a woman on the phone; she wanted to know how she could get in touch with a Captain Lee Robinson?"

"Do you know who it is? Is she still on the phone?"

"No, but she left a number, said it was very important that you call her. The number is from Hamilton, Ohio."

"Ohio? That's where Pat lives. I'll come as soon as I can put this band on this bale. Is the number next to the phone?"

Lee connected the band and then with a worried look at Lucy, rushed to the house and dialed the number in Ohio.

The phone rang for several minutes, and then an unfamiliar voice came on the line. "Hello! Who is this?"

"This is Lee Robinson; did someone wish to talk to me? Is this Pat's number, is she alright?"

"Lee, are you the Marine that once dated Pat in Hawaii?"

"Yes, she had my son. Please, what is wrong, and why are you calling me?"

"Lee she was in a terrible car wreck, her husband was killed, and we think she is dying. She wants to see you, can you come up?"

"Yes, I will leave in the hour, but it will take me six or eight hours to get there. What hospital, and give me an address. I can drive quicker than I can get a plane out of here. Tell her to hang on, I'm coming."

Lee got the address took a shower and changed clothes. Carl and Lucy came in, and he explained the phone call. Lucy packed a few things in his bag, and Carl offered him some money. "Please take it Lee; you don't know how long you may have to stay."

Lucy looked at his worried face, "Lee she will be alright and you be careful driving. And call us when you get there, and have the time."

Carl put his bag in the car; Lucy kissed him and again said, please drive carefully. He then got into the car, and was thankful that he had filled the car up with gas just yesterday.

He pulled out of the driveway and toward the highway that would take him to Ohio. He watched for the highway police, but where he could he stepped on the gas.

"Please God; don't let her die."

He drove all day, and into the night, only stopping to get gas, and grabbing a cup of coffee. He was glad he wasn't stopped by the police; he knew he drove over the speed limit most of the way. Seeing the city limits he pulled over to the curb and looked at his notes. The hospital should be in the next block.

When he had driven a short distance, he spotted the hospital, and then looked for a place to park. He pulled in a twenty four hour parking garage, and paid for all night. Looking at his watch, it was eleven p.m. He had made good time.

Going up the steps, he came to the front desk."What room is Pat in? I don't know her last name, but she was in a car wreck, and her husband was killed."

The nurse looked at him. "Are you a relative?"

"Just a very good friend; and she asked to see me."

"Go to room 214 and wait outside. I will have someone to come and talk to you."

He went up the steps to the second floor and went into the waiting room.

A voice came from the dark side of the room. "Are you Lee Robinson?"

Turning around at the voice, and saw a frail looking woman, with obviously lack of sleep looking at him. "Yes Miss, and who are you?"

"I'm Sara, Pat's sister. I think I met you before, but you were wearing a Marine uniform. Are you the father of Pat's baby?"

"Yes, I think so. How is Pat?"

"She's dying. She wants to see you?"

"Can I see her now?"

"I will check with the doctor. And what she wants, we have already talked about it, and I have no objections."

Twenty minutes passed, and Lee was getting worried. Then Sara came back with Pat's doctor. "I shouldn't allow this, but this is an unusual case. She was hurt real bad, she is all busted up inside. If she could live, she would be bedridden the rest of her life, and be on tubes most of the time. She does not wish to live like that, and has asked to die peaceful. Sara and you will have to make that decision for her. She has asked for her sister and me to leave the room, while she talks to you. We will watch her on our monitor. Please don't stay long."

Lee entered the room, and saw what once was an active and beautiful woman, now lying in bed, with tubes in both arms, blacken eyes, and the outline of a twisted, and broken body under the sheets.

"Hello Pat, did you want to talk to me. I'm Lee without my

uniform; don't think you have seen me without it. I'm not in the Marines anymore, I'm a farmer."

Pat held out her hand "Lee, kiss me. Tell me that you still love me."

He reached over the bed, kissed her and then held her hands." Yes Pat, I have always loved you. I wish things had been different, it was my fault."

"You couldn't help it, I should have waited. But the baby, he had to have a father. I did not love Ralph, he knew that. But he wanted to marry me anyway, said I may get to love him later. He was a good and kind man. I loved you, and you tore my heart out when I asked you to get out of my life. But I could not hurt Ralph; he was so good to me and the baby."

"You know he died in the car wreck?"

"Yes, and he doesn't have a family, another reason why I couldn't divorce him. Oh! Lee I have messed up everyone's life, please forgive me."

Lee kissed her," you are forgiven. Now what do you want to tell me."

"Darling, will you marry me? Sara has already spoken to the hospital Chaplain."

"Yes, but let's wait until you get well. You may change your mind then."

"Darling, I'm not going to get well. I know that I am dying. I have asked the doctor to take the tubes out; I don't want to live in bed the rest of my life. "

"Honey, you never know, I will help you to get well."

"Lee my darling, you have a son, and he need's his father.

Ralph has no family; Sara has three kids, and couldn't raise another. Marry me, and take your son home, he already has your name. When he gets older, tell him about me, and how much I loved him. When you hug him, you will also be hugging me. Find yourself a good woman and marry her, I want my son to have a mother and father. If you love me, please say yes."

With tears running down his face, he pushed the button on her control, and the nurse and doctor came running into the room. The doctor looked at her and gave her a shot. "Young man, I think she has talked enough," checking her pulse.

Pat opened her eyes, "No doctor, don't let me die now. We are going to get married, Lee ask Sara to come into the room."

"I'm right here Pat; I was standing in the doorway. I have asked an aid to get the Hospital Chaplain. I have already talked to him, and he has agreed to marry both of you. You're sure this is what you want?"

"Oh, Yes Sara. If Lee will have me, I want to be his wife. You do want to marry me, don't you Lee?"

Lee leaned forward and kissed her. "Pat I love you, and I want you for my wife. Yes, I want to marry you."

The Hospital Chaplain, with Sara as her bride's maid, and the Doctor as best man, said the vows that Lee and Pat were now married… Lee kissed the bride.

The doctor checked the monitor, removed a tube from the side of Pat's mouth, and with tears running down everyone's face, they all left the room. Lee stayed by Pat's bed, with his face next to hers, and he prayed.

Every few minutes the doctor went to the door and looked

at the monitor, she had her eyes closed, but she was still breathing. Lee still had his face next to hers, and his arm across her waist. They both appeared to be asleep.

Thirty minutes later, the nurse heard a beeping sound, she informed the doctor and they went to Pat's room. He looked at his monitor, it showed no signs that her heart was beating. He gently moved Lee aside, who had gone asleep, and checked her vitals. Pat was dead, with a peaceful look on her face, knowing that she had found her lost love, and little Lee was now with his true father.

Sara asked Lee to come to her house and meet her husband and her children. It was time for Lee to meet his son.

Lee followed Sara's car to her home which was only couple miles from the hospital, and then pulled into her driveway. Her husband Fred and the kids came out to meet them. "Lee asked about his son, was someone inside watching him?"

"Sara laughed, Lee you are acting like a concerned father already. Yes, my next door friend is watching him. Let's go inside and meet your son."

When they went inside, Lee saw a small boy playing with toys on the floor. He would be about four years old. He got down on his knees, and reached out to touch him. Hello Leland. My name is Lee; I am your new daddy."

"Lee, Pat calls him 'little Lee' after his father."

He stayed and ate with Sara and Fred, and held and played

with his new son. They planned the funeral for Saturday, that would give them two days, and Lee hoped that his brother Carl, and Lucy could come.

After supper he made reservations at the Holiday Inn for the next three days.

Lee went out with Sara and her husband Fred for supper Friday night, while her friend watched the kids. He had called Carl, and they were coming up for the funeral Saturday. Sara was keeping little Lee until he goes home.

Saturday would be a sad day for him. He went across the street and ate breakfast, at Jim Bo's. Before he finished his second cup of coffee, he saw his brother drive up. Carl and Lucy came inside, and hugged him; they had left the kids at home.

"Brother Lee, I can't wait to see your son. After we eat, can we go by and see him before the funeral?"

"Yes, we have plenty of time. The funeral is not until one o'clock. Are you driving back after that?"

"Need to Lee, I have to milk the cows. We brought a car seat with us, if you want the baby to ride back with us. That way you could stay another day, if you wanted too."

"Thanks Carl, yes I want to visit her grave after everyone leaves. I will come in Sunday."

"Leave your car we will go in my car. I will bring you back after the funeral."

They drove over to Sara's house and met all the kids. "He's

beautiful, Lee." as Lucy picked up 'little Lee'.

They stayed until time for the service, leaving the kids with the baby sitter. Lee was quiet as they drove to the church, he thought back to when he first met Pat. As he remembers, she stuck a needle in his butt. *What was it she said?*

She had seen better looking butts in the nursing homes.

The funeral home was full; Pat had made many friends since she had come back. The service was short, and then they drove to the cemetery, the pastor gave a short sermon, and then they lowered Pat into the grave. Lee watched with tears in his eyes, and said to himself. *The earth has her body, God has her soul, and I have her son. As long as I have him, she will always be with us.*

After the service, they went to Sara's home and picked up 'little Lee'. Sara hugged the baby and cried. She would miss him, but she had three of her own to care for. They promised to visit each other, and Lee and his family left.

He took Carl to his car, put the baby in the car seat, and they said goodbye. They wouldn't get home until late. Lee watched them go, and then went back to the cemetery, and sat at Pat's grave until dark.

Lee woke up early, took a shower and went out for breakfast. Then he filled his car up with gas and headed for Chattanooga. Winter was coming, and he and Carl had to get the hay in the barn. He no longer felt like a Marine, but a farmer.

CHAPTER 18

Mary Brown

Hearing "Old Sam," the red rooster crowing, Lee threw the covers back and slowly got out of bed. Looking at the clock, it was only 5 a.m. This is one thing that he didn't like about being a farmer. Carl said he would get use to it, *but when?* He thought. He was staying at his brother's house and looked out the window and his brother was feeding the cows. Then he smelled fresh coffee brewing on the stove, Lucy must be getting breakfast ready.

Getting dressed and grabbing a jacket, he went through the kitchen and picked up a cup of coffee. "Morning Lucy. Did little Lee give you any trouble last night?"

"Morning Lee, you know that boy never gives any trouble. It must be the Marine training in his little body. When you and Carl finish the feeding, come back in, breakfast will be ready."

"Thanks Lucy, I'll tell Carl to hurry up. I'm hungry for your pancakes."

It was a cold morning, and soon it would be Christmas again, "Where does the time go? Little Lee will be six years old in April. It's been about a year since his mother died. I wish she could see him now, he has grown so much. *Pat, I love you and miss you so much. I will do all that I can, to make our son be the man you would want him to be.*

"Hey Lee, give me a hand with this feed sack, I'm not as young as I used to be."

"Brother, you will always be younger than me. If you think you're getting old, think that your older brother is three years older than you. You just need some of Lucy's pancakes."

They unloaded the feed sack from the loft and carried it outside for the cows. Then they carried out a couple bales of hay. Took some water and poured it the pig trough, and added the slop that was left over from yesterday.

"Now," said Lee." Can we go and get some of Lucy's pancakes?"

"I'm with you brother, race you to the house."

After a good breakfast, Carl lit up his pipe, and Lee turned on the news. North Korea was threatening to invade South Korea. "I thought after WWII, there wouldn't be any more fighting. Well, I have done my fighting, let those two fight it out, that's no concern to America."

Lucy had gotten her kids off to school, and Lee put his son on the floor and played ball with him. "Carl, I noticed that the kid's bedroom was getting a little crowded, with them growing up like they are. Would you help me build a room on to my bunk house? Little Lee needs his own room, now that's he is growing up. It's time I took care of him at night, Lucy could give your kids more room."

"Sure Lee, but he would miss the boys at night. When do want to start?"

Winter came and then Christmas, Carl and Lee had built a small bedroom on the back of the bunk house. At first little Lee wasn't happy about it, he wanted to sleep with his cousins. Then Lee gave him a little puppy for Christmas, and let the puppy stayed in his room. After that everything was, "okie dokie."

"Lee, did you know that little Lee will be six years old next month. Have you thought about getting married, and giving him a mother?" said Lucy.

"Lucy! Stop being a matchmaker. When Lee meets the right girl, I'm sure he will marry her." Carl said laying down the paper.

"Thanks to both of you, but after loving Pat, no one else has interested me. I will find the right girl one day, but then I will be so old she wouldn't have me."

"Why are you bringing it up now Lucy?"

"Because you have been a bachelor long enough. I'm afraid my Carl may start thinking about it. Being single does have its advantages."

"Do you remember the Garners in our church? I think you have met them a couple times."

"Yes, I know them. Why?"

"Well Lora Garner has a sister who is coming to stay with her until she can find a house. She served three years in the Marine Corps, and getting out next week. She is around thirty, and never been married. She took care of her mother for years, and never dated. After her mother died, she joined the

Marines, said she wanted to see the world. Would you believe it, she never left the States."

Lee laughed, "That happens sometimes. But why are you telling me?"

"The reason I'm telling you Mr. X- Marine, and now civilian Lee Robinson, is that we have invited them over to the house for supper. I thought I should fill you in before they got here. I understand that she is a beautiful and lovely lady. So get out of those overalls, take a bath, and be on your best behavior."

Carl looked at his brother. "The woman has spoken Lee. You better do what she says. Never argue with a woman who is a matchmaker."

Around six p.m., a car pulled up in front of the Robinson's home. And Lora and her husband Bob got out and then opened the back door for Mary Brown. As they exited the car, Carl and Lucy went outside to meet them. The women hugged, and the men shook hands. Lee stayed inside of the house with the kids.

Once inside Lucy introduced Lora, Bob, and Mary and then Lee walked up and Lora said. "Mary this is Lee Robinson, a former Marine, who retired last year, and now a cattleman and farmer. "

Lee took Mary's hand and said."I understand that you were a Marine, and just got out of the service last month. Welcome to the civilian life. How long were you in?"

"Three years and four months." Looking at Lee then pulling her hand from him.

Then Mary said, "I would like to meet the kids, I

understand that you have a little boy?"

Lucy went into the kitchen and brought back Lee's baby. "You met some of mine outside playing when you drove up, but this is the youngest. His name is Leland, but we call him little Lee."

Mary looking at Lee. " May I hold him, he is so cute."

"Sure, he said. "He looks just like his mother."

"Lucy said that his mother was dead. I'm so sorry. .. Car accident she told me."

"Yes, a couple of years ago. Lucy is supper about ready?" Lee said wanting to change the subject.

Carl said the blessing, and then they ate the food which mostly came from the farm.

After supper they went into the living room. The women on one side with the men watching a ball game on TV. Lee got a little bored with the game, Atlanta was getting beat bad. He looked over at Mary, and it seemed that the other two ladies were doing all the talking. Mary looked over at him, with the look of, get me out of this.

Lee stood up and walked over to the girls and said."Mary, would you like to see the farm?"

Mary got up from the chair and said. "Yes, I would Lee. I have never seen a working farm, one with cows, pigs and chickens. Lucy said that you were a Captain in the Marines. I can't image you as a farmer. Do you make the cows stand at attention?"

"I tried, but like some of the men under me, I haven't had much luck. My old friends remembered me as a Sergeant for many years, and it was hard for them to salute me, and say sir.

But let me show you Bama, he is my favorite bull."

Carl overhearing Lee talking about Bama said. "Mary be careful around Bama. He thinks he owns this farm; no one can pet that bull except Lee. He is like a kitten to him, but anybody else, looks out. If he is close to one of his cows, I don't go near him."

"Thanks for the warning Carl, I will stay close to Lee."

There was a full moon out, and they had no trouble seeing. Lee pointed out the pasture, the barn and the pig pen. The night air was a little cool, so he took his jacket off and put it around Mary's shoulder. "But Lee, you may need the coat?"

"I'm used to it Mary, but if I get cold I have and extra one in the barn. Now what do you want to look at first?"

"You and Carl got me excited about seeing Bama. Can we see him at night?"

"He sleeps in the pasture next to the barn. I think he would like to meet a pretty lady; it's not far to the pasture.

They walked to the corner where the fence was attached to the barn. There in the corner was the largest animal Mary had ever seen. She shivered, and put her arms around Lee. "That's the biggest cow that I have ever seen."

"It's not a cow Mary, it's a bull. Be careful what you say, he is very sensitive; don't think he would like being called a cow. There is a difference between the two."

"Thanks Lee, I think I know the facts, I took Biology in high school. They also told me about the birds and the bees. Can I pet him?"

"Don't know, I'm the only one that he has let touch him. Let me talk to him." " Bama, this is a good friend of mine. Her name is Mary, and she would like to pet your head."

Bama snorted and then lowered his head, and Mary petted him.

"See Bama, I like to be your friend too," and she rubbed his head and neck.

"Well I be damn, I would never thought that I would see that." Said Lee

The two of them stood by Bama, and while Mary was rubbing his head, she wanted to know where he got the name.

"I met a Marine name Bama; he got his name from Alabama when we fought together on Guadalcanal. I was wounded and sent to San Diego Hospital. Later I was with the UDT in Hawaii, and he was one of the instructors. We have been friends ever since, I'm sorry to say that I haven't seen him since the war. He was a giant of a man, and a good friend. Patting Bama, Lee said, "Since he was such a big bull, the name fit."

"What was the UDT team, or can you tell me about it?"

"Yes. The war is over, and the UDT has been disbanded."

"Lee, you said that you were wounded on Guadalcanal? Did you get shot real bad?"

"Not too bad, that's where I met Pat, the mother of little Lee."

"Was she in the Marines? Can you tell me about her?"

"No, she was a nurse at the San Diego Hospital, I wanted to date her but she said she was married. Found out later she wasn't, her boss said for her to tell the Marines, and they wouldn't brother her. Later I ran across her again in Hawaii, this time she told me the truth, that she wasn't married. I guess that's where our romance started. It's a long story Mary, I will tell you about it another time."

"I'm sorry Lee; I didn't mean to pry into your life. We have been gone an hour. I think we need to go back, before my sister calls out the Marines."

"Mary, before we go. I have enjoyed talking to you, and I want to hear more about yourself. Do you mind if I ask you to have supper with me this week-end. I know that we have just met, but I feel like I have known you for a long time?"

Mary looked at him. "I think that I would enjoy that. What night were you thinking about?"

"What about this coming Friday night, I could pick you up at your sister's house around 7 p.m.?"

When they got back to the house, everyone had a smile on their face. "Big brother, we thought that you two might have gotten lost. We were organizing a search party; Lora was getting worried about her sister, with the Marine's reputation. "

Mary blushed;" I think I was in good hands. We just talked, while I was rubbing Bama's head, time sorted slipped away."

"You rubbed Bamas head? I have been around him for a year, and he won't let me get close." Carl said with a surprised look on his face.

"Maybe he is just a good judge of character brother." Said Lee

Lee looked at the address one more time. It was Friday night and he had a date with Mary. "Damn, I'm as nervous as a sixteen year old kid on my first date, taking a girl to the prom. Let's see now, how long has it been? Pat has been dead for two years, and before that I was shipwrecked for a year. Hell, it's been over six years, no wonder I'm as nervous as a prostitute in church."

That house on the corner with the porch light on, that must be the house. He pulled in front and checked the number. Lee got out of the car and went up on the porch and pressed the door bell.

"Good evening Lee. I see you found the house." Lora said opening the door.

"Yes, no problems. Lucy gave me a map. It was easy to find."

"Mary will be ready in about ten minutes, please come inside and wait. For April, the nights are still cold." " Sure is," Lee said. "Tell Mary to take her time, I'm a little early."

"Hello Lee." Mary had come up behind her sister." I don't need any more time. What you see is what you get. More time I don't think would help."

"Mary, you're beautiful."

"I think I'm going to like dating you, even if you are half blind." She said taking his arm." Now, Mr. Marine, wine and dine me," as they headed to the door.

Lee opened the door for her, and they got in the car and went toward town.

"Where are we going to eat? I'm starved." Mary said moving close to him.

"They have opened a new Shoney's downtown, let's go there."

After they had eaten, they sat around and talked. "I don't want you to tell me, unless you want to, but Lucy tells me that they could write a book about your many adventures. She told me that you were attacked by a shark and then washed up on a small island half dead. Said that you spent a year on the island, and when they found you, they had you listed as' killed in action.' You have had many adventures, during the war. Me, I spent three years in an office with a one star General and never left California. It wasn't what I wanted; I had hoped to go to Hawaii."

" Yes, it's a shame that you didn't get to Hawaii; It was the most beautiful place in the world. Then the Japanese came and almost destroyed it. They sunk our ships, destroyed our planes, and killed thousands of our service men, women and civilians. That was where I met Pat again, and we started dating."

"My friend Rodney and I were stationed there about a year, before I went native on a little island called Zamami."

"Tell me about your friend Rodney; Lucy said that the two of you have been friends for years."

"Yes we have, his name is Rodney Sweeny. We met each other in China before the war. At that time I was a Corporal and he was a Private, I had couple years in the Corps ahead of him. Later we went to Cuba to stabilize conditions there; it was a rebellion between Fidel Castro and another Cuban. Our country didn't take sides, but acted like a good policeman. We used the island to train for jungle warfare. I guess that was when we got to be good friends."

"Outside of Guadalcanal, we made all of our missions together, and we were both D.I's together at San Diego. Our friendship goes back almost twenty five years. He sometimes kept a notebook, said he was going to write a book about our friendship and adventures some day. "

"I think he should, you two have had more than your share of adventures." said Mary and asked for another cup of coffee.

"Lee are you still in the reserves?"

"Yes, for one more year then I can retire with twenty years of service. I'm getting a little old for the job I was doing, so I don't think I have anything to worry about."

Mary looked at him and said. "Things don't look good for South Korea. If the North invaded them, it may pull the U.S. into another war."

The waiter came by and left the check. They then drove back to her house, and as they walked up to the door, Lee stopped and kissed her. "Mary, I would like to take you out tomorrow night, I know of a great B.B.Q. place. Unless you think that I'm rushing you?"

"Lee, we are not teenagers anymore. I like you, and enjoy being with you. I think we both have some lost time that we have missed… Yes, I love B.B.Q."

And That Was How It Began

For the next three months Mary and Lee were together two or three times a week. A couple that was in love, and with years to make up. Their friends were counting the days that they would soon marry.

Little Lee was seven years old in April, three years after Pat had died, Lee asked Mary to marry him.

On May 15th 1951 a wedding took place at a little white church in Hixson. The brides name was Mary Brown, the groom was Lee Robinson. Two best men, Carl Robinson and Rodney Sweeny. Two bridesmaids, Lucy Robinson and Lora Garner.

After the wedding, the couple said goodbye to their friends and left for Hawaii, for a two week honeymoon.

CHAPTER 19

Korea

While in Hawaii Lee took Mary to all of the five islands, and was amazed how quickly Honolulu had been rebuilt. The beaches were now open, and they spent lots of time building up their tan to show their friends back home. He took Mary to Kauai and showed her where he had trained for the UD Team, which was now deserted and fence in.

But all good things must come to an end; so after two weeks, they decided to come home. They both were missing little Lee and knew the work that was ahead of them. Lee wanted to add another room on to the house, and a playground outside.

Carl, Lucy, and little Lee met them at the airport, and when all the hugs were over they drove back to the farm. "Lee, I have bought two more cows, and that gives us twenty. We are in the cattle and milk business… Mary, now that you're a farmer's wife, can you milk a cow?"

"Not now, but as a farmer's wife, I can learn." Mary said holding the baby.

After three months work, another room was added, and Lee had started on a playground for the kids. Mary had pitched right in, being a farmer's wife, and she had learned to milk a cow. Carl's oldest two boys were big enough to be a help on the farm, but there was still plenty of work to go around. It was a happy and good life on the farm, and to Lee, the war was a long way off.

Three months after the wedding, Mary told Lee that she was pregnant. That night they all went out and celebrated. "Now, I know why I built that extra room" and he couldn't wait to call his friend Rodney.

Rodney and Sue were thrilled with the news, but told Lee he had some catching up to do. They had two boys and one girl. They promised to visit each other soon.

"Lee, are you still in the active Marine Reserves? I'm afraid that North Korea may invade South Korea. If they do, our country will have to send troops there. We have an agreement to protect South Korea. I'm not in the Reserves, but if they activate the UDT, we both may be called. I'm worried Lee, I have a family now and it looks like you have started one."

"Rod I have only three months left of Active Reserve. I don't think anything will happen before then. I think we have done our share of fighting. Look! We are getting old; let the young men fight it out. No Rod, I don't think they would call us."

"Hope your right Lee. Let us know when the baby is born, and we will be there."

"I will let you know Rod, and bring all your kids. With Carl's, yours, and mine, we can have our own ball team. And by the way, we have couple of horses now. The kids would love to ride them. Bye for now old buddy." And Lee hung up the phone.

"Honey does Rod think that you two may be called back to the Marines, if South Korea is invaded?" Mary said with a worried look on her face.

"Just man talk honey, don't you worry about it. I will be out for good in a couple months, besides I'm getting too old."

In the next two weeks, the papers and the radio talked about a possible war in Korea. United States said, if it happened, they would only send a small Division of Marines. It wouldn't be a war, but a police action, and we would only keep our Marines there maybe for six months.

On June 25th 1950, North Korea invaded South Korea, and the city of Seoul was taken, and they moved across the country.

For the next two months America stayed out of the war, and tried through The United Nations to settle the issues. All of the active Marines, and those in the Reserves listened to the news, worried that they might be called. They had done their share of fighting; ... let America stay out of this one.

All of the men that were in the Reserves stayed close to the radio, they knew if America sent troops to Korea, they would be the first to go, because of their battle experience.

Lee kept busy around the farm, but listened to the news

every day. Mary was now five months pregnant with his child, and she hoped and prayed that he would not be called, but she knew that her husband was worried.

August 5th, 1950 Carl and Lee had been in the pasture checking for broken fences, when Carl's boy Chad, came running up to them. "Uncle Lee, Mom says that you have a telegram."

Carl looked at his brother worried."Maybe it won't be from the War Department, Lee."

"Who else could it be from? Does my wife know that I have a telegram Chad?"

"No sir, I don't think so. It came to our house. Aunt Mary is doing the washing."

Lee laid his hammer down. "Brother, I guess that I will just have to go and see what Uncle Sam wants?"

When Lee walked into the house, Mary was holding the telegram with tears in her eyes. "They can't, you have already done more than your share."

Lee opened the envelope and a plane ticket fell on the floor. Mary picked it up. It was a one way ticket to Pearl Harbor, Hawaii.

It was from Admiral Needy. "Captain Lee Robinson, we are re-activating the UD Teams. Report to Major Crown when you get to Pearl Marine Corps Base in Hawaii. You have ten days to report. "

Lee read the telegram twice, and looked at the date. Then he handed it over to Mary who took it with trembling hands.

After reading it she gave it to Carl who had just come in

the house.

Mary put her arms around her husband, hugged him tight and cried. "It's not fair, you have fought one war. Let someone else fight this one."

"Honey, I have been trained for that type of warfare. They don't have enough experienced men. Besides it will take at least six months to train another team. The war will probably be over by then."

"Can I go to Hawaii with you?"

"Don't think so honey, UDT is highly classified. I'm too old to do any fighting; my job will be the training. I will be back in six months."

"In six months, our baby will be here." Mary said crying.

"Darling, I'm a Marine and I have to go where they send me. I do not have a choice. Unlike a civilian job, I can't tell them I quit. I will do my job, and you take care of the baby until I get back. Pray for me and help Lucy around the farm. This won't take long; after all they call it a "Police Action."

Lee and Mary spent as much time together as they could, but on the sixth day he started packing. He would have to fly to Atlanta, then to San Diego and catch a ride on a military plane to Pearl Harbor, Hawaii. After reporting to Major Crown, he would go to Kauai and his old base.

Carl droved Lee to the airport at Lovell Field, and watched him get on the plane. Mary had said her goodbye's at home; she did not want to see him leave at the field.

The connections were good, and now Lee was on a B-17 heading to the Air Force base in Hawaii.

When he landed he had a soldier drive him to the Marine Base, and went to headquarters to see Major Crown.

He told the Corporal at the desk that he wanted to see the Major.

"Good afternoon sir." Lee said and saluted the Major. "Captain Lee Robinson reporting, sir."

"Great Captain, you made good time. I didn't expect you until tomorrow."

"Captain Robinson, do you know why you are here?"

"The telegram said that they wanted me to reactivate the UD Team. Who will be in charge, sir?"

"From the orders that I have, you will be. We have some men there now, cleaning it up. I have a plane to fly you to Kauai, then you will have men coming in for the next three or four days. Our time is on a short schedule, and they are trying to find all of the experienced team. You won't have lots of time for training. Cut out some problems, and work on their swimming and detonations.

"How much time do I have Sir, if we don't get enough experienced men, then it will take at least three months to train new people."

"Sorry Captain, but you don't have three months. If you're lucky you might get two months. "

"Then I guess I better get started. Where is the driver to take me to the air field?" Lee said saluting the Major.

"Corporal get a jeep and take the Captain to the airfield. Then the Major stamped some papers and gave it to him. My telephone number is in those papers, if you need anything, call. You will have high priority. Just get some men trained. It's urgent."

The Corporal came in and picked up his bags. "Are you ready to go sir?"

"Yes, it seems so. Do I have a plane waiting to fly me to Kauai?"

"Yes sir, the Major set everything up."

"I bet he did," said Lee as he followed the Corporal, and to the jeep parked outside.

When he arrived in Kauai, the same Corporal picked up his bags and loaded them in a truck, where three Marines were waiting. "Good evening Sir." And then the Corporal got behind the wheel.

"Corporal, mind telling me your name. And let one of the other men drive. You need to get back to the Major."

"Bill Beck Sir and I'm now working for you, Sir."

"What about the Major, Beck?"

"He had me transferred to your outfit Sir, said that you could use all the help you could get."

"He's damn right I do, shaking his hand. Glad to have you aboard Bill."

When they arrived at the Base, the sign saying UDT had been put back up in the yard. A Marine sentry was standing at the front door, and stood at attention and saluted the Captain. When Lee walked inside, no one was at the front desk but then saw couple of Marines cleaning up. "Good afternoon Captain," as they stood and saluted.

After returning the salute, he said "As you were. Do we have anymore Marines around private?"

"Yes Sir, we have two in the pool, shall I get them Sir?"

Lee, looking at the desk said, "Bill do you have your files with you?"

"Yes Sir" handing his files to Lee

He read the files of Bill Beck. He had been in the Marines for two years, high school education, and had worked as an orderly for Major Crown. "Sergeant Beck, you will now be a desk jockey. When the other Marines come in, check and file their papers. Stamp their hand, and send them to me, understand?"

"Yes Sir, but I'm a Corporal Sir."

"You are now a Sergeant. Send your files to me later and I will sign it."

Lee then went into the G-room, and saw two men in the pool, and a Master Sergeant shouting at them."Move Johnson, hell, you can swim faster than that. Reed, if you don't stay afloat longer than five minutes I will open the cage and let the sharks out. What have I got to work with, a couple of civilians, hell! We will never win the war."

He knew that voice, smiled and walked up behind the Sergeant, "Give them hell, Rod. You will make UDT men out of them, or kill them."

Master Sergeant Rodney Sweeny turned and seeing the Captain, stood at attention, saluted, and then they hugged each other, while the two Marines in the pool watched with surprised faces.

"When did you get here Rod? Could you not have gotten deferred? You were out of the Active Reserves, and you had three children?"

"A Major came by and said that they needed experienced UDT men as quick as they could get them. My job would be to train, and I wouldn't go to Korea. I would be a non-combatant. I guess I could have turned it down, but I asked who would be in charge. He looked at his list and said, a Captain Lee Robinson. That did it, I had to come. I'm the swim instructor, Lee. But if you want me someplace else, just let me know."

"For now, that will be fine. Do we have a gym coach? Be nice if they could get Bama?" Lee said.

"He was killed Lee. I understand it was a bar room fight. He was shot when he went out the door. He had married, but then divorced. After that he would get drunk and fight anyone. I had heard about it, and went to the funeral. He was a good friend, and we could sure use him."

"The two Marines that you now have. Will they be ready in a month?" Lee asked

"No way, but I understand we have Charles Goons, and Jim Stoop coming back. Both are experienced; just need a little refresher course. Why, the rush Lee?"

The next day five more men showed up. One a former

Ranger name Wallace Griffin. He was immediately given the job of Gym instructor. And now Lee had his team. Lee dropped the language class, and a couple of more, and worked on fitness, hand to hand fighting, and swimming and demolition classes.

Everyone trained ten hours a day and Lee now had ten good men, worthy to be on the team. He had sent five back home or to their old unit. They had their two month, and he was happy that the Major hadn't called.

He wrote Mary every week, and outside of a little morning sickness, she was doing fine. She was happy that he wasn't in Korea.

September 5th, 1950 he got a call from Major Crown, and asked Lee to fly to the Marine base at Honolulu.

On arriving, Captain Lee Robinson was taken to the Major's office where General Boxer, Charles Seems, and Milton Combs from the C I A were also present.

After the introduction, Major Crown looked at Lee. "Captain, how many good UDT men can you deploy right now?"

"Ten men are ready to go, and another ten in two months, Sir."

"The men that's ready to go, are any of them experienced?" Asked General Boxer.

"Yes Sir, six of them had been on missions in the war. Couple served at the Marshall Island, and the other four were at Saipan and Okinawa. They are good men, Sir."

"Can you have the other team ready in another month?" Asked Major Crown

"That's pushing it Sir, they need at least a month or two. They are young, and yet to be tested."

The Major pushed a buzzer, and Corporal Maxwell came into the room. "Max, take the Captain outside and fix him a cup of coffee. I will buzz you when we are ready for the Captain to come back in."

As Lee and the Corporal went outside, the door was closed.

"Cream and sugar, Sir?"

"Yes Max, that will be fine," as Lee found a chair and sat down.

Forty-five minutes later, Lee was called back into the room.

"Captain Robinson, you and your ten selected team be at the Navy airbase in forty eight hours, pack what you will need for thirty days."

Lee went back to his base with mixed emotions. He had told Mary that he wouldn't be in combat, but would only train the UD Team. Now he was sure he would be sent to Korea. If the U.S. made a Marine Landing, then the beaches and the bay would need to be checked out. I will leave Rodney here; he can train the other men. He won't like it, but hell, he has three kids.

Going to his office, he gave Rod the names of ten men, and for them to be in his office at O200.

When they were all present, he filled them in on Major Crown's meeting.

"Does this mean that we are going to fight the North Koreans?" Goons asked.

"Look's like it Sergeant. I don't know, but our job will be to clear the beaches, and check the bottom for depth." Write your letters home, tell them you're going on a maneuver and it may be awhile before you write again. Then pack your gear for thirty days, any questions?" He paused and then said, "A plane will pick us up in forty eight hours and fly us to Pearl Navy Base."

After the meeting, Rodney came up to Lee. " Why wasn't I on the list? We have always been together?"

"I would have liked that, but someone has to be in charge here, and train the other men. Maybe you can bring the other team in two months. This war may last awhile. After all, it's only a Police action."

CHAPTER 20

Inchon Korea

The 5th of September, 1950, Captain Lee Robinson and ten members of the UDT team boarded a small D E. (destroyer escort), and with several destroyers, battle ship and two aircraft carriers, left Pearl Harbor and headed for the open seas.

September 10th they landed at Tokyo, Japan. Captain Lee Robinson and his team transferred to a submarine that would take them to Inchon, Korea.

When arriving at the shores of Inchon, the submarine rose to the surface. Lee and his men had been briefed on their mission, and the UD Team went to the deck of the submarine and climbed into two rubber boats, manned by crew members.

Each man knew his mission, and Captain Lee had the hardest job. Watching his men leave the submarine, while he stayed onboard. He watched as his men were out of sight, remembering what Major Blake had told him. *When you are in command, you will watch your men go in harm's way, while you stay behind and wait.*

"Captain Sir. You will have to go below; we are getting ready to submerge."

"Thank you bosum mate." Lee walked to the Conning tower and went below.

Lee tried to sleep, but kept waking up. Then he got a book and read, but later couldn't remember what he had just read. He went to the galley got a cup of coffee, and was sitting there when the Captain of the submarine came in.

"Your first command, Captain Lee?"

"Yes sir, I should be with my men. I don't like this waiting." Lee said.

"In every war, someone has to stay behind, while his men go into battle and many will die. When in command, you have to make the decisions who will stay and who will leave and fight the enemy. It is the rules of the chain of command. "

"Yes sir; that was one reason I didn't want to be an officer. I don't like to wait when someone else is doing my fighting. Do you ever get used to it?"

"No Captain, you don't. You just live with it."

Then the two men talked about their families, and the new war. After the fourth cup of coffee, Captain Been looked at his watch and said to Lee. "It's 0400 I'm going to raise the submarine; the men are due back at 0430."

As soon as the submarine reached the top, the crew opened the hatch and Lee was the third man on deck. Again it would be a long wait.

The crew manned the guns, while they watched for any sign of danger.

A bosum mate brought Lee another cup of coffee while he sat on an ammo box and waited.

The night was pitch black, and you could only see a few

ED ROBINETTE

yards out at sea. Lee watched for that flicker of light that would tell him his men were returning. He continued to wait and said a prayer for his men.

It was now 0500 a.m. and they were overdue. "Wait! I think I see a light signal. Yes, that would be one boat, but where is the other one?"

In a few minutes Lee saw the other light from the second boat. Captain Been came out and alerted his crew.

Soon both boats appeared, and Lee counted his men, they were all accounted for. He thanked God and went to the side to help his men aboard.

All of the men were back safely, and went below, while the submarine descended below the sea.

It was a good mission, the beaches where cleared, and they only saw a few soldiers along the shore. They planted explosives on a couple of mines, that wouldn't go off until after 48 hours. The men were excited about their first mission, and Captain Lee Robinson was proud of his new team.

Lee gathered the information and pictures from his men while the submarine headed back to Japan.

September 15th, 1950. The first Marines Division landed at Inchon, Korea, and with heavy fighting pushed North Korea back and retook Seoul.

Later they were joined by the Army's 7th Division, 3rd Infantry, and Troops from the United Nations.

The Adventures of Lee Robinson

Since Seoul had been retaken, and the combined forces were pushing North Korea back, Captain Lee and his UD Team came back and made their base in a small school house, outside the city of Puscan.

Lee and his men would now be used to check the beaches for any mines, and report them to the Navy's Mine Sweeper ship. A month after landing, our forces went to Wonsan City.

The UDT was asked to check the Wonsan Harbor for mines, and informed the Mine Sweeper, so it would be safe for our ships. Captain Lee Robinson had a crew and a P.T. boat assigned to him for paroling the beaches and harbors. Every day they would go out and check the bays and coastline, in case of an overlooked mine.

After two month, Lee got a letter from Master Sergeant Rodney Sweeny. He and his ten men were coming to join him in Korea. Major Crown was closing the base down in Hawaii, and he had great news for Lee.

The next day he got a call from an Admiral at Wonsan Harbor; one of the cargo ships had hit a mine and had sunk in the harbor, blocking the entrance. He needed Lee and his men to come and blow up the sunken ship so other ships could come in.

Captain Lee had his men to load extra explosives on the P.T. boat and they headed for Wonsan Harbor. It was dark when they arrived, so they waited until the next morning. After breakfast, Lee put on a rubber suit and mask, and with a partner dove down and looked at the sunken cargo ship. It had sunk stern first, sinking in the mud with the bow up. At low tide, a large ship would hit the bow. It would have to be removed.

When he came up and started back to his boat, he noticed another boat was tied on. After climbing back on aboard he was approached by a Navy Admiral.

"Captain, I'm Admiral Garner."

"Captain Lee Robinson Sir", saluting. Are you the one that requested to blow up this ship?"

"Can it be done?"

"Yes Sir, it's standing on its stern. If we blow a hole in the bow it would sink to the bottom and be level, we checked the depth. We may blow the smoke stacks, and you would have a minimum of thirty feet. If you're not planning on putting a battle ship in the harbor, I think you will be fine."

"Captain, you have a deep water suit?"

"No sir, why?"

"The cargo hold is full of can foods. I was wondering if it was possible to remove the can goods before you blow the ship, our soldiers could use them."

"Sir, could you give me about a week? I have ten more UD men coming, and the leader is very excited, and I think I know why. The Navy has been working on an "Aqualung." It is a new device where we could go deeper and stay as much as an hour, maybe longer, before we would have to come up. I got a report that it was successful, but wanted to do a little more testing when I left Hawaii a month ago. My men can blow the bow, then when my other team, and hopeful an "Aqualung" arrive we can drop a cargo net from another ship, and my men will have the time under water to load the nets."

"Captain, if you can do that, our troops will be happy.

They need those canned goods." "When do you want to blow the ship?"

"I need today to set the explosive. Could you have the other ships stay clear tomorrow morning? I think we can be ready by 0900. I have got to make sure it goes down even, and not turn over."

"Captain I have to leave now, it is in your hands. I will get the word to the other ships to stay clear tomorrow."

After the Admiral left, he had a couple of his men to go down and place explosives on the bow. When they finished, he would go down and check.

He went to every ship close by, and told them to move further away if they could, because the explosives would cause some large waves. All small ships must leave the harbor.

Lee went down and checked, everything was as good as they could get it.

Three hours later, the ships had moved, and the small boats had gone out to sea. Lee gave the orders to blow, and with a loud explosion, the ship slowly sunk to the bottom.

When the waves settled down, Lee and a couple of his men went down to check. The ship was sitting on bottom in an upright position. They put explosives on the smoke stacks and blew them. The mission had been successful.

They went back to their base camp and waited for Rodney, his men, and what he had hope for an," Aqualung."

The next day Lee hadn't heard anything, so he left one man at the base, and if Rod did show up for them to take the truck and drive to Wonsan Harbor. He was going back and if he saw the Admiral, he would explain why he sunk the ship yesterday instead of today.

When they arrived, Admiral Garner was sitting in a small boat. "Captain I thought you were going to sink the ship today?"

"I had planned to sir. But when I went to the other cargo ship to tell him, he said he could leave that day. I had all the small boats move out to sea. I didn't know who would come in today. I had a perfect window... The ship is upright on the bottom. I want to check the ship one more time, and then we will have to wait."

"Very well Captain, I hope we can get the can goods up when your men come in. When you are ready for a boat with a net and crane, see the Harbor Master at the dock. I have already told him about it."

After he left, Lee put on his wet suit and the three of them went down to check the ship and look at the cargo hold. When they pulled the top cover back, then the ship could drop the net on the deck. He didn't see any problems if he had enough men, and hopefully with an Aqualung."

Coming back up to their boat, Lee said, "Let's patrol up the beach a couple miles. I see on the map there is another bay. We might be lucky and find a North Korean fishing boat."

He knew he had passed where our Marines had cleared out the enemy, but he didn't see anyone on the shore, or was fired on. It was another mile to the next cove.

He was in luck; sitting in the cove were two fishing boats. Looking through his glasses he did not see any large guns on board.

He turned around and went back toward Wonsan, but

after a mile he went into the shore, after scouting the beach for any activity. Seeing none, and with his two 20mm guns pointing toward shore, he pulled up on the beach.

"I need five volunteers to walk back to the cove, two to each boat, and one spotter. I will give you an hour to walk, and attach the explosives to the bottom of the boat. Then I will be at the entrance to the cove. Signal me if you have any trouble, and we will come in firing and pick you up."

He had no trouble getting volunteers; he wished he could have been one of them. The men got out of the boat with plastic 'stick on mines.' The fifth man carried a sub-machine gun and a mortar launcher. Again, he warned, if you have trouble, head for the sea, he would be close to the beach. After the men got out of the boat, he slowly followed them toward the cove.

Lee stopped before he got to the cove and waited. After an hour he started the engines again and slowly went to the entrance, this time with the motor running. He heard a rifle shot, then a mortar blast, and a machine-gun. Followed with a loud explosion as the two fishing boats blew up and started burning.

A hand appeared on the side of Lee's boat, and a voice saying, "Would you fellows mind pulling us in the boat?"

The four men climbed into the boat, and then Lee went into the cove for the fifth man, who was waiting on shore.

"What was the rifle shot?" Lee asked

Sam said, "After we planted the mines, one of the men must have seen me swimming out to your boat. The water was real clear; I guess I didn't go under far enough. "

"Good job men. Two fishing boats sunk, means no fish for the North Korean troops tomorrow. Let's go home and just maybe, Rodney might be there."

When they arrived back at their base, a Marine truck was sitting outside. Captain Lee checked with his sentry who said that the men inside were UDT members, and had the correct papers. Going inside Lee was met by his friend.

"Good Morning Captain," said Master Sergeant Rodney Sweeny standing at attention, and saluting.

"Good Morning Sergeant," returning the salute. Rod I'm damn glad to see you and your men. I hope you brought me some good news about the Aqualung?"

"That I have, In fact I have one for each man, and a couple extra ones. The problem was with the breathing device. The French Naval Officer Jacques-Yves and Elmile Gagnan now use two hose regulators, instead of one. They strap on your chest. One gives the diver oxygen and nitrogen, and the other one release the exhaled air into the water. One or two tanks of the oxygen are strapped on your back. A regulator attached to the hose controls the release of the air."

"Have you tried it out Rod?"

"Yes, we have sir. We have in our pool and in the ocean. We can stay down for several hours with two tanks. The deepest we have been is a hundred feet, but I think we could go deeper, if we had to. They are working on a better 'wet suit', one that would keep us warm at a greater depth."

"Rod introduced me to your new men, then we will have breakfast and you can fill me in."

After they had finished eating, Rod said that they were

closing down the base in Hawaii, and they would establish a unit here, for the duration of the war. They now numbered eighteen team members. They would not be adding more men.

"Rod I have a job for all of you tomorrow, it's a good opportunity to try our new equipment out. My team has been up all night, so we are going to bed. Make yourself at home, or take a tour of Seoul, but don't let any of your men get lost. Breakfast will be a 0600, and be prepared to leave at 0900.

All of the new men got back from their sightseeing, and nobody got lost. At the required time for breakfast, the men were up and excited. After they had eaten, Lee said for them to get their gear and head for the truck.

Eighteen members plus Sergeant Rodney and Captain Robinson, made a team of twenty, more than enough to do the job.

Arriving at the P.T. boat, Rodney was surprised. "Captain Lee, you have your own Navy,"

"Our job is to patrol the beaches for mines, and sink all of the North Korean fishing boats, so we had to have our own boat. They also loaned us a driver and a gunner." Then he introduced the men to the navy personal, Chuck and Billie.

They pulled out from shore and headed for Wonsan Harbor, a two hour trip. "Captain where are our troops located?" asked Rod

"Sergeant, our U.N. forces are chasing them back so fast, the North Korean don't have time to stop and take a crap. They are above a place called Chosin Reservoir on our map.

General MacArthur wants to run them back to the sea, but there's a problem with the Chinese. They have an imaginary line we are not supposed to cross. So our President, MacArthur, and the Chinese are haggling about it. It will be a shame if our men are caught up fighting the North Koreans, and the Chinese."

Chuck, the Navy driver of the P.T. boat, looked at Lee and said, "Another ten minutes sir, where that ship is now coming out, that's Wonsan Harbor."

"Men, we are about to arrive, but first we have to go ashore, and I will have to find a boat with a crane and a net to bring up the can goods. In the meantime check you're gear and tanks."

When the P.T. boat went to the dock, Lee got out and went to the shack where the Harbor Master stayed.

In thirty minutes, Lee came back, got into the boat and said. "Chuck, take the boat to the sunken cargo ship, and drop your anchor."

Lee and Rod donned their wet suit, and put on an aqualung, and he showed Rod what he should do. Since they had time to wait for their boat, they went down to check on the ship. It was still sitting on the bottom upright. They then went on the deck and checked the storage compartment. The two men slid the cover back, and saw the hold full of boxes. They then went to a second hold and it had assortment of boxes. After breaking one crate open, it had winter coats. Lee nodded his head. "Yes, they need to get those too."

Going back up to their boat, Lee saw a small tug boat coming from shore.

"He turned the job over to Sergeant Rodney to go down

and supervise the loading, and have the men be careful. Tell the men not to go under the boxes, but to take them one layer at a time. And Rod you or one of your men report to me every hour."

The divers went below and spread the cargo net next to the hold. They then placed the boxes in the net.

It took all day, and some of the men came up and replaced their tanks, everything went smoothly, and by nightfall, the sunken cargo was empty of its cargo of cans and coats. Another good mission completed by the UD Team. When they finished, they headed back to their base, while Billie cooked their supper in the galley. It had been a long and tiring day.

CHAPTER 21

Toktong Pass

November 2nd 1950, the U.N. Forces under General MacArthur were to push the North Korean Army all the way to the Yalu River, which borders China. From his headquarters in Tokyo he commanded two separate United Nations columns moving north toward Manchuria. In the western half of North Korea, was the U.S. Eighth Army, augmented by South Korean, British, Australian, and Turkish troops, totaling more than 120,000 combat soldiers, who were overstretched in a thin line from Seoul to the Chosin Reservoir.

On the eastern side of the Korean peninsula was MacArthur's X Corps, 35,000 strong marching north to meet up with the Eight Army along the Yalu River. Commanded by the Army's Major General Almond. X Corps was a fusion of two South Korean Army divisions; a unit of British Royal Marines, U.S. Army Seventh and Third Divisions. Plus the First Marine Division commanded by Major General Oliver Smith. All told General Smith had about 15,000 Marines, stretched sixty-five miles to the Chosin Reservoir, "Changing-or the frozen Reservoir."

MacArthur's plan was to sweep the North Korea Army all the way to the Yalu River, and the American boys would be home for Christmas. This would be over in four months.

But a month earlier, the foreign minister of China, had issued a public warning to the Americans to keep their distance from the Yalu River. Mao Testing backed up his Minister's threats by massing several armies on the far side of the river. MacArthur brushed off Mao's move as "diplomatic blackmail." He told President Truman on Wake Island that he had no fear of Chinese intervention. Maybe a few volunteers may crossed the Yalu, barely enough to make up a division. But in fact rumors were running through the American lines that the Chinese had in fact begun infiltrating North Korea in mid-October.

The first Marine division had taken Hamhung, and Fox Company was told to take Sudon Gorge, a small village held by the North Koreans, It was here the Marines saw their first Chinese soldiers. Before Sudong, no more than a handful of Marines had ever seen a Chinese soldier, and others wouldn't have been able to tell the difference between a Chinese and a North Korean.

Fox Company had prepared a Thanksgiving dinner, and the men said that they hadn't seen a hostile Chinese soldier in four weeks since Sudong. The Chinese had simply disappeared, and a good feeling was slowly returning to the company. Maybe they would be home for Christmas.

Many in Fox Company believed that they were going to a small village, Yudam-ni at the northwestern tip of the Chosin Reservoir. There they would rejoin the bulk of their Seventh Regiment, and commence the final push to the Yalu River.

But word filtered down that they were headed not to the reservoir, but to Toktong Pass—seven miles north, between

Hagaru-ri and Yudam-ni. There they were to dig in along the lower ridgelines of the highest mountain, the 5,454-foot Toktong-san, where it cut through the pass. It was the only road into or out of the Chosin.

The mountains around Chosin and the Toktong Pass was the coldest places in North Korea, sometimes the temperature would drop to 25 degrees below zero. And that winter December 1950, would be the coldest on record.

The Marines of Fox Company were swathed in bulky layers of winter clothing. Each man wore a pair of "windproof" dungarees over a pair of puke-green wool trousers and cotton long johns; a four-tiered upper-body layer of cotton undershirt, wool top shirt, dungaree jacket, and Navy issue, calf-length, alpaca-lined hooded parka; a wool cap with earflaps and visor beneath a helmet; wool shoe pads and socks worn beneath cleated, rubberized winter boots, and heavy-duty gloves covering leather or canvas mittens. Some men had cut the trigger finger off their gloves.

Captain William Ed Barber a veteran of World War II was the new CO for Fox Company. Fewer than 250 freezing weary Marines would guard this pass, from the Chinese Ninth Army Group, a force of fifteen divisions totaling about 100,000 men planning to trap the 8,000 odd Marines at the Chosin Reservoir, and the weary Marines at the pass.

November 27th 1950

Lee and Rodney had just gotten up and were fixing breakfast when his UD team came in from their mission of patrolling the coast line. "Good morning men, breakfast will be ready in thirty minutes. Did you see any Chinese soldiers?"

"Captain we did see some, maybe a battalion camped out around the town of Hamhung. When they saw our boat they moved back into the woods. They had white uniforms on, and when they moved back in the snow bank we lost them."

One of the men spoke. "MacArthur said that only a few volunteers had crossed the Yalu River. What we saw was more than a few."

The Ranger, Ray Gaines then said." When coming back around Wonsan Harbor, I think I saw another group."

Rodney looking at Lee said. "Captain could this be the beginning of World War III?"

"I hope not Rod, but I'm concerned about it, don't care what MacArthur says.

After breakfast the men that were on patrol filled out their reports and went to bed.

"Lee, have you heard from Mary, her baby will be due soon. If we got back for Christmas like MacArthur says. You will be there when he is born?"

"Got a letter from her yesterday, said that she is having morning sickness. She said that the news is that we are pushing the North Korean soldiers back to China, and we were coming home before Christmas."

"Rod, I'm worried. The Chinese says if we cross the 38th Parallel line, they would fight with the North Korean Army, and I don't think Russia is happy about what we are doing. If that happens Truman said. That he wouldn't rule out dropping another Atomic Bomb. Things don't look good."

Lee heard voices outside, and then his Sentry came inside. "Sir, you have a Major and three other men that wish to see you, sir. Can I send them in?"

"Yes, send them in Corporal."

Lee and Rodney saluted the Major, and then they introduced each other.

Major Phillips, from the First Marines Headquarters. C.I.A., Director, Bill Sheets, Major Sam Woodstock, Army Rangers Company, and Lieutenant Linn Chan from the South Korean Army.

Lee asked the Major if Master Sergeant Rodney could stay. "Yes, he may be one of your team. Can we go somewhere more private Captain?"

He took the men into his school house office. "I think we can talk here Sir, my men were on a patrol last night, and are sleep in the school's cafeteria.

"Captain Lee, I'm sure you have heard the rumors that the Chinese Army are crossing the Yalu River and will fight with the North Korean Army. MacArthur said it's just a few volunteers."

"It's more than a few volunteers sir. My men saw about a battalion of Chinese surrounding the town of Hamhung, and some more at Wonsan."

"That Report is popping up in many places, and that is what we want to talk to you about, Captain."

"Colonel H.D. White had been hearing this for quite some time, word was sent to MacArthur but again he said that China wouldn't fight, it's just a few volunteers. "

"This didn't sit well with the Colonel, so he found a small

plane with a radio man and said he would take a map, and pinpoint every Chinese soldier he could find this side of the 38th Parallel line, then he would send it to MacArthur."

The Colonel did not want fighter planes with him, said the Chinese would just hide. He didn't think they would hide or shoot on a small plane.

"But they did. They were shot down around the Toktong Pass. We heard from the radio man, they had crashed but neither one was injured. He was excited about the map, said he had pin pointed hundreds of groups of Chinese soldiers. The radio man has given us the exact location where they went down, and where they would stay until help came."

"Isn't Fox Company close by sir?" asked Lee

"Fox Company and the 8th Army are surrounded. The First Marines are at the Chosin Reservoir, and from what the Colonel says, they may be cut off. We need to get that map, and then we can use our planes to bomb the S.O.B."

"What can my men do sir?" asked Lee

"Captain, if we send a large unit in to the mountains, the Chinese would meet us and we would have a big fight. Hell, we don't know how many they are, we may be outnumbered, and they would see us coming and set up their defenses. No, it has to be a small group, slip in there, get the two men, and then get the hell out."

"How can we find them sir?" asked Lee.

"The radio man gave us the location where the plane went down. After we confirmed our plans to him, he would set the plane on fire, and then they would go north pass the plane and find some place to hide. By them going north, the Chinese wouldn't look for them until they got to the plane, then they would look south for them, he hopes."

"You would go in at night, they have a red lens flashlight, and you would contact each other."

"I'm assuming you want me to go sir, how many men should I take?"

"Captain Lee, I know you and your men are professionals working at night, but you will need some fire power if you are discovered."

"This is my plan. Major Sam Woodstock is an Army Ranger, and fought at New Guinea and Guadalcanal. He will be in charge, with four of his men with Thomson machine guns, two men with a mortar, and a Navy Corpsman. Lieutenant Linn Chan knows the country and the location; he can also speak Chinese if it is necessary. That is nine men, plus you and how many men you think you will need. We need a small group, but enough to fight your way out if discovered. It would be nice if we can get the men out without alerting the Chinese."

"Now, show me a table and let's look at the map. Linn showed us where the plane went down."

"Captain, can you and your men be ready tomorrow at 0900?"

"Yes Sir, as soon as they wake up I will select the men."

"Good, you will ride in a truck with Fox Company; they are going to take a small town called Sudon. While they are fighting and clearing out the North Koreans, your group will slip out on the back road, and go on your way unnoticed. Linn knows of a trail that's off the road. He said it would be a ten mile walk to the mountains, then five miles to the plane crash. That's the plan Captain, give me a list of the men you are taking, and may God be with you."

After Major Phillips and the C.I.A. man left, Major Sam Woodstock said to Captain Lee. "Captain when will you have your men selected? I would like to talk to them before we go tomorrow."

"Major can you have supper with us at 1800 I will have the men assembled that are going."

"That will be fine Captain, and if you have enough food I will bring my men, we need to have our men meet and find out what supplies they will need. Lieutenant Chan said it could drop to 25 below zero in the mountains, and we must be prepared for the cold. I hope Colonel White and his pilot has warm clothing."

"I will see you at 1800 "the Major said, and he and Lieutenant Linn Chan walked out the door.

"Well Rodney, what do you think?"

"Don't think it will be a cake walk sir. If we run into a company of Chinese, someone is going to get killed. And Captain, 25 below, our guns will freeze up, and we will have to wear so many clothes to keep warm, we won't be able to walk."

"Rod, get me the men's roster, we need to pick five or six good men and then I'm going to ask for volunteers."

"You know they all will volunteer sir. And I hope my name

is at the top of the list."

"Rod, do you think that both of us should go? Why don't you stay here and lead the men on shore patrol, besides you have three kids at home. Anything happen to you, Sue would kill me."

"Captain, we have always been together, you watch my back, and I will watch yours. It's Semper Fi, Lee." (Always faithful)

Lee agreed for Rod to go, and he went and got the men's roster.

"The first man I want is Army Ranger Ray Gaines. He could take down a squad of Chinks. With his fighting experience, he will be handy."

"Next man is Marine Raider, Carl Fox. Another good Marine in a fight."

"And the last man is the 6ft 4' Ash Baker, from the mountains of Tennessee."

"Counting you and me that will give us five men, and with the Major's men we have a total of fourteen good men."

"Rod, when those men wake up, tell them I want to see them. Now go find some hamburger meat, we will have hamburgers and cokes for tonight."

After Rodney left, Lee went to the Marine Base and signed for five Thomson Machine guns, with ten clips for each man. His men had already been issued a Colt 45. M-1 rifles and Carbines. He picked up another box of hand grenades. Then he called Major Woodstock, told him the number of men and his Thomson's, and then asked him about the winter clothing.

"Captain, give me their height and weight, and shoe size. I

will have them sent over tonight."

When Lee got back to his headquarters, most of the men were awake, and he asked Rodney to send to his office, the men that had been picked.

He asked each man, told them of their mission, and said it could be very dangerous, some may be killed.

Every man selected was willing to go, in spite of the danger.

The rest of the men would be on patrol, and would have the P.T. boat out in the bay, from the town of Hamhung, and stay there for three days.

At 0600 Major Woodstock and his men showed up at Lee's headquarters. After supper, the team of 14 men went into one of the school rooms.

"Major, is 14 men enough? More of my men would be glad to go." Said Lee

"Captain, I think that we have all that we need. Small enough to slip in and some good men for a fire fight. Have you planned for an evacuation, if needed?"

"Yes sir, I have. My P.T .boat and crew will sit in the bay outside of the town of Hamhung, for three days. If we can get the Colonel and his pilot out. And then to town, we can drive back to Sudon by sea. That is, if we still own it."

"I will call the Colonel White to have Fox Company hit Sudon in two days. It should be cleared by the time we get there. And if they have enough men, to clear Hamhung again."

The Major looked at Lee's men, and nodded approval. "Men, I have brought some cold weather gear, check and see if they will fit. "Captain, you said that you have some Thomson machine guns, and Carbines? Have your men stripped them down and put bear grease on the working parts, and some on the ammunition, the cold will freeze the guns, and the bullets will jamb. If you use the carbine, aim for the head, they are wearing a heavy vest, and our carbine won't penetrate. Have one or two of your men carry the M-I rifle instead of the carbine, heavier but more fire power."

The meeting lasted for hours, and every man knew what he was to do. Then the Major asked every man to memorize the map in case they got split up. When no one could think of another question, the Major called the meeting to a close.

"The trucks will be in front of your school house, tomorrow at 0900, the man that's late will be left. Get a goodnight sleep; it may be your last one for the next two days."

It was a cold morning in November when the trucks arrived at the school house, and Captain Lee and his men got into the truck behind Major Woodstock. Lee and Rodney got into the cab, while his men got into the covered back. It would be a six hour drive to Wonsan, then another three hours to Sudon. It would be dark when they got there, but that was the plan.

After six hours they arrived at Wonsan, and everyone was pleased that it was still in U.N. Forces hand. But they were told that the Chinese were in the hills surrounding the town.

They filled up with gas, and after thirty minutes they were on the road again. Just outside of town they picked up a platoon of R.O.K. (South Koreans) and in another ten miles, they met the Marines Fox Company. Together these two platoons would hit Sudon, clearing out the North Koreans, and the Chinese if they were there.

It was getting dark, and they were five miles away and no one had seen any Chinese. The Marines were pleased---maybe they went back to the border, and the North Koreans wouldn't be any trouble.

South Koreans were on one end of town, and Fox Company Marines would go into the middle. Then all hell broke loose, Chinese soldiers came running out of the trees, and hills. They blew their bugles, lit flares, and shouted," Death to the Americans." Major Woodstock had Captain Lee and the team pulled their trucks to the side of the road, while the fight for the town raged on.

The Chinese came in waves, not fearing the guns, and were dropped one after another, later it was said that they were on drugs, and fighting like they wanted to die. They came by the hundreds, and died the same way.

"Major if these are just a few volunteer stragglers, and then we are in trouble." said Lee.

The fight lasted about three hours, then a Lieutenant came up to the Major and said they owned the town, and it was time for them to go.

CHAPTER 22

Rescued from the Toktong Pass

Major Woodstock, motioned for his team to get out of the trucks, and asked Captain Lee Robinson to see him.

"Captain, I want you behind my men, if we get hit then maybe you won't be shot, and you can carry on with the mission. We need to rescue Colonel White and get that map. From tonight's fight, I'm sure the Chinese are here in great numbers. Tell your men no talking, and not to bunch up. Travel in a single file when possible."

Lee started to salute, but stopped. "Thanks Lee, tell your men that there will be no mention of rank. Everyone will address each other by their first name only. We can't have the Chinese picking off the officers."

With Lieutenant Linn Chan in front of the column they followed one man after another, each man watching both sides of the trail. They had walked about an hour, when Sam called a break for ten minutes. The trail had now begun to twist and get steeper as they approached the mountains. Every man took some water and ate a candy bar for energy.

"How much longer Linn before we start up the Toktong Mountains?" Sam asked.

"Another two hours Sam, and when we start up the trail, that's where we may be spotted from the road above. When we get there, have the men to walk next to the tree line, and slow. "

They arrived at the trail that goes up the mountain, but the woods which gave them cover ended. There was a field, with waist high grass that they would have to cross for about a quarter mile, before they could pick up the tree covered path again.

It was getting close to day break, and Sam thought that they need to stop here, and get some sleep before going across the open field. He gave the order for a 50/50 watch. (One man awake, one man sleep)

"Lee what do think our chances are of finding the Colonel?" Rod asked while they were eating a can of beans.

"Less than 50 percent Rod. It's been three days. Unless they found cover, they probably frozen to death, or the Chinese caught them. Rod you get some sleep, I will take the first watch."

It was 1700 p.m. and the sky was getting dark and the wind was screaming out of the arctic and across the Manchurian plains. It was the fiercest any man had ever encountered. The area around the Chosin Reservoir was said to be the coldest place in Korea, and the wind was blowing in a cold blast, and then it started snowing. Sam looked at a thermometer that he had in his back pack, it showed ten below zero.

Lee made some coffee with his thermos stove, and then he had his men put on some dry socks, and check their toes, they had to be careful of frostbite.

It was 1900, and the snow had already put three inches on the ground, and Linn said it was time to go. Each man lay on the ground so that the snow would be on their backs and would cover them, as they crawled through the grass of the open field. It was a tiresome and slow trip, but with the blinding snow they hoped they weren't spotted.

The rescue team made it across the field without any contact, and reached the path that goes up toward Toktong Pass.

Linn warned the team that their path was about a hundred yards below the road, and where some of the Chinese soldiers may be hiding. He told Sam and Lee that they could stay on the path for another hour, but then they would have to get on the road to find the wrecked plane, and then go past the plane another mile where the Colonel and the pilot may be hiding.

The snow and wind continued, and Linn kept a close watch on his compass, and they had missed their path several times. Twice they had to double back. Lee told Rod how lucky they were to have Linn, without him they would be lost.

In about an hour, Linn held up his hand, and pointed up to the road. The team checked their guns, and then climbed up the path to the road that leads to the Pass, and hopeful to the plane crash.

The snow was deeper on the road, at least a foot. Sam looked at his watch, and it was 0200 a.m.

They walked for another hour, and then Linn held up his hands, and pointed around the curve to Sam and Lee. Both men gave the signal for the men to attached their bayonets, and have their guns at ready.

As they walked around the curve, they saw the wrecked plane. They stood still and waited for five minutes, and then with the men on both sides of the road, Sam and Lee slowly walked toward the plane.

A shot was fired from the trees, and Major Sam Woodstock fell to the ground with a bullet in his head. Everyone started firing at where they thought the shot came from, and Lee crawled over to where Sam was lying. His friend was dead.

There weren't any more shots, so Lee had his men to go into the wooded bank and check. They found a dead Chinese soldier, who must have been left to watch the plane. He was dead, but Lee knew that others had heard the shots, and their mission would be known.

Lee took charge and had a couple of the Major's men wrap up the body and carry it back to the wrecked plane, then find a place on the side of the road and hide the body the best they could, and then cut a notch in a tree so he could be picked up later.

They would go another mile forward, maybe the Colonel had heard the shooting and would come out of hiding, but he alerted the men that he was sure that the Chinese heard, and may come running.

They walked down the road, split up with a man on each side of the road, and criss-crossing every few minutes, never standing still where they might be a target. They had covered about a mile without making any contact with the two missing men.

The Army Ranger Ray Gaines and Marine Raider Carl Fox had the point about a hundred yards ahead of Lee and his men, when they came to a stop. Ray came back to see the Captain.

"Sir, we have company. Carl and I hear a truck coming down the road."

"Thanks Ray. Then Lee had his men to go on both sides of the road and hide in the woods, no shooting unless spotted."

In another ten minutes a big truck appeared, carrying about thirty Chinese soldiers in the back. They passed Lee and his men and went down the road toward the plane crash. "

When the truck was out of sight, Captain Lee mustered his men at the side of the road.

"Men we have gone a mile further than we were told that we would make contact with the Colonel. I think that they are dead or captured. Since we know that a truck full of soldiers is behind us, we don't know how many of them are ahead. My plan is to go forward another five miles and see if we can find their camp. They may just have the two missing men there. Any questions or other plans?"

"Captain, what if we come across a large force, or maybe a Battalion?" asked Ray.

The Captain looked at Ray. "That's Lee, no mention of ranks, remember. If we find a small group we look for the Colonel, if too large, we turn around and go back, and again look around the plane's wreck. We have come too far to quit. "

Again the men scattered about, no one within in a yard of each other and walked slowly up the road toward the Toktong Pass. Lee looked at his watch, it was 0400 a.m. soon it would be daylight, and they would have to find a place to hide. The snow began again, and the wind would cut through their clothes, as the temperature dropped. Lee had never felt so cold; the South Pacific war was never like this. Here you were fighting two enemies, the Chinese and the bitter cold.

Ash Baker who was now at the point came walking fast and approached Lee.

"Sir, we can smell smoke, and the sky is lit up in front of us."

Lee had his men to stop, and he and Rodney went forward to check it out, after about a hundred yards they looked down into a meadow, and saw a dying wood fire and about forty tents close by. Five or six soldiers were sitting by the fire. Down and behind the tents he saw a wooden building, with a guard standing outside. He motioned Rodney that they might be holding the Colonel in the shed.

"Why would they need a guard, if someone wasn't inside?" asked Lee

"I think you're right Lee. Someone or something important is in that building."

"Rod most of them are asleep. I think we have the surprise and the fire power to take them out and check that building. Let's go back and talk to the men."

Lee gathered his men and told them of his plans. " The mortar men would set up their gun to hit the center of the tents, while half of the men would go to the left and kill the men that came running out of the tents. Lee and the others would go to the right of the tents, and catch the ones on that side. During the fire fight, he and Ray would slip down to the building and check it out. It is now 0500 a.m. everyone get in position, check your guns and make sure they are not froze up. We will start firing at 0600. Any questions?"

Everyone moved into their position and at the set time open with the mortars, and then the Chinese soldiers came running out of their tents and into the deadly fire of the Marines. The fire fight lasted about ten minutes, and then he and Ray went down to the building, where two men were out front.

As they got close they saw that one soldier was an officer, both were looking at the fight on the hill. Lee motion that he would take the officer, and Ray the guard. Then they would both rush inside.

Both of the soldiers went down as they opened fire, and then they rushed to the door, with Ray spotting another guard inside, and slamming him against the wall, and cutting his throat. Lee looked over in the corner and saw an officer bound with tape and lying on a cot.

"Colonel White?" Lee said loosening the tape.

"Yes! Thank God. I had about given up hope."

"Colonel, I'm Captain Lee Robinson, the big Marine with me is Sergeant Ray Gaines. We only have a small unit, but we are going to get you back. Where is your pilot?"

"They shot him, but they thought I may be of some use to them. They don't know what I was doing."

"Do you have the map sir?"

"Yes, but it's hiding at the plane crash."

"Good, we can pick it up on the way back. Colonel, pick up the dead soldier's gun and follow us.

The three of them ran up the hill where the team was just ending the battle, and Lee had J.R., the Corpsman, exam the Colonel.

It was 0700 in the morning and the snow was at least 8" on the ground and it was still snowing. Lee had the men to throw more wood on the fire, and have the men to put on dry socks, and exam their feet for frostbite. When checking his men, only one man was injured in the hand. They were lucky that they caught the Chinese by surprise.

After breakfast they found some more mortar shells and a case of 'potato masher' (grenades). They were preparing to leave when Rodney came up to the Captain.

"Lee, I believe we have company coming for breakfast." Pointing up to the top of the hill.

On the hill were at least a hundred Chinese soldiers looking down on them.

"Rod, that's more than we saw in the truck, where did the rest of them come from?"

"Well we can't get around them, and they are in the Pass between us and Fox Company, so I guess we will have to dig in and wait on them to charge us" Lee said.

"Rod, have the men meet me here. We have got to make some plans, then looking over to Colonel White. Sir, you are the ranking officer, do you want to take the command?"

"No Captain, this is your mission, I was not in a combat division. We abide by your decision.

When the men gathered around Lee, he asked if they still had plenty of ammunition, and what he wanted them to do.

"Men we are outnumbered at least ten to one, but that is nice odds for a Marine. But we will have to make sure every shot fired will hit a target, or we will run out of ammunition. Look around the area and pick up any guns or ammunition that you can use. Then pick your spot, and most of the Chinese soldiers are frozen by now, so use them to fortify your position. Put three bodies in front, two deep, then two on each side. Make a square from the dead bodies. The snow will cover them up in twenty minutes, so you won't have to look at their faces. The ground is frozen, so we can't dig fox holes, and that is the only choice we have."

"Captain, I just thought of something. When I was captured, I remember that they took our radio. If it's still in the shed, we can call for air support."

"That's great Colonel, take Lieutenant Chan with you, he will know our location."

The Colonel left to check on the radio, and the men started gathering the dead bodies, while Lee checked on their positions. The two mortar men taking the point, and the divided Marines on the right and to the left.

Lee looked up on the hill and the soldiers had a fire going, and were eating breakfast, they were in no hurry to slaughter a few Marines, that had no place to go.

The Marines had set up their position, and were now waiting for the attack, that Lee knew would come at any time.

Then a Bugler blared, and loud shouting of "death to the Marines" and the Chinese soldiers came running down the hill, side by side, without any regard to our guns.

At a hundred yards Lee shouted fire, and the front row went down, but others stepped over them and kept coming. It reminded him of the Japanese Bonsai attack in World War II. They seem to have no regard of their deaths.

They kept coming in waves, even as the Marines mowed them down, and only a few made it close enough to throw their potato mashers. Lee watched two jump in the box that Rodney was in. But in five minutes, Rod gave him the okay sign.

The fight hadn't lasted thirty minutes before the Bugler sounded again, and they retreated and went back up on the hill.

Lee checked with Rodney, and his men were okay. And then he checked on the mortar crew, and found both of them dead. He was now down to eleven men and one wounded. He knew that there would be other attacks, and wonder how long could his men hold out.

The Colonel and Chan came running up the hill. "Great news Lee, we found the radio, and planes are coming to our aid.

Lee and the men said, "Amen, the Fly Boys are on the way."

Two of the men volunteered to man the mortars, after they found out that it would still work. They pulled the two dead Marines out, and lay them outside their gun emplacement; even in death they may stop a bullet, and save a Marine.

Thirty minutes later the Bugler sounded again, and with the clanging of drums, and the shouting of" Marines, you die."

Again they came rushing down the hill, side by side, with no regard to their safety.

Lee had the men to wait until they got within a hundred yards, and then shouted" Fire." The front row went down, but to his amazement the enemy stepped over their fallen comrades, and kept coming. The Colonel and Chan were firing as fast as they could, then he saw a Chinese throw a grenade into Rodney's hole, but just as fast he picked it up and threw it back, killing two. They were now in their fox hole and one stuck a bayonet into Linn Chan's chest, and Lee's gun was now empty, so holding the hot barrel he swung and caught the Chinese soldier on the side of the head.

He was now using his 45, the only weapon that had any bullets left, when he heard a roar as an Austrian Mustang came in flying low with guns firing at the Chinese. Other planes soon appeared, and they drove the enemy back. And then two F-4-U Marine Corsairs arrived and dropped napalm bombs as the Chinese retreated back up on the hill.

Lee checked on Chan, but he was dead. The Colonel had a head wound, but wasn't life threatening. Then he went over to Rodney's fox hole and found him lying on the ground holding his leg. Only four other Marines were alive.

"Damn Lee, they shot me in the same hip that I was wounded at Iwo Jima. Are you okay Lee?"

"Yes, I think so, but if it wasn't for our planes, we all would have been killed."

"What about the Colonel, Lee?"

"He's okay, had a bullet glance off his head, but Linn is

dead, got stuck by a bayonet in the chest. What about Carl and Ash?"

"Both dead Lee, only me, the Corpsman and Ray Gaines are left. "

"Well I guess that only leaves the five of us. When the planes leaves the Chinese will be back. Do you have any more ammunition?"

"Two more clips for my machine gun, but maybe we can find some from our dead friends."

There were no more signs of the Chinese, but our planes kept strafing and dropping their bombs, and then a Marine plane came over, dipped his wings and then left.

Again, Lee and his men were alone. He knew they could not take another attack, with only five of them left. J.R. the Corpsman checked Rodney's hip and told him that the bullet had gone through his hip. Then he stuck a morphine cap into his mouth to thaw it out, and then stuck it in Rod's leg.

"The good thing about this cold weather he said, the cold has stopped the flow of blood."

"Well I'm glad it's good for something, because I'm freezing my butt off." Said Rodney.

"Men, they will be back, so add some more bodies around your bunker, and we all will stay together. We will fight and die together,"

"Captain, I'm sorry to have gotten you and your boys into this situation. You should have let me alone."

"Colonel, it's not your fault. We wanted to save you and the map, but now I don't think any of us will get back alive.

We aren't dead yet, so maybe we can take a few more Chinese with us."

"Lee, it's been an hour, what the hell are they waiting on?" said Ray stomping his feet.

"Ray, do you have any more dry socks?"Asked Lee

"No Captain and I think my toes are frostbitten."

"J. R., Check some of the dead men, and see if you can find some dry socks, then check Ray's feet"

"Aw Hell Lee, what difference does it make, we all will be dead before the day's over."

"We're not dead yet Ray. J.R. do like I said."

"Lee, I hear firing. It's coming from up in the Pass. Who are the Chinese shooting at?"

Lee and the other Marines listened, yes there was a fire fight, but with who?

Now there were sounds of a big gun. "That's a 155 Howitzer. Only the Marines have one of those. I believe we may have some help."Lee said

The Colonel had been looking through his glasses in the opposite direction, and said. "Don't get your hopes up men, I see nearly 1000 soldiers heading our way. May God help us!"

Lee took the glasses and looked, and saw at least a thousand men walking and trucks pulling large guns. He wiped the snow off his glasses and looked again, and this time he was smiling. "Colonel, those are Marines."

The two men watched as they kept coming toward them, and by now you could tell that they weren't marching, but walking in a staggering file.

Lee and the men watched, for the first time in history, the proud Marines were retreating. It was the First Division and the 8th Army pushed back by 100,000 Chinese, from the Chosin Reservoir.

CHAPTER 23

The Retreat

It was a sad sight for the men to watch, the First Division, heroes of Guadalcanal and other battles, now wounded, and exhausted walking toward the Toktong Pass. Later war correspondents, visiting the rear areas, asked the commander of the First Division, General Oliver P. Smith, about the Chosin withdrawal. His response was "Retreat, hell," he was quoted as saying. "We're just attacking in another direction."

Meantime the battle in the Pass had quieted down and Marines were approaching Lee and his men. He commanded his men to hold their guns over their heads, with both hands. When they got close, he shouted out. "American Marines."

Colonel White and Captain Robinson went forward to meet the Major who was in charge of the rescue company.

They saluted and shook hands and then Lee introduced his men to Major Brown.

"How many men do you have Major?" asked Colonel White

"A full Company, Sir. Approximately one hundred men before our fight. We lost ten men and twenty-two wounded. We have a couple of Corpsman tending to them now. Do you have any wounded sir?"

"Yes Colonel we do. We have a corpsman, but he needs some supplies."

"I will have my men get right on it sir."

The rest of the company started coming down the hill. Captain Green saluted the Major and said."We have the pass secured sir, we counted a hundred and twenty Chinese bodies, and some had been dead for several hours he said, looking at Lee."

"We just had a fire fight an hour before your men came." Said Lee

"Just the five of you?"

"Well we started out with 14 men on a rescue mission four days ago. We lost some good Marines."

"When have you and your men eaten Captain Robinson?" asked the Major.

"Had a couple cans of beans this morning, Sir."

"Captain Green have your cook fix these Marines a hot meal, and tell our Corpsman to check them out. I understand their Corpsman is out of supplies."

"Yes sir, I will get right on it. Which side do you want me to set up our 155 Howitzer sir? I see a long line of soldiers behind you?"

Lee laughed. "I hate to say it Major, but that's the First Marine Division, with the Eight Army behind them. They have about 300,000 Chinese chasing them, from the Chosin Reservoir. They are about ten miles away."

The Colonel, and Lee took the Major aside and told him of their mission, and that he had to get back to Hagaru-ri with his map. The last he heard, we had an airfield there.

"Yes Colonel we still have the town, and there is an airfield, but don't know how long we can keep it. My job is to get you there, and then help Fox Company hold the Pass, and keep the back door open. When your men have eaten and gotten a little rest, I will send a platoon with you, and the Captain with his men. I think the Pass is clear now, but there may still be some snipers that we missed."

The Captain, looking at Lee. " Whenever you and the men are ready, Sir."

Lee assembled his men, told them to pack light, and only take what was needed. We still may do some fighting, so make sure you have plenty of ammunition.

Captain Green had two men carry Rodney on a stretcher up to the top of the hill, where two trucks were parked. "You mean we don't have to walk back?" said Lee

"No sir, If we don't run into some Chinese you can ride all the way back to Hagaru-ri , that is if we still own the town. " The Captain said

As the trucks drove down the road, a shot would sound and a bullet would hit the cab, but then the Marines would open up with their machine guns, and all would be quiet again. They stopped at the wrecked plane, and Colonel White found his map, and then looking at Lee said. "Some good Marines died for this, and now I hope we can bomb some Chinese bases."

It took six hours to get to Hagaru-ri by truck, Lee and his men had taken two days, after the fight at Sudon City. When the trucks exited the mountain and approached the town, Captain Green had Lee's men to lie down on the floor, and the trucks came to a stop. Then he and his men went forward and checked out the town.

Lee didn't hear any firing, and in thirty minutes the Captain came back and told him that they still own the town, but the Chinese came around every night, and would fire on the town.

"There's a C-47 plane waiting on the airstrip that would fly them to Seoul, and take off the wounded, and then fly Lee and his men to their base at Pusan." said Captain Green.

When they got to the plane, Lee asked if Captain Green was coming with them.

"No sir, I wish I could, but my orders are to bring the Colonel and your men here to the airfield, then get my ass back, I think that's what the Major said."

"My men have got to help Fox Company to keep the back door open for the Army and the First Marine Division. " And then he shook everyone's hands.

"Good luck Captain, and thanks for the ride."Lee said shaking his hand.

The plane landed at the airfield in Seoul, and the wounded were taken off and were then loaded on another plane, heading for Japan. Lee went over to Rodney's stretcher and shook his hand. "Rod old boy, looks like you are going to beat me home. How does your leg feel?"

"Doesn't hurt much now, the medic give me a morphine shot on the plane. But I guess I will be like 'Chester on Gunsmoke.' You know the one that limps, with Marshall Dillon?"

"Be sure to call Sue when you get to Japan, she may want to stay with you there."

"Lee do you want me to call Mary?"

"No, I will call her when I get back to our base. Hell I may be a new daddy by now, she was due a months ago."

"Lee I hope the First Division gets out of the Chosin Reservoir, MacArthur has gotten lots of our Marines killed."

"Rod did you not hear what Captain Green said? He said that President Truman fired him. He had told the President three times, that China wouldn't enter the war. Said there may be a few volunteers, but they wouldn't be any trouble. "

"Good, serves him right. He got lots of good men killed. Got to go now Lee, they are getting ready to close the door. See you in the States in a couple months."

Lee watched the C-47 leave for Japan, and then he walked over to his plane, that would take him to Pusan City and to his UDT unit.

He was met at the airport by a couple of his men."Afternoon Captain, glad to have you back." Said D.B. Reeves

"Where's Rodney sir?" Jim Wilson asked

"On his way to Japan, his fighting days are over. With two purple hearts, a soldier will no longer be in combat. He got wounded in the same leg again." Lee said.

Lee climbed into the truck that would take him back to his base. He asked D.B. if they had been making any contact with the Chinese."Yes Sir, we have been up to Wonsan Harbor a couple of times. You can see them in small groups along the shore. We sunk four North Korean fishing boats, and rescued some Army soldiers that were cut off from their unit."

"Captain since the Chinese has come into South Korea; will we be in another war?"

"I hope not D.B. President Truman fired MacArthur, but it may have come too late. I understand there are over 300,000 thousands Chinese in North Korea. The Colonel, we brought back, has a map of most of their locations, and we hope to bomb them. We lost some good men on our mission D.B."

"Yes sir and we will miss Carl, Ash, and the other men. But we are glad you and Rodney made it back. What about our unit, Sir? We have been hearing some scuttlebutt that they may do away with the UDT?"

"I heard the same thing, D.B. I guess it depends on what the Chinese are going to do."

"Well it looks like I made it back, is the mail on my desk?"

"Yes sir and you have couple of telegrams also." D.B. said

Lee went to his desk and found the two telegrams, and began to read the first one."Dear Lee I have written several letters, but you have not answered, I hope it was because you were away someplace and couldn't write. Please write and tell me that you are alright. I worry so much. Our baby may come at any day."

He then opened the second telegram written three days later. "Dear Lee, my darling. Please let me hear from you. You have a 7 pound girl, born yesterday. I had to have a name to put on the birth certificate. Your son," little Lee" wanted to name her Patricia, or Pat, said he wanted his new sister named after his mother. I hope this will be alright with you? If not, tell me another name. Please let me hear from you, the news said that the Chinese has entered the war, and it may be World War III. The President said he might drop an atomic bomb if the Chinese takes all of Korea." Love Mary

"D.B., come in here."

"Yes, Captain?"

"D.B. I'm a father of a 7 pound girl, tell the cook that I want something special tonight, maybe a cake or something."

"Congratulation Sir. Is the baby and mother alright?"

"I think so. Have one of the men take a letter to the post service, just as soon as I can write one."

Lee sat down at his desk and wrote a long letter, and told Mary that he thought that Pat would be a good name for the baby. He was glad that "Little Lee" wanted to name her after his mother. He told her about Rodney, and since he had been gone about a year, he hoped he would be coming home soon, but again it may depend on what the Chinese would do. Love, Lee

The bed mattress felt good, it was the first time in a week that he had a good night's sleep. He showered and went in the mess hall for breakfast. The table had been set up for twenty-two men, but he notice that four plates and cups had been turned over, in honor of the men that had been killed.

The men stood at attention as he walked in, and saluted

him. He felt humble and proud of his men. "At ease men," then looking at the cook, said "Cookie what are we having this morning?"

"Your favorite Sir, blueberry pancakes, bacon and hot coffee."

"Thanks Cookie, I was hoping it wouldn't be K-rations. It's good to be back home."

He sat down next to Sergeant Miller. "Captain, there are reports that some of our Marines are pushed to the sea around Wonsan. Do you want us to go up there and check?"

"Sergeant, if you unloaded some of your gear, how many men can you get on the boat?"

"Maybe fifteen or twenty, I think that would be it. We could pick that many up and drop them downstream in a safe zone, and then go back for more. We would only take the Captain and the two machine- gunners, maybe five crew members total."

"Do it Miller, but call us if you make contact, or see any large group of Chinese. I can call an air strike from here. "

"Yes sir, after breakfast I will gather the men."

"Sergeant you and your men be careful, I don't want to lose anymore good men. "

After breakfast Lee went to his desk which was piled up with paper work, and Sergeant Miller picked his men and went to their P.T. boat.

About 0900 a.m. Colonel White called and said that he had sent air strikes for the men at Chosin Reservoir and Toktong Pass. Lee then told him about his patrol, and if they spotted large concentrations of Chinese they would call him for an air strike.

It was a long wait, but then at 1700 p.m. he got a call from Sergeant Miller. "Captain, we have picked up twenty men, some are wounded. But behind them are about five hundred Chinese. Lat' 40'x 36'N by Long' 20'x W. Ten miles south, of Wonson Harbor."

"Thanks Miller, I will call for an air strike. Get the wounded men back here to the Aid Station."

For the next two weeks Lee's boat patrolled the coast, picking up wounded, and reporting large concentrations of Chinese Troops.

The third week after Lee got back he got a call from Colonel White. "Captain Lee, would you have all your men present tonight at 1800, Major Phillips, C.I.A. Director Sheets, and I would like to see you and your men."

"Yes Sir and I will have my cook fix up some snacks."

At 1700 the officers showed up and Lee had his men stand at attention, then after a brief meal, Colonel White said. "Captain Lee, the men that were with you on the rescue mission have them to stand up."

Lee and his men stood up, and the Colonel pinned a silver

star on each of the Marines, plus a purple heart for Rod that was wounded. "I will leave you the medals for you to send home to the men that were killed."

After the ceremony they sat down and the Colonel brought them up to date. "Three days after we arrived at Hagaru-ri and flew back to Seoul, Maj. General Oliver Smith and Commanding General of the 1st Marine Division had Lt. Colonel Raymond Davis 1st Battalion, 7th Marines took his men to the Toktong Pass. He contacted Captain William Barber, Commanding officer of what was left of Fox Company. Together they kept the pass open for Gen. Edward Almond U.S. Army Commanding General of X Corps, and General Smith of the 1st Marines for their men to fight their way the fourteen miles to Hagaru-ri."

The Chinese were on both sides of the column, and it was a fire fight all the way to town. But when they arrived at Hagaru-ri the wounded were flown out to Japan. After what was left of the X-Corps, and the 1st Marine Division. They headed for Koto-ri. And after repairing a bridge that the Chinese blew up, they finally made it to Hungnam harbor on December 15, 1950.

"What happens now, Sir?" Captain Lee asked

"Captain our war is over, we are all going home. The Air Force will continue to bomb the Chinese where they find them, hopeful all of our troops are out of North Korea, and down to the 38th parallel. No one won, but we took a beating, the worst defeat in American History. Secretary of State Dean Acheson called it the greatest defeat suffered by American arms since the Civil War battle of Bull Run. But

Historian Edwin P. Hoyt called the Marines' march from the Chosin Reservoir "one of the greatest retreats in the course of military history."

"Lee, the Marines have nothing to be ashamed of. They were outnumbered ten to one. One division of Marines against six or more division of Chinese, an estimated 25,000 killed, and 12,500 wounded between October 15 and December 15th. The Marines casualties, 700 dead and nearly 200 missing, 3,500 wounded, and there were more than 6,200 mostly frostbite victims, of which one-third will return to duty."

Now it is up to the U.N. to do the talking. It is considered a cease fire, and will probably take years to settle.

"Captain, I have some papers for you to sign, then you and your men will fly to Japan, and then to Camp Pendleton, where they will be discharged from the Marines."

"Thank you sir. But what about the UDT Unit?"

"Captain the unit will no longer be active. Your boat will be turned over to the South Korean Navy. Now if there are no more questions, we will have to leave."

Lee called his men to attention, and Colonel White and Major Phillips saluted and shook every man's hand. "The truck will be here at 0900 for the men to board, and go home." said the Colonel.

When the officers left, the men let out a big shout."We are going home. Be home for Christmas" and everyone was hugging each other, including Captain Lee.

"Men, you can start packing, and I will do the paper work. They will be ready tomorrow morning at breakfast time." he said heading for his office. The first thing will be to write a letter to Mary and tell her the good news.

By 0600 the men were packed and ready to go. Cookie the" South Korean" had cooked them a big meal. After breakfast they took up a collection and gave it to him. The truck was on time and saying goodbye to Cookie they got on the truck.

When they got to the Pusan airport a C-47 was waiting for them. The plane landed in Japan, and a couple hours later they were on their way to Camp Pendleton, and it was there that they said their goodbyes. Each man promising to see each other again.

Captain Lee was now on a plane without his men, and was flying toward Chattanooga, Tennessee. He leaned back and took a long nap, dreaming of home.

CHAPTER 24

Home Again

"Daddy, Daddy, wake up. Today is my birthday, I'm ten years old today." said Pat, pulling the covers off of his bed.

Lee half awake looked out the window and saw the snow coming down, "Rod, grab your gun, the Chinese are coming again."

"No Daddy, you're home. That was a long time ago, please wake up. Today is my birthday."

Lee rubbed his eyes and then looked across the bed, and seeing Pat his daughter said."Sorry sweetheart, but Daddy was having one of his old dreams. When I see snow it reminds me of a long time ago. Did you say that you were ten years old? How could you grow up so fast, it seems like yesterday you were just a baby, and now you are a pretty young woman."

"Daddy, Mommy is going to bake me a cake; do you have a present for me? I love you Daddy."

"Now Pat, that sounds like a bribe, and I do love you. What kind of present would you like, a small expensive one, or a large smelly one?"

"A large one Daddy. Is it in a big box?"

"Part of it is in a box, it's on the porch. Not sure where the other part is. But you're not going to see either one unless you give your Daddy a great big hug and a kiss. You see I can bribe too."

"Hey you two in there, breakfast is going to get cold." Mary said hollering from the kitchen.

Lee kissed little Pat and carried her into the kitchen.

"Good morning honey, sorry I over- slept on such an important day." He then put Pat down and kissed Mary.

"Darling can you believe that this little girl is ten years old, and she wants a big present?"

"Mommy, Daddy had another one of his bad dreams. He thought he was fighting the Chinese again."

"Lee you still having those dreams? I told you several years ago to see a doctor."

"You mean a head shrink don't you Mary. It will just take time."

"Darling that was ten years ago." She said.

"Yes ten years, and lots of good men died, for what? They still call it a truce, both countries standing at the 38th Parallel line, same place as before. Asked the men that fought there, it wasn't a Police Action, but a real war."

"Honey don't get upset it's over, and you aren't in the Marines any more, now breakfast is going to get cold, let's eat and then I'm going to lie down, I'm not feeling good."

"Honey, you haven't felt good for some time. You're not pregnant are you?"

"No Darling I'm just tired. But it's no wonder I'm not. The many times you had me in bed, when you first came back from Korea." Mary said, smiling.

Lee leaned over and kissed her."I had lots of lost time to make up, remember?"

"Yes, and I think you did." Mary said smiling again.

"Mommy, Daddy let's eat, and then look at my big present" said Pat pulling on Mary's apron.

After a good breakfast of blueberry pancakes, Lee got up and went to the den to read the morning paper, while Mary and Pat were doing the dishes. But before he could read the sports page, Pat was back, and climbed into his lap.

"Daddy put that old paper down, I want to go and see my present, please Daddy."

Lee kissed her and said, "Just as soon as Mommy gets through and little Lee is finished feeding the cows."

"Hey Dad, the horse kicked old Bamba, thought they were going to get into a fight." Little Lee said coming into the house.

"Hush Lee, you can tell me about it later, now go and see if your mother is ready, if not I will never get to read the paper."

"Little Lee looked at the front page, it said that North Viet Nam had invaded South Viet Nam. Daddy, are we going to have another war? Isn't that what happened in Korea ten years ago, the war you were in when my little sister Pat was born?"

"Yes little Lee and it took three years to sign an Armistice after the fighting was over. And the history books still calls it a "police action." Tell that to my friends who were killed."

"Lee, quit talking about the war, it's over. You know it bothers me, and now little Lee is talking about It." said Mary coming into the room.

"Mom if war breaks out, I will go. I will join the Marines, like Dad."

"Son you're too young and I hope you will never have to go to war. I think America has learned a lesson about Korea; surely they wouldn't make the same mistake again. Now let's go and look at that big box your sister got for her birthday."

"Dad, Mom, before we go I would like to say something, and I hope you won't get mad."

"What is it son?" Mary asked

"I would like for you and Dad to call me 'Leland' instead of little Lee. I get confused with Dad, and I'm not little any more. I'm fifteen years old, almost a man."

Lee looked at him and said to Mary. "By golly he's right honey, he is almost a man. Yes it's alright with me, it was your true mother that wanted to call you little Lee. Leland does sound manly, don't you think so honey?"

Mary leaned over and kissed him," Yes Leland but give us time to get used to it. Sometimes we may forget."

"Now that the three of you have gotten that done, can we please go and look at my present. After all, it is my birthday," Pat said putting her hands on her hip.

"Sorry Sis, but I thought that this was the best time, you can call me Leland too you know."

"I will call you more than that, if we don't go and see my present."

Their first stop was the back porch. And with great expectation Pat ripped off the paper on the big box. About half way through she saw part of a saddle, and her eyes got bigger, and with a renewed furry she tore off the rest of the paper. "Putting her arms around her Mom and Dad, she cried and said, "I love you."

Brother Leland looked at the saddle and then at his sister. "Don't mean a thing Sis. You will get the horse on your next birthday."

"Dad, he is kidding isn't he, I do have a horse someplace?"

"Yes honey, you have a horse. He is in the barn, next to Leland's horse."

"Dad you mean I have a horse too? But I have only seen one, and that was Pat's horse. Where is mine?"

"Your uncle Carl has been keeping it in his barn, for the last week. We were afraid one of his boys would tell you. He and Lucy have put both horses in our barn while we were eating breakfast."

"I saw that horse, Cousin Luke said his Dad was keeping it for someone. And it was mine all along. Just wait until I see my cousin."

"He didn't lie to you son. He just didn't know who his Dad was keeping it for." Now let's all of us go to the barn.

When they opened the side door to the barn, Pat saw a beautiful American Saddle horse, that was about five years old and with a shade of red hair. When she went up to him, he nudged her and grunted.

"Dad, Mom, he's beautiful. Thank you, I love you. It's the best birthday present in the whole world."

"We are glad you like him honey, but he comes with responsibility. You will have to feed him and clean up his stall. He only had one owner, and I don't think he has a name. What do you want to call him?"

"That's easy Dad, his name is 'Big Red,' and that's what I will call him."

Now Leland was getting impatient. "When do I see my horse?"

Lee looked out the door and said. "Well, I believe there's my brother Carl and Lucy coming with a horse to our barn. You reckoned that could be your horse?"

Leland ran out of the barn and rushed to his uncle Carl, saying. "Is that my horse uncle? He sure is pretty, what breed is he?"

"Yes little Lee, he is your horse, we have been keeping him for you. Now you and Pat can ride together. I guess Luke will still ride the old mare. And your horse is a Quarter Horse, about six years old. I believe the previous owner called him 'Jim Bo' he comes to that name. Luke get your mare, and the three of you go riding. I need to talk to my brother.

They all stood around and watched the kids riding their horses and Lee was surprised how good Pat could ride. He knew that his son had been riding the old mare that belonged to his brother but didn't think that Pat had been riding him. He stopped the kids and warned them about old Bama, his bull.

"Listen kids, please stay away from the cows, or you will have Bama to contend with. They are his cows, so please have your horses stay clear of them. "

"Well I could stay here all day, but I have some cooking to do, and then bake a birthday cake, so if you all will excuse me" said Mary and started walking back to the house.

"Wait Mary, I go with you and help. I think Carl wants to talk to Lee." Lucy said looking at her husband.

"Brother, lets walk over to the watering trough, I have something to give you."

"Sure Carl, what do you have? Did you buy me a horse too?"

"I wished it was," pulling a telegram from his pocket and handed it to Lee.

With a surprise look on his face he took the telegram and read it. "Damn, I do not believe this."

"What is it brother?"

"Carl I have been ordered to Washington. Have to be there Monday, two days from now."

"Have you been recalled back into the Marines? We are going to be involved in another war it looks like? The President has already sent some Green Berets to South Viet Nam, for advisors only, he told the paper."

"I really don't know Carl. I'm forty eight; too old for an enlisted man, but not for and Officer if they called me back. Hell I can't let Mary and the kids go through this again. I have been in two wars, and have served my twenty years."

"Don't tell Mary or the kids Carl, today is Pat's birthday and I'm not going to think about it until Sunday. I will have to tell Mary then, because I will be catching a plane in Atlanta."

"My son Luke can handle the farm, Lucy and I will drive you and Mary to the airport."

"Thanks brother, now let's go to the house and get ready for supper. I haven't read the paper yet."

They got to the house and Carl and Lucy went to their home. "I thought Lucy was going to help you with the cake?" he said to Mary

"She will be back; one of the kids came over and said that she had a phone call. Lee the kids are riding their horses, why don't you take a nap before supper."

"Think I will, but I want to finish reading the paper first. He went into the den and picked up the front page. Heavy fighting around Da Nang, the South Viet Nam soldiers are retreating." Throwing the paper down, he went to the bedroom and lay across the bed, and said a short prayer. 'Please LORD, not again.' "

"Wake up honey, Lucy says you have a phone call over at her house. Now don't be late, we will have an early supper so we can eat the birthday cake later."

Lee got up and walked the short distance over to his brother's house.

"Hi Lucy, did you say that I had a phone call?"

"Yes Lee, I wrote the number down, it's Rodney and he wants you to call him as soon as you can." "Rod? Oh hell. Now I know it's not good news," and he went to the table and picked up the number, and dialed. The phone only rang twice, and Rodney was on the line. "Lee? We have been drafted again. Hell, we served our time, and I have two purple hearts to show for it. They can't do this to us, can they?"

"No Rod you won't have to go. They don't take anyone that has earned two purple hearts. But me as an officer, they can take me if they desire to. Maybe they don't want either one of us. What did your telegram say?"

"Fly to Washington Monday December 17th, and a plane ticket, but nothing else."

"Well there is no point worrying about it now. I will meet you in Atlanta Monday, maybe we can have lunch together, see you there old buddy," hanging up the phone.

He turned around and Carl and Lucy were looking at him. "Everything is ok, Rod and I have been called to Washington, doesn't mean anything. But I will wait until Sunday to tell Mary. Now let's go back over to my house and eat some cake."

It was a great birthday party for Pat, and she and Leland loved their horses. Sunday, Lee told Mary the orders and told her not to worry, but with tears in her eyes she promised that she wouldn't. That night he made love to her and she fell asleep in his arms.

Monday morning he was awake at six a.m. and after a quick cup of coffee, Carl was waiting at the door, and the four of them headed to Atlanta.

When they arrived at the airport, Sue and Rod were at the gate. Everyone hugged each other and Lee and Rod got on the plane.

They arrived in Washington and were met by two Marine M.P. Who escorted them to a black limo, which had a sign in the window that said, "Official Business."

Then the limo drove into Washington and to the Pentagon Building, where they were escorted by two Marines to a room filled with officers with Navy and Marines present. Someone shouted attention, and then President John F. Kennedy walked into the room.

The President looked over at Captain Lee and said. "I understand that you were in charge of the UDT in Korea, and

The Adventures of Lee Robinson

Master Sergeant Rodney Sweeny was your training officer."

"Yes Sir, and eighteen other good men, some which didn't come back with me."

"I have read your records, it was quite impressive, not only in Korea, but in World War II. You and your men did an excellent job, and our country is proud of you, and your team. The U D Team was deactivated after Korea, and no longer exists.

"Captain I want another unit like that again. We need someone to check out the beaches, and rescue hostages. I want it called the NAVY SEALS.

(Se , Air, Land) and will be under me and the War Department." How long would it take to train a unit of twenty men?"

"With good recruits. About six months, Sir."

"Captain, to ease you and the Sergeant's minds, you two won't see any combat; you both have done enough for your country, but however I need your help. We have set up a base in Virginia Beach along the coast. We have twenty five miles of posted fence beach. We want you to find your former crew, if they are still physically able, see if they will help. It won't be an order, for this will be an all volunteer unit. You will be permitted to move your families close by, if you wish. Gentlemen will you give us six months of your time to train an elite unit of NAVY SEALS? Your country will appreciate it?"

Lee looked over at Rod, and with the nod of his head he stood up."Mr. President we will be glad to train another unit of men, and they will be called NAVY SEALS, just give us six months and they will be ready."

"Thank you Major. Now I will have to go, but before I do

I have a little ceremony that I would like to hold. Would all of you stand up?"

Then the President of the United States pined a ' Navy Cross' on the front of the jacket of Captain Lee Robinson and Master Sergeant Rodney Sweeny and then shook their hands. Then the other men in the room salute both of them.

After the President left, Colonel Sellers told Lee that he would report to him, and informed him if he needed anything." Were there any questions the two of them wished to ask?"

"Yes Sir, a couple. The President addressed me as Major. I was a Captain when I was discharged. And if we bring our families to Virginia Beach, will they get a housing allowance?"

"Captain Lee the position calls for a Major; I already have the papers signed. Put these on your uniform when you go to the base," sliding a small box over to him with a couple of bronze oak leaves inside.

"And Yes Major, you and your family will get a house allowance, and both of you will be paid service pay, along with your retirement check. Do you have any questions Sergeant, the same applies to you and your family?"

"No Sir, You have answered my questions. We will have you a team of Navy Seals within six months."

The meeting lasted all day, Lee and Rodney were dismissed and they were relieved that they would remain in the states. They would only do the training for six months, until they could find another qualified leader. Both were awarded the Navy Cross for their action in WW II. They were then taken back to the airport and got on a plane going back to Atlanta where their family would be waiting for them.

CHAPTER 25

Navy Seals

Lee woke up early the next morning and went to the closet and pulled out his old Marine uniform and tried it on. The blouse was too tight and he couldn't button the pants without sucking in his stomach. Then he tried his dress blues, and found the same problem. While still struggling with his pants he went into the kitchen.

"Mary, my uniform has shrunk do you think that hanging in the closet all of these years caused that to happen?"

"No dear, I think that you have gotten bigger, too many of my blueberry pancakes. Come and let's eat, and then I will see if I can let out some places, you can't go around holding your stomach in."

After breakfast, Mary thought the job would be too much for her." Honey let's get both uniforms and your dress blues, and then go to town and finds a good tailor to refit all of your uniforms."

Lee took his dress blues and his two green uniforms and put them in the car, while Mary looked up a tailor in town, and then they were on their way.

"Honey, I may take the first couple weeks to get settled in and get the men started, but then I will try to come home every weekend, it won't be that bad a drive. But when school is out, you and the kids come down and stay for the summer. I should have a house by then."

"What about Rod and his family, is he going to do the same thing?"

"Not sure, he is a couple hundred miles further away; He may just wait until school is out."

They arrived in town, found a good tailor and after fitting him up, said it would take two days to do a good job. Lee left the clothes and he and Mary had lunch and did a little shopping.

When he pulled into the Naval Seal Base, he saw that it was an old World War II Coast Guard Station that had been abandoned years ago, with the exception of two new buildings. He saw four men dressed as Sea Bee's working on the roof of one of the barracks, and at least two more was working inside.

Major Lee parked his car and went inside, where four of the Sea Bee's dropped what they were doing and saluted him. "As you were men." And then seeing a young Lieutenant who was still standing at attention, Lee said. "At ease Lieutenant, how many men do you have with you?"

"Ten Sea Bee's, Sir. I'm in charge. Lieutenant Bill Glasscock Sir, we have been here for two days."

"Lieutenant, I am Major Lee Robinson, and expecting a

Master Sergeant Rodney Sweeny coming in today, and a few other Marines. Am I the first? Or has some more of my men showed up?"

Lee looked at him, fresh out of Officers School and he couldn't be more than eighteen years old. "You are the first Sir; can I show you to your room Sir?"

"That would be nice Lieutenant" as Lee reached for his bags.

"Private Gopher, Pick up the Major's bags and come with us." The young Lieutenant said.

They went into the new barracks and Lee saw an office, adjoining a bed room and a bathroom. The private carried the bags in the bedroom and set them down. The Lieutenant then saluted the Major."Will there be anything else Sir?"

"No Lieutenant, you go back to your work, but if any of my men shows up bring them to my office."

He then went to his desk and opened his briefcase and removed the list of names that would be his instructors, and was pleased that he knew half of them… men who had worked with him in Korea and Hawaii. But there was one name that was missing, that he wished he had. Master Sergeant Bama, who was killed years ago in a bar room fight, shot in the back.

Then he looked at the new men who would be the Navy Seals. They were the top of their unit, but he couldn't believe how young they were. "Was he that young when he became a UDT member?" Some of them were young enough to be his son. And now he would train them to kill, and some would not come back from their missions.

He sat at his desk with tears in his eyes, as he remembered

the men in his old unit that he had sent out and they never came back. And now here he was again, training young men to fight and die for their country. Why can't we learn to settle our differences over a table, and not have our young men die?

"Sir, there is a Master Sergeant Sweeny outside. Should I send him in?" the young Lieutenant said.

"Yes, by all means, send him in." Lee said getting up from his desk.

Rod walked in and saluted, and then the two men embraced each other.

"Major, it looks like we will have another adventure together, how long has it been?"

"Too long Rod. About ten years since Korea. But we did meet in Washington. How are Sue and your family?"

"Great Sir. Mary and your two kids?"

"Doing fine, she and the kids will join me when school is out. Damn, it's good to see you again."

By the middle of the week everyone had shown up and they began their training.

"They are a good group of men Rodney." Lee said as they watched the men train."

"Yes they are Major; almost as good as we were when we trained for the UDT"

"Better, and more educated, they are quick to learn," Lee said as they watched a Seal thrown down on the mat.

A Marine Corporal came running into the gym. "Major Sir, I think you ought to go into your office and watch the T.V. The President has been shot."

Lee and Rod ran into the office, and saw the President,

The Adventures of Lee Robinson

John F. Kennedy slump over in a car, while F.B. I. agents were looking on both side of the road ... looking to see where the shots had come from.

"November 22nd 1963 John F Kennedy was assassinated and pronounced dead in Dallas, Texas."

The world was stunned, and Lynden Johnson was declared President.

In 1963, North Vietnam invaded South Vietnam. The new outfit, called the Navy Seals, involvement in Viet Nam began almost immediately and was advisory to the South. The Seals began the UDT style training course for the Commando platoons in Danang.

February 1966, a small Seal Team One, detachment arrived in Vietnam to conduct Direct action missions.

Major Lee Robinson and his men were disbanded, and he and Rodney went back home and became veterans again. The Navy Seals still use Virginia Beach as their home base, and are very active in their missions.

In June 1971, the last Marine leaves Vietnam, Nixon was President.

Leland was too young to fight in Vietnam, but Rodney had two sons that went to the war. Jimmy the youngest came back home, but Earl, the oldest was missing in action, and would not be found until ten years later, dead.

Pat and Leland were at the University of Tennessee, and after graduation Leland wanted to go to medical school and become a doctor. Pat met a boy in school and planned on getting married when they finished.

Mary had contracted Tuberculosis and spent some time in

a Sanitarium, but would continue to take her medicine. Lee lost all interest in the farm, and had become restless again. The doctor told Lee that the mountain air would be good for Mary, so he started looking for a home around the Smoky Mountains.

One day while he was in the barn, he saw an old newspaper in the trash can, and read an article that said, "Wanted, a veteran to be Sheriff of a small mountain town, near Asheville, North Carolina." Lee read it twice, and then looked at the date. The paper was only a week old. He finished his milking and then went into the house. Mary was in the bedroom sleeping, so he went to the phone in the kitchen and called the phone number in the paper.

The phone rang twice and then a rough voice said. "Hello, how can I help you?"

"My name is Lee Robinson I was a Major in the Marine Corps, fought in World War II, and the Korean War. Have you filled the job as Sheriff in your town?"

"No we haven't, but we were thinking of running elections, but I don't like our candidates. Did you say you were a Marine?"

"Yes, retired with twenty five years of service. I was a Major and helped trained the Navy Seals at Virginia Beach five years ago. My wife is sick, and I'm looking for us a place to live in the mountains."

"Well we have plenty of mountains here. Rockdale is a small town, surrounded by the Blue Ridge Mountains. Six blocks long, with three stop lights. Getting to be a Tourist town, the job is mostly putting drunks in jail and ticketing the tourist, for speeding. How old are you?"

"I'm 58, birthday is in April. By the way, who am I talking too?"

"Harry Cobb, been Sheriff here for twenty years, I'm seventy now and time to retire. You interested in the job?"

"Yes I am. When can I come up and talk to you?"

"Today is Wednesday, can you come up Thursday or Friday. I'm off this weekend?"

"Yes I think so, what about Friday, and will you be at your office?"

"Friday will be fine; I will be here all day cleaning the junk out of my desk. When you get to town our office is in the second block, if you get lost asked anyone, they know where the Sheriff's office is located. By the way, the small police department is in the same building."

"Thanks Sheriff, I will see you Friday around noon. I figured it will take me about six hours to get there. Can you line me up with a room in a motel; I won't go back until Saturday."

"Can do. See you Friday" and then Harry hung up the phone.

"Who are you talking to Honey? I could hear part of it in the bedroom. Are you going somewhere Friday?"

"Yes sweetheart, I need to see a man in a little town called "Rockdale" twenty miles from Asheville, North Carolina. It's about a six hour drive, so I will spend the night and come back Saturday. Pat will be here, she doesn't have a class Friday. You don't mind, do you?"

"I guess it will be alright, just come back Saturday or call me. I haven't felt good lately."

Lee left at six o'clock Friday morning after telling Pat and Lucy to check on Mary, and gave them the number of the Sheriff's office. Very little traffic was on the road after he left Knoxville.

He stayed on I- 75 until he got to the turn off, to Asheville. Then when he pulled in to Asheville, he stopped for gas and grabbed something to eat. After lunch he looked for the road that would take him to Rockdale.

Around twelve o'clock he pulled into a beautiful little town, with large old houses built before the war. There were mountains on both side, and one lane going through the town. He counted the red lights, and saw the Police Building on his right. The Sheriff's office was in the same building.

He pulled to the curb, and there were no parking meters. He went inside and asked the receptionist if he could see the Sheriff, Harry Cobb.

"A tall man around seventy came out to greet him. "I'm Sheriff Cobb. Are you the ex-Marine named Lee Robinson?"

"Yes I am sir, but there is no such thing as an ex-Marine. Once a Marine, you will always be a Marine. Yes, I'm Lee Robinson."

"Hell, I should know that. I have a son who was a Marine in the Korean War."

"Yes Sir, I was there too. It was a hell of a war, but the Government called it a "Police Action," but anyone that was there would tell you different."

Harry introduced him to the Police Chief and to a man in his fifties name Cliff Bylow, who was the town's Mayor. After everyone was introduce they all went into the Sheriff's office, and talked.

After a couple of hours, they asked Lee to go out to the front office and get a cup of coffee, while they discussed his qualification. In less than an hour, they asked him to come back into the office.

"Lee we won't run the elections. If you want the job, we all agreed that it is yours. When can you take the job?"

Lee got up and shook everyone's hands. "I thank you for your confidence in me, and yes I do want the job, however I will need a couple of weeks. I have not told my wife of my plans, and I will need to look for a house. I wish to bring her up here next week, and let her see what a pretty town Rockdale is. She is in poor health, and I don't want to be far from town."

"Mr. Robinson, my daughter is a realtor. Let me give you her name, and you call her when you are ready to look for a house." said Cliff Bylow, the Mayor.

"Lee, if you have the time let me show you around the town, and introduce you to some men that you should know. Be my guest for supper tonight, I will call my wife, and she will look forward to seeing your wife when you come back." Sheriff Cobb said.

"Yes Harry, I would like that. But tell your wife not to go to any trouble about supper. I can eat anything Sheriff. Do you not have a Deputy?"

"Did have but he quit six months ago, wasn't enough pay for a family of six. He was a good man. I tried to get him more money but the board turned it down. But we still have his salary in the budget, so if you know of a good man that doesn't have a large family, we could use him."

"Yes, I think I might. Like mine, his family has moved

on and now it's just the two of them. We both served in the Marines together for over twenty years."

"That would work out great, that way you could split up the hours. That's one reason I'm retiring, too many hours for one man, and a dispatcher. Did you meet Joe Black?"

"Yes I did, and you have Mrs. Karen Baker the bookkeeper. Does she work full time?"

"Yes, the day shifts only. We have an older man name Jim Wilson that fills in for Joe at night. You have a staff of four counting you. The budget is for five. Hope you can get your friend to be your Deputy. The dispatcher is also the jailor, and does the booking, which isn't very often."

"Mrs. Cobb, the chicken was delicious, and the apple pie is one of my favorites. When I bring my wife up, we will give you a call."

"You do that young man, and I think your wife will like it here. With Harry retiring, we are hoping to do a little traveling."

"My wife was a Marine, and I have done enough traveling, now that the kids are gone, we just hope to relax in a small town, and take it easy."

Lee had seen the town and met several people, and now after a good meal he was ready to find a motel and go to bed.

"Harry, I'm ready to go. Did you line me up in a motel?"

"Yes I did Lee, small but very clean and quiet. Takes about

ten minutes to get there. And by the way, do you like to fish?"

"Love it. Do we have some trout nearby?"

"We have a Park called Lulu Lake, full of Bass and the river that flows in the lake is full of trout. Only the locals know about this place."

"That, I think would bring my friend up, he loves to fish."

Harry drove Lee to a little motel at the end of the road. "Lee if you like pancakes, the café across the road has the best. Sherry owns the café, and the best food in town."

"On arriving at the motel, Lee called Mary, told her about the town and that he would leave tomorrow morning, and then he went to bed.

Lee got up early and thought he would try Sherry's pancakes. As she came to the booth he saw a very attractive woman about fifty coming to his table.

"Good morning." She said setting a class of water on the table. " Don't think I've seen you around here before."

Lee stood up and offered her his hand. "I am Lee Robinson from Hixson, that's just outside of Chattanooga, Tn. And I may be your regular customer in a few weeks. Sheriff Cobb told me about your place. I'm staying at the Ridgeview motel across the street."

"You know Harry? I understand he is thinking about retiring, everyone likes him. He's been our Sheriff for years. Will you take his place?"

"I have been offered the job, but I need to see if my wife will move here. Her health is bad, and I think the mountain air here would be good for her. I told Harry that I will let him know in two weeks. I will bring my wife up Wednesday, and stay a few days, and look at some houses."

Lee got ready to leave and asked for a check. "No charge on your first meal, and I hope you take the job. Be sure to bring your wife by, I would like to meet her."

Lee pulled in the driveway and Mary came out to meet him. "Did you get the job honey?"

"Job! How did you know about a job?"

"I heard you talking on the phone and then I found the marked newspaper. It's in the mountains, close to Asheville, the paper said. And I know that you are tired of the farm. You weren't cut out to be a farmer. The kids are grown and don't need us anymore. Where you are happy honey, I will be happy too."

CHAPTER 26

Rockdale

Monday morning Lee got up at five o'clock and went to the barn on a cold and brisk day and fed the chickens and' Big Red,' Pat's favorite horse who was now eleven years old. With school and her boy friend Ed she didn't ride him anymore, and he was happy just playing in the pasture and pestering the cows. Now that Bama the bull had died, Big Red could do what he wanted with the cows.

Lee after feeding the stock opened the gate to the pasture but kept Betty their one cow in the stall until he could milk her. He had the pail almost full, when Betty decided to back up, knocking the pail of milk over." Damn you Betty that does it. I'm giving you to my brother Carl. If Mary likes the mountains, then I will let Carl have the farm too."

"Good morning honey, did you bring any milk from Betty I am almost out." Said Mary, pouring him a cup of coffee.

"No," Lee said." Damn cow turned the pail over. We will be leaving after breakfast. Pat can get some from Lucy if she needs some. Did you tell her we may be gone for a week?"

"Yes and they will look out for her and Leland. I need to pack a couple of more things, and then I will be ready. Are you sure you will be happy with a new job, and away from the farm?"

"Damn happy" said Lee

When they got to Knoxville the sun had come out, and it was a beautiful day. Then they began to see the mountains, and he lowered the window and said to Mary. "Take a deep breath honey, you soon will be breathing good clean air."

They arrived in the little town of Rockdale; Mary looked out the window and saw the large houses that were built before the war. People would wave at them when they slowly drove down the street to their motel.

"Honey, I love the town and the mountains, yes I think I could be happy here."

It was one o'clock and they had not stopped for lunch, "Before we stop at the motel, let's go to a little café that I found. It's called Sherry's the best food in town."

They parked the car and went inside and were greeted by the owner, Sherry.

She looked at Lee and said."You did come back, and this must be Mary, your wife." After the introductions Sherry took them to a table, and took their order.

After lunch they went to their motel room, and unpacked. Later that day he drove her around town and to the park at Lulu Lake camp grounds. That night he called Harry Cobb and was invited over for pie and coffee. It was a long day, and they both were exhausted. But before they went to bed he asked her. "What do you think?"

"It's beautiful honey and if you will be happy here, then

I will be. I know that you weren't cut out to be a farmer, and you worked hard for me and the kids and, now with the kid's leaving, we will build a new life together. Yes, I think I will love it here."

As they got into bed, she turned over and said. "Lee have I told you today, that I love you?"

"Yes, but you can tell me again, I won't get spoiled." Then he puts his arm around her body and kissed her and then turned out the lights.

The next morning they had breakfast at Sherry's café and Lee tried her pancakes, and graded them A-plus. Then they drove down to the Police and Sheriff building, and met everyone and told Cliff Bylow, the Mayor, that he would accept the job. Then he told Cliff to call his daughter, who has the Realty Company to meet them at Sherry's Café, and they wanted to look for a small house.

They had just finished lunch when a young girl in her twenty's came in the door. Seeing Lee, she went to his table and introduced herself, and said that her name was Tonya. Sherry brought her a cup of coffee, and she sat down at his table, and began showing them pictures of the houses that were for sale.

Most of the houses were too big; Mary said they wanted a small place, with not more than two bedrooms. They got the list down to three, and then went out to look at them. The first house they turned down because of the location and the price. But when they got to the second house, both of them agreed that this was their house. A small white house nestled in a valley with the mountains in front and back.

It would only be three miles to the Sheriff's office, and a mile to a small mall, where Mary could shop until she dropped. The house had about half an acre of land in the back, where Lee could make a small garden. They would have only one house close by, with an older couple about their age.

After talking to Mary, he put a deposit down on the house. He would call his brother Carl, and tell him that he would sell him his share of the farm that they had agreed on. With that money, they could pay off the mortgage of the house in five years.

They went back home, told the kids they had bought a house, in a small town, but Lee would keep his house on the farm. The kids could live in it when they came home on school breaks.

Everyone pitched in to pack, and within three days they were ready to leave. Lucy was going back with them to help Mary with the new house, because Lee had to report to work.

Lee woke up at five a.m. but told Mary he had no chores to do that early in the morning, so he was going to sleep until six. After eating breakfast with Mary and Lucy, he got into his truck and drove to work.

"Good Morning Sheriff Robinson," his staff of three said, handing him a cup of coffee.

"Good Morning" he replied, taking the coffee and going to his desk.

Looking at his dispatcher, he asked."Joe, will you bring me

up to date on what I should know, and Karen do I have any papers to sign?"

Joe Black filled him in about a couple of speeding tickets, and a drunk that the Police had brought in and jailed.

"Why would they bring him here, instead of the Police Station," asked Lee.

"It was out of their district, he was drunk outside the city limits. They only book the ones in town. But we both have the authority to arrest someone, if they break the law."

"Thank you Joe, Karen do you have some papers for me?"

"Yes Mr. Robinson, I have three papers for you to sign." handing him some papers.

"Please," Lee said to the three people that made up his staff." Call me Sheriff or just Lee, we are more like a small family than a large company."

"Want another cup of coffee, Lee?" said Joe

Lee stayed in the office until lunch, and then asked Joe what was Sheriff Cobb's duty.

"He would check the mall for any complaints, and then drive down to the city limits of Asheville, then the back roads to Lulu Lake Park, and watch for speeders at the intersection of interstate 75 and 40. Kind of boring job, Lee. Not the kind of action you had in the Marines."

"After the war Joe, I worked on a farm for over ten years, wasn't much action there either. I can live with a little peace and quiet."

Lee stopped at a B.B.Q. restaurant that Joe had told him about and had a sandwich and a coke. Then taking the Sheriff's car he made the rounds that Harry would make, and arrived back at the office around five p.m.

He asked about his car, and Joe said it was assigned to him and he could take it home. He left his truck at the office and he would bring Mary back later to pick it up.

When he got home, Mary and Lucy had done a great job placing the furniture. Since this was his first day at work, and the women had worked so hard on the house, he would take them to supper, and buy them a steak at the Long Horn Restaurant.

After a good meal, Lee drove back to his office and Mary drove the truck home. It had been a long and good day.

It had been a week since Lee had taken over the Sheriff's job, and he had written about thirty speeding tickets, and arrested a couple of drunks. School was out and the trout were beginning to bite.

"Mary, I'm going to call Rodney and see if he and Sue can come for the weekend, I don't have to go into the office and Rod and I can do some fishing."

"That would be fine honey, and maybe he will take the Deputy Job and move up here. It would be nice to have them to live here, and you two could do lots of fishing together."

Lee went into the hall and dialed Rodney's number. The phone rang twice and Rod picked it up. "Hello there 'Leather Neck' this is the Marines calling. This is Major Lee, and I need you for some 'active service.' Will you be available for this coming weekend?"

"Hello yourself 'Bell Hop' what do you mean impersonating an officer, don't you know that you can get into trouble. I have a friend who is a Sheriff in a little hick town, and I may just call him."

"Damn you sound good. Did you get over the flu?"

"I got over it Lee and then Sue came down with it. But we are both over it, and looking for some fishing. When are you and Mary going to invite us up?"

"That's why I called, good buddy. Can you and Sue come up this weekend? The fish are jumping on the banks."

"Lee, school is out, and Charles can stay with his grandmother. Let me talk to Sue and call you back."

He hung up the phone and told Mary that Rod would call back.

Hour later he got a phone call. "Lee if you have a place to put us, we will leave Friday, and come back Sunday. That will give us a full day for fishing."

Friday afternoon Sue and Rod drove in the driveway, and the long time friends hugged each other.

After looking around the house, they went out for a ride, and stopped by to see Sherry and have supper. "Sherry… Rod, Sue, and I go back for at least thirty years. That was years before I met Mary. We fought all over the Pacific in the war, and at Korea. We have shared many adventures together."

"And as I have said before, I'm going to write a book about it someday." Rod said.

Sherry grabbed herself a cup of coffee and pulled up a chair next to the table. "You both are heroes, and Rod please write a book about your friend and the adventures the two of you had together. I would love to read it."

They sat and talked about two hours, and then Lee took them down to his office, and then drove through town and to the Lulu Lake camp grounds. It was getting dark, so he drove them back home.

Mary looked at both of them. "And then asked if they liked the town?"

"Love it, I have always loved the mountains," Said Sue.

"Rod, what do you think?"

"Like Sue, Mary, I love the town and tomorrow if I catch any fish, I will sell our house and move up here."

"That's what we were hoping you would say Rod. I need a Deputy, and you have the job if you want it."

"Are you serious Lee? I think Sue and I would love to live here."

"I'm serious Rod, you won't get rich on a Deputy pay, and the work may be boring, but we will be together again, and catch lots of fish."

"Lee you are serious. Sue and I would like nothing better, for us to be together again. Charles will be in college in the fall, our other kids are married or in school. When school starts Sue and I will be all alone in a big house with four bed rooms. We don't want that. Like you and Mary, we want a small house."

"Rod would you and Sue think about it? Now let's go to bed, we need to get up early and catch some fish."

Lee woke up early and knocked on Rod's door." Wake up my friend I have coffee and donuts on the table."

"Be right with you Lee, I'm still on Southern Time. Pour my coffee and I will be right out."

The door opened to Lee's bedroom and Mary walked out. Then in five minutes Sue came out rubbing her eyes.

"What's with you girls, why are you two up so early?" Lee asked

"We smelled the coffee", Mary said. "And we also want to get to the mall when it opens, when the men are out to play, the wives shop."

They all drank their coffee, and Lee ate three donuts. Mary was over at the counter fixing the men sandwiches to take with them.

It was getting daylight and Lee told Rod that it was time to go. It would take about an hour to get there.

Saturday morning there was very little traffic and they made good time, arriving at Rock Creek a little after sunrise. Lee then took a dirt road up the mountain to a wooden bridge. "This is where we start," said Lee." There's a few rainbow trout in here, but it's known for the big browns. Sometimes they go up to three pounds."

Rod had his line in the water first, and it wasn't five minutes before his fly reel began to hum. "Lee, I think I have a big fish on the line, get the net ready."

He worked the fish toward the bank, and Lee picked it up with the net. "Go at least two pounds. It's a big brown. Now you just wait and I will catch his spouse." throwing his line next to a big rock.

Lee had walked down from under the bridge when he heard Rod. "Lee, I will need the net, I just caught his spouse."

Walking back he saw Rod walking back and forth, fighting a big brown trout. "Watch the rocks; they are slip-p..."as he watched his friend fall down, hitting a big rock and falling into the water.

Checking his friend and seeing he wasn't hurt said. "Rod, if you had told me you wanted to go swimming; I would have taken you down to the lake"

"Zip it Lee, I may do it the hard way, but I have a big fish on the line. Now get your net ready."

Rod brought the big brown to the shore, and like a Pro, Lee gently slides the net under him and dipped him out of the water. Looking at the big brown, they both agreed it would go over three pounds.

"Well my friend, are you going to catch some fish for supper, or do I have to do all the work?"

"If you quit falling into the water and scaring the fish away, I think I have one on my line. I felt him when you hollered, and I put a big rock on my rod, now I'm going to pull him in." Lee said.

He went back to his rod and removed the rock, and watched

his line head out to the middle of the pond. "He is a fighter, but I don't think I will need the net." as he slowly pulled him in to the bank. The trout wouldn't go a pound, but one of the best eating fish in the pool. It was a twelve inch 'brook trout.'

The three fish were their limit for now, so they climbed up on a big rock, and ate the sandwiches that Mary had packed.

"Lee, I think this mountain air has helped Mary. She looks better than I saw her last summer at your farm. What does the doctor say about her T.B.?"

The doctor said that she was negative for the time being.

"What does that mean Lee?"

"It means she doesn't have active T.B. It's not positive; no one can catch it from her. But she still has it in her lungs. She is allergic to the new medicine, and there's nothing left but bed rest. You know she stayed six months in a sanitarium in Chattanooga, last year. I was hoping that the mountain air would help, and I think it has."

"It will mean a lot if you and Sue can come here to live, and I could use your help in the Sheriff's office."

"I want to talk to you about that. If in a year you haven't done anything but give speeding tickets, and haul a few drunks to jail, why would you need me?"

"Well one, we would like you and Sue for neighbors. Two, I have a budget for another officer. Three we could rotate our hours. Right now I'm working five days a week, and on call twenty four hours a day. And four, I would have a fishing buddy."

"Lee, Sue likes it here, and you know you and Mary are our best friends, we talked about it last night. Our son Charles will be going to U.T. this fall, and he and a friend want to live in a dorm. That means we would be living in a big house with four bedrooms. When we get back, I'm calling a Reality and put our house up for sale. I will have a month to sell the house before he goes to school. Hope we can be here and look for a house in about a month."

"Then it's settled, let's go to the lake and catch some more fish, we are two short."

CHAPTER 27

Fight in the Cabin

"Sheriff Lee Robinson pleases," the voice said, and the Dispatcher gave him the phone.

"Sheriff Robinson here, can I help you?"

"Hi Lee, this is Rod. I just wanted you to know that I'm bringing Sam Watson in again."

"What has he done this time?"

"He was at Lulu Lake campgrounds, drunk and took his clothes off in front of some young girls, and made some obscene remarks. I had to handcuff him. I will bring him in and let him sleep it off."

"Thanks Rod, this makes the third time this month. Give him a couple days in the cell; we got to cure him some way."

Lee turned to the Dispatcher, and said. "Rod will be bringing Sam in, lock him up. He's at Lulu Lake again taking his clothes off."

Joe laughed and said. "If it wasn't for Sam getting drunk, Rod wouldn't have much to do. Lee, isn't Lulu Lake where your wife Mary was kidnapped, and you had to kill a Mountain man?"

"Yes Joe, that was almost five years ago and it was something that I will never forget. I have never had a man hit me so hard; if it wasn't for Mary he would have killed me."

"Lee, I have heard some of the story, but not about the fight. If I make us a pot of coffee, would you tell me about it?"

"Make the coffee Joe; I've got another hour before I can go home."

"Deputy Sweeny and I went through the war in the Marines together, and I retired two years before he did. I went back to Chattanooga, and that's when I met my wife Mary Wilson".

"I was half owner of a farm that my brother had worked on for years, while I was in the Marines. So when I retired I built a small house on the farm and learned to be a farmer. Mary and I got married, and I had already had a son by another marriage, and then we had a daughter name Pat. So I became a farmer and we lived on the farm for seventeen years. We were happy, but I was getting bored with farm life."

My son was away at college, and after that he went to Medical School and became a doctor. My daughter Pat, was now seventeen and enrolled in the University of Chattanooga, but wanted to live in the dorm at school. So for the first time, Mary and I were alone, just the two of us. Her health was bad, so I started looking for a place in the mountains, thinking that the mountain air would be good for her.

"I looked in the newspaper, and saw this job for Sheriff in Rockdale, so Mary and I drove up here, and we both loved the mountains.

The Adventures of Lee Robinson

The next day I called the Mayor of the town of Rockdale, and told him about my Marine experience, and that I was an M.P.(military police) in China for couple years. He was impressed and asked me when I could come, and see him. Well the two of us got in the car and drove to Asheville, then to the little town of Rockdale. Mary fell in love with the town and the mountains at first sight. The town only had four red lights.

I saw the Mayor, and I got the job. Then we looked for a house, with a big back yard. And like I figured, the first six months were drunks and speeding tourists.

Mary and I loved going to Lulu Lake Campgrounds, we would go about every weekend that I was off. The fishing was great, and Mary and I would go to the pool. We never had any trouble. I didn't get many weekends off, so Mary would go with her friend. The Mayor said I could hire a Deputy, so I would have more time off.

I called Rodney Sweeny at the Marine Base, and offered him the job when he retired in about six months. He said he would love it, he had two children that were still in school, and when they left to go to college, his wife Sue and he would come up. They loved the mountains.

About a month later we had planned to go to the lake with Louise and her husband Fred, our friends that lived next door, but the dispatcher called me and said that I needed to be in court that morning. Mary and I had forgotten about it. So I told her to go with Louise, and Fred and I would go to court and would come later.

They left Saturday morning, at ten, and I went to the

court house. In a couple hours I got a call on my phone, hysterical screaming from Louise. Lee please come quickly, Fred has been shot, and a man has taken Mary. Please hurry, hurry. Then the phone went dead.

I asked the Judge if I could leave, that I had an emergency, and for her to call the Mayor that I may need help. But I was heading for Lulu Lake, and to send an ambulance. I thought I might need Rex my dog, if I had to go into the mountains, so I swung by the house and picked up Rex, a big hound, part shepherd, and headed for the campgrounds.

I saw a crowd gathered at the pavilion and made my way there. Louise came running to my truck, crying.

"Lee it was the mountain man, he was drunk and came up to Mary and said he wanted a kiss. She slapped him, and then he hit her. Fred came running up to help and he shot him. He's still alive, but hurt bad. Then the mountain man grabbed Mary and dragged her up the mountain."

"Which way did they go, Louise?"

"The Coon path, you know the one that leads up to the top of Raccoon Mountain. They have been gone about an hour." She said.

"I want to check on Fred, and then I'm heading up the trail. Tell Fred there's an ambulance coming, and help from the Highway Patrol, but I'm not waiting on them; just tell them where I'm going."

Fred was shot in the shoulder, and he would live. I took Rex and we headed for the Coon path that went up the mountain.

Rex and I ran about a half mile, then the trail started going uphill and I had to slow down. My dog picked up the scent and started barking. As I followed I thought of the stories told of the mountain man. Those that saw him said he was a giant, and lived in the mountains, very seldom coming down to the valley.

The trail got steeper, and I began to get tired. For the last two years of putting drunks in jail, I have let myself get fat and lazy. I wish Rodney was here, but he won't come for another month. It's up to me and Rex; I've got to keep going.

I thought of Mary and if he has done anything to her, I will kill him. But since he took her with him, I don't think he would harm her.

Rex started barking and moved into a circle. He must have stopped to let her rest for a minute. Then Rex started back up the trail, I took five minutes rest, and followed him saying, "Old mountain man, I'm coming to get you."

I made a call on my walkie-talkie phone to the Mayor and told him where I was.

"Lee, we got the Highway Patrol here, please wait. You can't handle him alone; he's a giant, and crazy."

"Can't wait Mayor, he's got Mary. Is Fred alright?"

"Fred will be okay, but Lee I wish you would wait until we can get there."

Rex then came to an intersection of three paths in the woods, sniffing at one path, and then to the other two, he looked at me confused. I knew what someone had done. They would use different paths to throw the dogs off their trail. The only thing that I could do was to go up each trail until I would find the right one, or call for more help to follow all three paths. But that would take too long and several more hours, because I was at least ten miles from my base.

I had my dog,' Rex' for several years and he was a good pet and hunting dog, but tracking another person he lacked experience. I would let him pick out the trail and we would follow it until it got cold. Then instead of going back to the beginning, I would cut straight cross and hoped that I would run into the other path. After about a mile, sure enough I ran across another path.

This time Rex picked up the scent again, and we walked another mile and came to a small stream. But here, he lost the scent. I looked for foot prints in the creek bottom going up stream, thinking he would head toward the top of the mountain. After another half mile I found a foot print, and I knew that I was on the right trail. A little later, I noticed the prints went toward the bank, and figured that this was where he got out of the water.

Rex and I followed the scent for another mile, and then he began to bark and I knew I was close, but his barking may have given my surprise visit away. I put my hand over his mouth, and I think he understood because he didn't bark again, but kept looking at me. I checked my gun to make sure it was loaded, and quietly we went up the path, and then I saw a small cabin.

I looked around and didn't see anybody moving, but Rex was growling so I knew that someone was watching me.

I went toward the cabin, but sent Rex to a small shed and he disappeared inside, and later I heard a small" yep" and then a thump.

My thoughts were should I check the shed where Rex went, and see if he was alright? I couldn't call him and give my position away. And if Mary was not in the cabin and I cannot prove that she is there, and then legally he could shoot me for trespassing or for a false arrest.

I decided that I would go toward the cabin and stayed behind the trees to hide myself from the shed. I slipped around the back and looked inside; saw an empty bedroom with a bed and two chairs. Mary was nowhere in sight. I had to be sure that she was here, before I could confront the owner. I found an open window and crawled inside. "Mary," I softly cried out," are you inside?" I heard some scraping noises from the kitchen, and with my gun in hand, I crouched and went through the door. Mary was tied to a chair and had a washcloth stuck in her mouth and she couldn't speak.

I began to untie her from the chair and removed the rope from one hand, when I heard a noise behind me. I had put my gun back in my holster when I was untying Mary, which was a big mistake. I turned around and saw a giant man, at least 6'4 or 6'5 and over 300 pounds. He was headed toward me with a 2x4 in his hand, I got my 45 half way out of my hostler when he hit my hand and the gun slid across the floor. He rose the 2x4 again at my head, but I ducked and as hard as I could hit him in the gut.

He relaxed his grip on the board, and I drove my knee into his groin and then I hit him in the jaw. He shook his head, looked at me and grinned. He laid the 2x4 down, and smiled again, he intended to finish me off with his bare hands.

I was only 6' and 175 pounds, and he was the largest man I had ever seen. He was a giant, and I knew that I couldn't whip him in a fair fight, so I had to use my wits and the experiences that I had learned in the Marines.

He came at me again. I waited until he was ready to swing at my face and side stepped to the left, and with my foot I kicked his knee cap. He staggered and then I kicked the other knee and he went down cursing me. When he hit the floor, I kicked him under the chin and with both hands I pounded his face with my fists. But somehow he got back up and came at me again, and this time he caught me on the jaw, and I went backwards and hit the wall. "The only other time that I was hit that hard was by an Austrian in a bar in Honolulu, when I was in the Marines."

I was sitting against the wall when he came after me again. I waited and when he got close I then rolled across the floor and got back up. His knees were hurting him and had slowed him down some, but he still had plenty of fight left.

With his knees hurting it gave me a little advantage. Again he swung at me, and moving aside I hit him in the mouth, followed by one in the gut. He grinned and came after me again, he would not go down. Since I now had the speed, I could side step him, and I would use Judo chops to his face and neck. Normally one hard Judo chop in the neck would stop a man, but not this giant. His neck was like a tree stump, and he just kept on coming.

I was getting exhausted and I knew I couldn't keep dodging

him, and once he had me in his arms I would be a goner. And with his strength I would not be able to escape. I had to keep out of his reach, but I was getting tired and my body ached all over where he had hit me. Again he came at me, I side stepped and caught him in the mouth, but this time he grabbed my hand and hit me in the jaw, and I would have hit the floor, but he held on to my hand and tried to pull me toward him where he could get both hands around me. I knew I would be in big trouble if he did.

I turned my body toward him and with my knee I hit him in the groin. I looked over at Mary and she was free from her ropes and was looking for the gun. I hit him again in the groin, and then I stomped his foot, and kicked his shin, and then with my fist closed I drove my knuckles into his throat. He released my hand and swung at me and hit me in my chest. I heard a rib pop, and I was knocked back against the wall and slid down to the floor.

He came over and kicked me, and I heard another rib break. Then he pulled his leg back again, but this time I grabbed his foot, and with a hard jerk, he fell down. I then roll over and looked for the gun, but couldn't find it. I got up and motioned for Mary to hunt for it. When he got back up he wrapped his arms around me, I knew that this would be it, I had no fight left in me.

I had one arm free, but the other one was pinned against my body. Again he started to squeeze me, and I felt the breath leave my body. But with my one free arm, I took my elbow and as hard as I could drove it in his stomach. He grunted and bent over, and I turned around facing him, and again drove my knee into his groin.

He released me, and hit me with his fist again knocking me down and against the wall. The room started spinning, and I knew that I was going to black out.

I shook my head, trying to stay conscious, and saw him pick up the 2x4, and this time he was going to finish me. I tried to move but couldn't get up. I looked over at Mary, and she had found my gun and slid it across the floor toward me.

I picked up the gun and fired just as the mountain man started to swing. The bullet caught him in the chest, and he just stood there looking at me. Then he pulled back the 2x4 again, and this time I fired two more bullets into his chest, he cursed me and then fell to the floor.

Mary came over and helped me get up, and with my gun pointed at his head, I made sure that the mountain man was dead. She then helped me to the kitchen, and I sat in a chair while she took a wet towel and washed the blood off my face. Then she took a sheet off the bed and wrapped it tight around my chest.

We looked around the room and found my walkie-talkie, and called for help. It would be at least three or four hours before they could reach us, and I asked for a stretcher to carry the mountain man out. They said that if we could build a small fire they could spot the smoke and lower a chair down from a helicopter for Mary and me.

It would be a long wait either way, so I asked Mary to go to the shed and check on Rex. After twenty minutes she came back and said that he was dead. He had choked him with his hands. She tried to make me comfortable and found some coffee and made a pot. She said he didn't molest her, but he tried. She clawed his face so much that he left her alone, and made her cook for him. It could have been much worse.

It would be the next day before they could get a helicopter to us. Mary would not let me move and found blankets and we slept on the kitchen floor.

The next morning she made a small fire, and then threw water on it so it would smoke. They heard the helicopter and they spotted the smoke and then a couple of agents was lowered and helped Mary and me in the lift. And then took us to the hospital in Asheville. They would come back later for the body of the mountain man. Two agents would stay and wait on the land party.

"And that Joe was the way it happened. I've never let Mary go there again without me. But that was almost five years ago, and I haven't had any trouble there since, except for a few drunks."

Looking at the clock, Lee said it was time to go home. Mary was making him an Apple Pie.

Joe set looking at him, "Whew, what a story, and what a fight that must have been.

CHAPTER 28

Mary

Lee left the office thinking about the fight in the cabin, and it was hard to believe that it happened five years ago. If the mountain man hadn't been drinking, he may have never acted like that. Several people have talked to him, and said he was just a harmless old man. Well, that's what whiskey will do to you. I haven't taken a drink since I married Mary, almost twenty years ago.

He pulled into the driveway, and was surprised that the back door was locked. She usually unlocks it when she knows that I'm coming home. Pulling his key from his key chain, he went into the kitchen. "Mary, you in the bathroom?"

Getting no answer he went into their bedroom. On the floor, with the phone off the hook, he saw Mary lying on the floor. The carpet was stained with blood, and more was running from her mouth. "Good God! Mary what's wrong. Did you fall?"

Mary slowly opened her eyes, stared at him and tried to talk. "Lee I tried to call you, but I must have passed out. Honey, I am sick."

"Just lay still, I'm calling an ambulance. Mary I'm so sorry, but we will get you well."

It wasn't more than fifteen minutes until the ambulance showed up. The medics put her inside, and Lee got into his car and followed her to the hospital.

They took Mary to E.R. while he stood in the hall and waited.

It was only twenty minutes, but to Lee it seems like hours before the doctor came out, with a grim face." Sheriff Robinson, your wife has had a hemorrhage, and has lost lots of blood. We are giving her more blood now, and think we have stopped the bleeding. Do you know why she was bleeding? Did she ever have Tuberculosis?"

"Yes Doctor, ten years ago, maybe longer. She was in Chattanooga, but they said it was healed. She hasn't had any problems in years. Said it was arrested, and no longer active. Is that why she is bleeding?"

"Yes Lee, we think that's the reason. There is nothing else we can do here, but I would like to call The University Hospital in Knoxville and have her flown there by helicopter. They would know what to do; you could follow in your car. Do you want me to call?"

"Yes please do. I will contact my office and start driving to Knoxville. Should be there by the time they exam her."

Lee called the Dispatcher and told them what happened and to tell Rodney that he was taking the week off, but would call him when he knew anything. Then he got into his car and headed for Knoxville.

On arriving at the U.T. hospital, he ran inside and asked the receptionist where he could find his wife. He was then sent to the fifth floor, and again talked to the Desk Nurse. "Mr. Robinson please go to the waiting room, and the Doctor will see you in a few minutes. They are still running some tests."

He waited a good hour, and three cups of coffee later a young doctor came into the room and asked Lee to come to his office.

"Mr. Robinson. Sheriff?"

"Just call me Lee, Doctor. What's wrong with my wife?"

"Lee I am Doctor James Howell, and your wife now has active Tuberculosis and it has jumped over to her other lung. She is in serious condition."

"But why Doctor? She spent six months in a sanatorium in Chattanooga, and they said that it had been arrested. It's been over ten years and she hasn't had any problems. And she had a check up every year, with no sign of active T.B."

The Doctor leaned over to his intercom…"Nurse, asks Jim Howell to bring me the records of the bone scan of Mary Robinson."

In about ten minutes a clean cut middle aged man came into the room, carrying some files…"Is this, what you need James?"

"Mr. Robinson, this is my father, Jim Howell, nurse and perfusions. He normally works with heart patients, but this morning we asked him to do some bone scans of your wife. These are the pictures."

"Look at the bones, see all of those black spots? That means that the T.B. is now in her bones, and here is a picture of her lungs. She now has the disease in both lungs."

Lee took the x-ray pictures and looked at them for several minutes. "Doctor, what can we do? I can't let her die."

Doctor Howell took the pictures and gave them back to his father. "Thanks Dad, for doing the scans, I know you have a busy schedule." and Jim went back to his office.

"Mr. Robinson we would like to keep your wife here for about a week, we will have to put her in an isolation room, and you will be the only one allowed to see her at this time. She is a very sick woman."

"Can I see her now?" Lee asked.

"Can you go and get something to eat and then come back later. We have sedated her and she will sleep for a couple hours. When you come back let the nurse know and then go to the waiting room. When she awakes, we will let you see her, but only for a few minutes. I'm sorry Mr. Robinson."

Lee got up to leave, but was stopped by Doctor Howell. "Mr. Robinson I saw from your records that you are a Marine and served our country in World War II, at the Marshal Islands and Okinawa?"

"Yes Sir I did, and a few more islands."

"Thanks for what you did; my grandfather was also a Marine on those same islands. And if you don't mind me saying it, you look a lot like my grandfather, who lives in Chattanooga. Mr. Robinson, pray for your wife and us, and we will do everything that we can to make her well again. We doctors can only do so much, but then it is up to God."

Lee went down stairs and called Sue and told her he was staying at the hospital for the next couple of days. Then he called his daughter Pat, and left word for Leland who was in class. Then he called the office and told Karen and Joe that unless it was an emergency, give all calls to Rodney. When all the calls were made, and then he went to lunch, he had missed breakfast.

After he had eaten he went back to the desk and informed the receptionist that he would be in the waiting room.

He had fallen asleep when the nurse came into the room and awakened him.

"Mr. Robinson your wife is awake. You can see her now, but please don't stay long, she needs complete rest."

He was shocked when he first saw her. She had an I.V. in both arms, and a tube in her mouth. "Hello honey, boy have they got you wired up. I hope you are feeling better. He then put his hand on her shoulder, and said." I love you dear, but where is my apple pie?"

Mary tried to laugh; it's on the floor I think. I remember making it, but then I fell. I don't know what happen then. I tried to call you, Lee, I was so scared. I will be okay won't I honey?"

"Sure, you just need a little rest, and then everything will be alright." Then he kissed her on the cheek.

Leland and Pat arrived at the hospital the next morning Three days had passed and Leland and Pat took turns staying at the hospital, and tried to get their father to get some rest. Mary had been moved to a private room, but everyone that went into the room had to wear a mask and gloves.

After ten days, Doctor James Howell came into the room and asked Lee and his daughter Pat to come to his office. With a grim face he asked them to sit down." Where is Leland, her son?"

"He had some classes he had to take, he will be here later."

"Mr. Robinson, Pat, I have bad news. Lee, your wife, and Pat your mother is dying. There is nothing else that we can do. The Tuberculosis has spread through her body. Her disease is no longer active, but I want you to continue to wear your mask, and wash your hands every time you are in the room. "

"How long will she live doctor?" Lee asked

"It could be a month, or three months. This is what I suggest. You could put her in a nursing home, or you can place her under Hospice Care and take her home. I would take my wife home. Hospice would have a nurse come by once or twice a week; a doctor would be on call when needed. You would have a social worker, to come by and bathe her. That would be my suggestion."

Lee looked at Pat who was crying and with tears in his eyes said. "Doctor, I'm taking my wife home. If she dies, then it won't be in a nursing home, but it will be in her own bed. When can I move her?"

"Wait until tomorrow, and I will have the medicine and an ambulance to take her home. You do mean your home in Rockdale don't you?"

"Yes doctor, Pat wanted to take her back to Hixson, but she has two small kids at home."

"Take her to your place Lee; little kids should not be around her. Hospice will know what to do. And may God bless and comfort you and your family."

Pat put her arms around her Dad and they walked out of the doctor's office, and went downstairs for a cup of coffee and talked. "Dad give me the house keys, and I will drive to the house. I want to clean up the house and her bed room before Hospice comes out tomorrow. "

"You plan on staying the night there?"

"Yes, I will call my husband Ed, and tell him we are going to bring mother home. He wanted to come, but he needed to stay with the kids. Do you want me to move your things into the other bedroom?"

"Yes, and get Fred and Louise to move her bed out on the back porch, Hospice will order a hospital bed, and move what furniture that you don't need in the room. Pat, please call Sue and Rod, I don't think I could do it. Damn, I love that woman; she thought I could do everything. Now she is dying, and there's not a damn thing I can do to prevent it. "

"Dad I love her too, but just remember you had twenty-five years together. Lots of married couples don't have that many. She would want you to remember the good times you had together, and go on with your life."

"I guess I better be going, I want to get there before dark, are you going to follow the ambulance tomorrow?"

"Yes honey, and please be careful. We should be there by late noon. Be sure to call Rod and Sue."

"I will Daddy, are you sure you will be alright driving, just think that she may live a year or longer. "

"I hope so honey, oh I hope so."

When the ambulance and Lee got home there were two other cars he didn't recognize in the yard. They carried Mary into her bedroom and he was met by two women from Hospice. The nurse was named Lily, and a social worker named Julie.

Both of these lovely women would be compassionate, and a great help to him and Mary.

They gently put his wife in the bed and the nurse immediately began to check her vitals while Julie made sure that we had everything that we needed. Lee had never been around anyone from Hospice before, and was amazed of their love and caring for his wife, and their professionalism.

Pat came into the room and kissed her father, and leaned over and kissed her mother on the head. The women from Hospice stayed about an hour, and on leaving told Pat that someone would be out tomorrow and bathe her mother, and then they left.

"Did you get hold of Rod?" Lee asked Pat

"Yes Daddy, but they said they would wait until tomorrow to come by and visit."

"Good, did you call Ed and the kids?"

"Yes Daddy, everybody knows that mother is home. Now when have you eaten? I have some stew on the stove, please sit down and eat."

Pat gave her mother some milk and went to bed. "Dad its eleven o'clock, please go to bed."

Lee ignored her and set by the bed and held Mary's hand, kissed her and then he went to bed.

Lee woke up at two a.m. with a chill running through his body. The house was quiet, and not a bird or any animals could he hear outside. He knew that death had entered his house; he had felt this feeling before when one of his friends had died. "Mary!" He shouted, and jumped up and put his pants on and went into her bedroom.

Reaching her bed, he knew that she was dead; lying there with a peaceful look on her face, knowing that she would never suffer again. He held her hand and kissed her, dropping to his knees beside the bed, and screamed. Then the tears came. Pat was awakened by his screaming, and went into the bedroom and saw her Mother dead. She put her arms around her Dad and held him close until he fell back asleep.

Lee was awakened by a knock on the door; he had fallen asleep again in Pat's arms. Going to the door he saw Lily the Hospice nurse, who took one look at him and then rushed into the bedroom.

Lily called the Hospice Doctor, and then put on a pot of coffee. "Lee she has found peace now, Mary will never know any more pain, please accept that, and remember the good times you both had together. Death is only a temporary time on this earth; she has left one door, and now she will enter another. I promise you that you will see Mary again."

Mary was buried in a small cemetery in Rockdale, a few miles from town surrounded by mountains. All of Lee's family was there plus many of his friends. Half of the population of the town of Rockdale attended the funeral.

The Mayor and Rodney were standing next to the grave. "Lee, take the week off, longer if you need it" the Mayor said. "And take your grandkids fishing."

CHAPTER 29

Red Dog Tavern

It was the fifth time that Rodney had heard the phone ring without getting an answer. Then he called Lee's next door neighbor, "Louise, have you or Fred heard from Lee?"

"No we haven't seen him since he left to see his daughter in Chattanooga. Have you called her?"

"Yes, she said, that Lee had called, and one of her girls was sick, and he said he would come later. That was two weeks ago, and Pat hadn't heard from him since."

"Rod, have you called his son, Leland in Knoxville? Maybe they went fishing together?"

"Yes, he hadn't heard from his Dad either. Louise I'm getting worried."

Rodney hung up the phone and told Joe the Dispatcher that he was going to Sherry's Café, she might know something.

The café was busy so Rod nodded to one of the waitresses and went to a booth. She brought him some water, and asked if he wanted to see the menu?

"No, but tell Sherry when she has the time to come to his

table. And you can bring me a cup of coffee."

"Good Afternoon Rod. Betty said you wanted to see me," putting the cup of coffee on the table.

"Yes Sherry, have you heard from Lee?"

"Not since the funeral, we talked for a few minutes, and he said that he needed to get away. Maybe go to Knoxville and go fishing with his grand children. Is anything wrong?"

"He is not with his children in Chattanooga or Knoxville. Nobody has heard from him in over two weeks. He was supposed to come back to work two days ago. Sherry, I'm worried."

"Rod, there is a cabin on Rock Creek that he told me about one time. I think it is above the bridge, and no one owns it. Said he went there a couple of times to just get away. He was very depressed after the funeral. Could he have gone there?"

"I never been there, it's a long ways up Rock Creek and don't think anyone lives in it. But I've looked everywhere else, so if I don't have a call I will go there tomorrow."

"Rod please let me know something; you know I think a lot of him."

"We both do, Sherry. Yes, I will let you know if I find him."

He drank his coffee and went back to the office, telling Karen and Joe that no one had heard from Lee.

"Joe, have you been to the cabin above the bridge on Rock Creek?" asked Rod

"Yes one time. You can drive a mile pass the bridge, but then you have to walk the rest of the way. The fishing is mostly Brook Trout, but a long ways to find them. I think there is an old cabin there, but in bad shape. Do you think Lee might have gone there?"

"Don't know, but if I don't have any calls, I'm going there tomorrow."

The next day Rod packed a lunch, called the office and told them he was heading to Rock Creek. After driving for about an hour he came to the bridge that spanned the creek. The road was narrow but continued on up the mountain, then it almost became a path, and after another mile, it ended. Looking around a large boulder was a field and then he saw Lee's car.

He checked the car and made sure there were no blood stains, and then he looked across the creek and saw a small cabin. Wading across the creek he carefully watched the cabin, and making sure no one was watching him. He found a window on the side and looked inside. At first he saw no one, but then he spied a cot, and someone was asleep on it.

"Lee if that is you, I'm coming in." With his gun in his hand, Rodney pushed the door open and rushed inside.

The person on the cot jumped up and started for his gun, hanging on a nail on the wall.

"Lee, it's me, Rod."

"Rod? Hell I almost shot you, what are you doing here?"

Then Rodney looked on the floor, beer and whiskey bottles were everywhere, and the room stunk with vomit. "Lee you're drunk. Why?"

"My wife died Rod."

"Yes I know, but that's no reason to get drunk and get lost. Your friends and family were worried about you. I have never seen you take a drink since you married Mary. She would be ashamed of you, if she saw you like this. Lee, you are not the only one that lost someone that they loved. Now sober up, we have got some work to do, and we need you."

"What are we going to do Rod? Are the Chinese coming?"

"Lee, that was over twenty years ago, you are a Sheriff now and we need you to catch some bad guys. Do you have a change of clothes in your bag?"

"Think so, why?"

"Take your clothes off, strip down and go outside and get into the creek, the cold water will sober you up, and clean some of that puke off of you. I will look for a bar of soap, if there is such a thing here, and then I will bring you some clean clothes. Please go Lee; I need to talk to you sober. We have some serious work to do."

While Rod was looking for some clean clothes he looked out the window and saw Lee naked and lying in the cold water. If that doesn't sober him up, then nothing will.

"Rod bring me some dry clothes, I'm freezing."

"Okay you got me sober and froze my balls off, now what's so important, that you came up here to get me?"

"Lee if you have a razor, shave some of that beard off, then we will go to Sherry's and get you a big breakfast. I bet you haven't eaten in several days. On the way back I will fill you in about the job."

The Highway Patrol has been putting road blocks on I-75 and has arrested several drug smugglers, but then they started using our road bypassing the highway. They are driving straight through Rockdale going to Asheville, Chattanooga, and into Atlanta. It's a long drive from up north, so we found out that they are stopping and spending the night at the "Red Dog Tavern" owned by Red Wilson, who has ten rooms in the back where they can stay for the night, for a fee to Red."

"Is Red Wilson in the drug business too?"

"Yes, our Feds think so. They have had a couple of agents staying there at nights. Red let tourist stay there to make it look legal. But we think its a million dollar operation."

"What will our job be Rod?"Asked Lee.

"They are forming a task force led by you and the Feds. It is out of the Highway Patrol district, but they will have two cars and four troopers present. The Feds will be in charge, along with us, because it is in our district. Four troopers, two Feds and the two of us are planning to gather at the rest area ten miles from the Red Dog Tavern, we will meet at 5 p.m. Friday, and then surround the Tavern at 7 p.m."

"We hope there will be no visitors present. We have asked restaurants that see tourists who would be traveling late, to tell them that the Tavern would be closed, and not to stop there Friday night."

"Thanks Rod for finding me and sobering me up. This action is just what I need, to get me back on my work, and quit feeling sorry for myself. I have had two women that I loved die, and I guess I couldn't handle it. But getting drunk wasn't the answer, and forgetting my friends, and family was worse. I'm okay now, and there's Sherry's Café, and I'm hungry."

As they entered into the Café, Sherry saw them and ran

to Lee, hugged and kissed him. "I should slap you, scaring all of us like you did. Now sit down and I will bring you some coffee."

"What do you want to eat, Lee?"

"Let's start with two eggs, two bacon, and three of your blueberry pancakes. Then if I'm still hungry, I will look at the menu."

Sherry brought the food to the table, kissed him again on the head, and said." Lee, don't ever scare us like that again, this town loves you, and Rod and I are your closest friends."

"Thanks Sherry, it won't happen again."

Lee had been on the phone with the other law officers most of Friday morning, and after lunch he and Rodney would ride down to the staging area and wait on the others.

"Rod, I'm surprised what these young kids are doing today. It was only in the Vietnam War; that I even heard of marijuana. Now the kids are pushing meth, cocaine, and even prescription pain killers. Where have we gone wrong with our kids?"

"I think it's the time that we are living in today. At our young age, our parents would have worn the belt out on us. We are having wars about every ten years, unemployment, and lack of the respect for our parents and the law. And if they keep passing laws in Congress, we won't be saying prayers in school, or at the ball field." Rodney said checking his gun to make sure it was loaded.

Two Highway Patrol cars rolled into the parking area, and in several minutes two men from the Feds showed up. Everyone was present, and they went over their plans again.

"Sheriff Robinson, this is your district. If we find drugs in the club, do you want us to padlock it?" One of the Feds said.

"Yes, or burn it down. It's been a trouble spot for us for a long time. I've given 'Red' a warning ticket several times. If we find drugs inside, that is all the proof that I will need to shut him down. There was a killing in his place a couple years ago, but we didn't have enough evidence to shut him down."

"Everyone check their guns. Mr. Gules do you have the search warrant?" It's about time for us to go. It will take about thirty minutes to get there, maybe we can interrupt their supper," said Lee heading for the car.

With sirens blowing, the lawmen pulled into the Red Dog parking lot, blocking as many cars as they could. They went inside and ordered everyone to get up and face the wall.

Some had to be forced to stand against the wall, but after showing their badges and with a nudge from a gun, there was little argument left. The lawmen went from man to man, checking their I.D.

Red Wilson came running from the kitchen and demanded to know what was going on? Seeing Lee he said. "You again? I'm going to have your badge. Wait until I see my lawyer."

Mr. Gules stepped up in front of Red Wilson. "Is this what you want to see? It's a search warrant to check your place of business. I would suggest that you don't interfere."

While the other lawman was checking the I.D. of those against the wall, Lee and Rod went into the kitchen and the back office. "Rod, you check for extra storages places, I'm going to check his office."

Lee opened the drawers to Red's desk, and then spotted a large safe. "Tell Red I said to come in here, now."

Red came in, saw Lee looking at the safe, and then grabbed for a gun that was hidden behind some books.

"No you don't," Lee swung and hit Red on the jaw and knocking him into the wall. He reached again for the gun and Lee kicked the gun under the desk and hit him again."

Rod came running into the room, "Do you need help Lee?"

"No, I'm just having fun with an old friend," and delivered another blow to Red's chin and knocked him over the desk and onto the floor.

Picking Red up, he said. "I will give you five minutes to open that safe." Red reached into his pocket and pulled out a piece of paper with numbers on it and then he looked at Lee. "I'm going to have you killed for this."

When the door to the safe was opened, Lee saw about six shoe boxes inside.

"Mr. Gules, you need to come and see this."

Both of the Feds came into the office and looked inside the safe. One ordered Red to pull a couple of the boxes out and open them. When the lid was taken off, they could see that it was full of money. "It's my money, from the club" Red said.

The Feds pulled the other boxes out, and all of them were filled with hundred dollar bills." We will take these and check the serial numbers," Gules said.

"Lee, you and the Feds need to come in the kitchen." Said, Rod.

After they put handcuffs on Red Wilson, and gave him

ED ROBINETTE

over to one of the troopers, the two Feds and Lee went into the kitchen.

Rod was standing next to a storage door that went downstairs. "Lee I thought our UDT days were over. I started to open the door when I saw a small wire leading to that box on the wall. He has the door booby trapped. If I had opened it, I would have blown me out of the kitchen."

"Have you disconnected the wire?"

"Yes, but I haven't opened the door. I thought that the Feds might want to look downstairs."

"Open the door, and let's see what's so important that he would put a explosive on the door."

The four lawmen went down stairs and saw ten suitcases lined up on the floor, each with a name tag. Mr. Gules opened one of the cases and it was filled with cocaine and other drugs. "Well with the name tags, it will make it easy for the Judge. "

"This ought to keep your friend Red in jail for a long time. Sheriff will you see that this place is padlocked."

The next morning it was front page news, and Lee and Rod were at the office reading about it. "Well that should be the end of the Red Dog Tavern," Lee said drinking his coffee.

"Yes but they are still using our road for a short cut to Chattanooga and Atlanta, last week I stopped two kids traveling through town, and when I opened the trunk I found four sacks of marijuana, they were going to Chattanooga." Said Rod

"Lee I have the shift today, why don't you go to Sherry's Café and you have a big lunch. I think I will drive down to the Red Dog Tavern and see if anything is going on."

Red Wilson got ten years in prison, and the men that were delivering the drugs received five years and a heavy fine. The Red Dog Tavern was padlocked for six months, and then later was burned to the ground. No one was charged.

CHAPTER 30

The Last Adventure

Lee had the day off, but after leaving the office he was restless and decided to drive down to Lulu Lake Campgrounds and maybe do a little fishing. It was Wednesday, so it was almost deserted, except for a few campers.

He pulled into a parking space and opening the trunk, got out his fly rod, and started walking up stream. He saw a dimple in the water next to a large rock. Casting his fly nearby, he saw the line tighten and with the sound of the spinning reel, he watched his line head to the middle of the stream. Placing his thumb on the reel, he made a short jerk, and the fight was on.

In less than five minutes, he pulled to the shore a two pound rainbow trout. Pleased with what he had done he tried another spot, and again he had a fish on his line. This trout would only go about a pound, but the two fish would be supper tonight. The next hour his luck had ran out, and he decided to get some ice from the ice bin and take them to Sherry's Café who would cook them for him tonight.

Driving back to Rockdale he took the short route to Sherry's Café, and carried his two fish inside. "Howdy, Sherry, will you cook an old man supper tonight?"

"Hi Lee, yes you know that I would be glad to. How many fish do you have?"

"Two, but with your slaw and fried potatoes that should be enough. What kind of pie have you made for today?"

"Today is apple pie day, topped with ice cream. How does that sound Lee?"

"Honey, you sure know how to get to a man's heart. Have I told you that I love you?"

"Not yet. But you better before I cook your supper." She kissed him and brought him a cup of coffee.

"Lee, someone burnt down the Red Dog Tavern, did you see it in the papers?"

"Yes, I saw that. Rod and I was talking about that this morning. I'm glad that eye sore is gone. And Red won't be dealing in drugs for a long time."

"Sherry how long have you been running this café? I have been eating here for at least ten years. My wife loved to come here to eat."

"I think around fifteen years, I bought it right after my divorce, been here ever since."

"Have you thought about getting married again?"

"Thought about it, but I don't think I want to go down that road again."

"What about you Lee? Your wife has been dead what… three years, think you will ever marry again?"

"Doubt it Sherry, we had a wonderful marriage together. That is unless you will marry me?"

"Lee, if I ever married again, it would have to be a man like you. I wish I had found you before your wife did, but again that's the story of my life."

There was a loud blowing of a horn, and screeching of breaks, and Sherry looked out of the window.

"Lee that car almost hit that woman, and then hit the car in front of him; he is now on the sidewalk.

Lee lay down his cup of coffee and started out the door. "See you around six p.m. Sherry" as he race toward his car. He saw the red car in front of him, weaving and picking up speed. He turned his sirens on and called Rod to join the chase.

"Lee, this is Joe, the Dispatcher. Rod is down close to Asheville. Do you want me to contact the highway patrol?"

"Yes do that, tell them that I am chasing a red car, with two men heading toward Bristol. The car is out of town and speeding. I think the license plates are from Ohio. They are around exit ten, and traveling over one hundred miles an hour."

After about ten minutes, Lee could see two patrol cars blocking the road a couple of miles up.

But the driver in the red car saw them too, and made a right turn into a field knocking down fences as they drove from field to field.

Lee knew that it was important that they wouldn't be stopped. They must have something in the car that was valuable, so Lee turned and went into the fields behind them. The chase continued until the field was ended by a creek.

The red car saw the creek and made a quick turn and flipped the car over. The two men were climbing out of the windows when Lee drove up. He ran to the car pointing his gun at the two men. "Just hold it right there, and put your hands on the car. Both hands damn you."

The other two patrol cars drove up, and the officers pulled their guns, and walked over to the two men.

The two highway troopers put cuffs on the men and searched them, finding that both men had a gun.

After they took their guns away, Lee asked one of the men to open the trunk. "We lost the key," the tall dark man said.

"No problem" said Lee. Taking his 45 and firing at the trunk lock several times until it opened. "Now it's open."

Inside was a shoe box, and when they opened the box it was filled with hundred dollar bills. Then he saw at least ten bags that contained cocaine and marijuana.

"Well gentleman, just where were you taking this? Atlanta or Chattanooga?" Lee asked

"None of your damn business you country hick?" said the short chubby man.

One of the troopers stepped up, stuck his gun under the man's chin and said. The sheriff asked you a question, now answer him."

"We don't know, someone was going to contact us at a rest stop when we crossed the line in Virginia, they know us, but we don't know them. Honest that is all we know."

The trooper looked at Lee and said. "Sheriff that is out of both of our districts, if you want, we can take these two boys in, with the drugs and then contact the Highway Patrol in Virginia."

"That would be great fellows, thanks. They interrupted my lunch, but I have a date for supper."

Lee was getting back into his car, when the tall, dark man

said. "Sheriff, you're a dead man. Our boss gets upset when someone takes his money and drugs. I will tell him what hick town you're from."

"You do that, but tell him that we have an extra cell, just for him." and he got back into his car and drove back to Sherry's Café, and a fried trout supper.

That weekend Lee went down to Chattanooga and saw Pat and the grand children, and stayed Saturday night, and then drove to Hixson to spend the day with his brother Carl.

"Lee you're getting too old to be chasing drug pushers, and wrestling with drunks. Your grandchildren want you to take them fishing. What age will you be next month, sixty eight?"

"Carl you may be right, sometimes I ache all over. And last week, I was chasing a car down highway 40 at ninety miles an hour. That was crazy. I didn't think about it until later, and then it scared the crap out of me."

"Lee your house is still empty, Pat and Ed lived in it until the kids came, then they had to get a bigger house. Brother we need some time together. Hell we haven't gone fishing together in years. "

"Carl you may be right, I'm getting too old for the job. I could quit, and let Rodney be Sheriff, he is several years younger than me. I think I will go back and tell Rod and the Mayor that I'm stepping down. I would even marry Sherry if she would have me."

"Brother, it would be good to have you here, I can't do farm work anymore, but my kids have taken over the farm. Hell, we can fish every day, and if you can talk Sherry to come with you, then that would be great too. She is a fine lady."

"Now let's go in the house and eat supper, I think Lucy has baked a chocolate cake for you."

That night when Lee went to bed, he thought about the idea of retiring, and he and his brother could do some fishing. And there were his son Leland and his boys. He had let everyone down, it was time to quit and take them fishing.

"Yes, that is what I will do, tell Rod tomorrow, I …tel tomor." And he fell asleep.

Monday morning Lee woke up early, and thought what he would say to Rod. They had been together for years. I remembered that we met in China that was almost fifty years ago. We fought side by side and shared many adventures together. But again, we would still see each other; we can go fishing and hunting.

Then again, I hate to break up a good team. I will ask him to come over to Sherry's and have coffee with me, and then I can tell him.

Lee drove to Sherry's Café and when he met her he asked if they could step into the kitchen?

"You want me in the kitchen?" She said." What are you up to Lee?"

"You will be safe with me." He said.

"How do you know that I want to be safe with you? What's wrong Lee?"

"Sherry I want you to be the first to know. Rodney will be here in a few minutes. Honey, I'm hanging it up, quitting, retiring, or whatever you call it. I have had enough, last week I was chasing a car down Highway 40 at ninety miles an hour. I could have killed someone. I want to quit and go fishing with my brother and grand kids. Hell Sherry, I'm sixty eight years old."

"I and this town will miss seeing you every day. I know I will."

"Then marry me, and we will be together. We will do some traveling."

"Wow! You come in here and tell me you're retiring, and then ask me to marry you. What can I say?"

"You could say yes."

"Lee, I love you, but I think we both have been down the road to the altar before. I wished I had met you a long time ago, but you had a wonderful wife and family. I think that we are both too old to make that trip again. Let's just be good friends." I have worked hard to get this place, and don't owe a penny on it. I love cooking and I love my customers, I would be lost without it."

"Good friends? Does that mean kissing friends?"

"Yes, good kissing friends."

Lee grabbed her in his arms and kissed her.

She removed his arms and looking at him said."I think you better go and set down; you're getting an old woman hot and bothered. And I may change my mind and marry you, and then what?"

"Am I too old for you, is that the reason?"

couple of punks. All because we took the drugs away from them, a couple of paid hit men."

The ambulance drivers came in bringing a stretcher, followed by the Chief of Police. Blood was now running down from the table and covering the floor. The two men picked Lee up and laid him on the stretcher, and put a sheet over his body, but it was soon soaked with blood.

Rod took his arms from around Sherry, and went over to his friend, and placed his hand on his shoulder. "Good Friend, this will be one adventure that I won't be going with you, but I bet when you get to heaven and approach the gate. All of our friends that were killed will be waiting on you. They will be standing at attention, and singing the Marines Hymn. Goodbye old friend."

FROM THE HALLS OF MONTEZUMA, TO THE SHORES OF TRIPOLI.
WE FIGHT OUR COUNTRY'S BATTLES, IN THE AIR, ON LAND AND SEA
FIRST TO FIGHT FOR RIGHT AND FREEDOM, AND TO KEEP OUR HONOR
CLEAN, WE ARE PROUD TO CLAIM THE TITLE OF UNITED STATES MARINES.
OUR FLAG'S UNFURL'D TO EVERY BREEZE, FROM DAWN TO SETTING SUN.
WE HAVE FOUGHT IN EVERY CLIME AND PLACE,

Ed Robinette

WHERE WE COULD TAKE A GUN.
HERE'S HEALTH TO YOU AND TO OUR CORPS,
WHICH WE ARE PROUD TO SERVE;
IN THE SNOW OF FAR OFF NORTHERN LANDS,
AND IN SUNNY TROPIC SCENES,
YOU WILL FIND US ALWAYS ON THE JOB- THE UNITED STATES MARINES
IF THE ARMY AND THE NAVY, EVER GAZE ON HEAVEN'S SCENES
THEY WILL FIND THE STREETS ARE GUARDED, BY UNITED STATES MARINES.

ALSO BY Ed Robinette

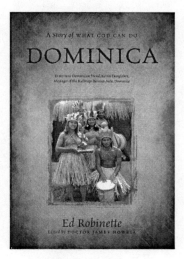

Dominica

    This story is about the life of a young man, named Jim Baxter who is injured in the War and tired of killing decides to go to medical school and become a doctor to serve his fellow man. While in school he suffers a life threatening accident that leaves him scarred and deformed. Ashamed of his appearance, he decides to live on the island of Dominica, where he hopes that no one will care about his appearance. In his quest to still practice medicine, he devotes himself to the Carib Indians, a native people that live on the tiny island. As the story unfolds, Jim touches the lives of others, as his life is touched by the hand of God.

    Ed Robinette has done an excellent job with sharp visuals to bring the reader right into the story. In no time you are there following the characters as they move around the island. Robinette has that rare ability to make a movie inside the head of any reader. I loved the fact that it was so easy and fun to read. I am sure he will have many more as he clearly love to tell a story. Lantz Powell. President Chattanooga Writers Guild

Learn more at: www.outskirtspress.com/dominica